ISBN-13: 978-1544231266

ISBN-10: 1544231261

Cover design: LA Johnstone Graphic Design, www.lajohnstone.co.uk

Formatted for Kindle and paperback by www.publishonkindle.co.uk

Contents

Author's note

This might be a true story, because all of this might've happened.

It is set in a real place at a real stage in British history.

The Kent coastline is one of the most exciting and extraordinarily diverse features of the south-east. The county is bounded by water on three sides. There are the famous towering White Cliffs, there are marshes, rivers, creeks and inlets, there are islands. There are soft sandy beaches, mighty cliffs, sloping shores of pebbles. Here is the wide mouth of the Thames, the North Sea and the English Channel. A fabulously beautiful, enchanting, dramatic, extensively varied and thrilling coastline.

Always an ideal setting for dark mystery, intrigue, espionage and crime relating to the sea.

This is not a book about smuggling but inevitably the free traders have a role to play. A great deal of literature on the subject is available elsewhere, both in fiction and fact. So too on the history of the Cinque Ports and the Kent coast.

Smuggling in bygone days tends to have a romantic lean, thanks largely to works of fiction, and often first thoughts head towards the coast of Cornwall. There was nothing very romantic about smuggling, often violent, brutal and ruthless, and the real hotbed of activity was Kent, closest to Europe and therefore ideally located.

Whole communities could be involved in landing contraband, and smuggling was never simply about 'goods inwards'. In fact smuggling wool out (owling) probably preceded the reverse traffic!

Nonetheless I hope this work does convey some idea of the extent of this illegal activity around the period in which it is set. Kent appears to have been Premier League. Today's smugglers deal in drugs and people. Nothing romantic at all.

The phrase Preventive Services basically covers anyone, including the military, fighting against smuggling. For simplicity I call one of these characters a Revenue man, but Excise, Customs, all will do just as well. 'Revenue' is my oft-employed choice of generic term.

There had been other assassination plots in this era, and Kent was no stranger to the thirst for rebellion, so the concept is not unique, but history is not the mainstay of this tale, merely its essential backdrop.

The knowledgeable may well discover flaws, but I hope these won't detract from any enjoyment of the novel.

For this might indeed have been a true story......

***

Map of East Kent

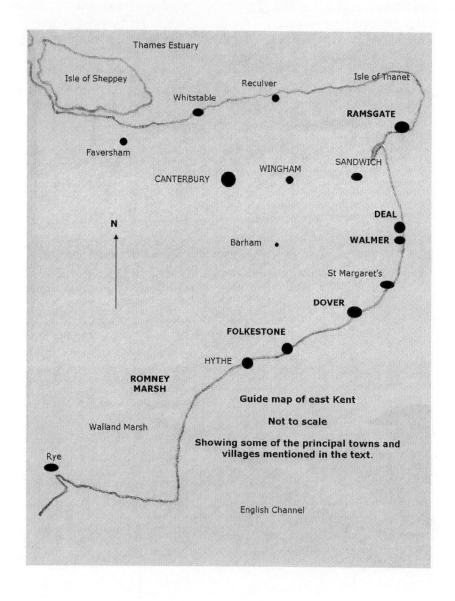

Thames Estuary

Isle of Sheppey

Reculver

Isle of Thanet

Whitstable

RAMSGATE

Faversham

WINGHAM

SANDWICH

CANTERBURY

DEAL

N

Barham

WALMER

St Margaret's

DOVER

FOLKESTONE

HYTHE

ROMNEY MARSH

Walland Marsh

Rye

English Channel

Guide map of east Kent

Not to scale

Showing some of the principal towns and villages mentioned in the text.

Introduction

It is the late 18th century, in the reign of George III.

Major events such as the American War of Independence, the French Revolution and the Napoleonic Wars belong to this era. Indeed, even now Napoleon is rising to power.

The fear of war is bringing uneasiness to Kent as it is elsewhere.

Now the mysterious Oliver Kindale is on his way to Dover.

His destiny is aligned to the activities of a Frenchman and an English outlaw. Threatening developments in France seem to be at the centre of his critical mission.

But Kindale is not an officer of the law, nor is he a military man. Indeed, little is known about him.

The east Kent coast has been a hotbed for smuggling but Kindale is not pursuing the free-traders, although their paths will inevitably cross. Which side of the law does Kindale operate on? What are his motives? Why is he in Kent at all?

And what of the man himself?

Death hangs in the air. These are dangerous times and Kindale will face danger and other challenges, some that will test him heart and mind, body and soul.

Could the very fate of England be in his hands?

Prelude

She was ready for the game, this most deadly of games.

"Où est Douvres?" she whispered loudly in her native tongue, loud enough to be heard by those closest to her.

The man kneeling by the fire, poking it with a stick, raised his arm and pointed aimlessly and carelessly into the pitch dark, the blackness that surrounded them all this cold winter's night, a night so bereft of moon and stars and any other sources of light. No words passed his lips.

He might have been pointing to heaven or to hell for all he knew.

Ignorant oaf!

She was tired of their ignorance and stupidity. At least she would be rid of it for a while now she was moving into the second act of this terrible drama, the first act complete and the curtain down.

Veronique Descoteaux was playing a part and had made sure Chastain chose her for her next role.

He chose her for many reasons but principally her beauty (which he could not resist), her noble bearing and her near-perfect English. Now they would be a respectable English couple, Mr and Mrs Copwood, living quietly in Dover while he unleashed his heinous conspiracy.

Tonight she had been led here, to this bleak and neglected stretch of the French coast, to await the vessel that must take her to England and to Chastain. All she had been told was that an English seaman called Hapling, who knew these waters and inlets thoroughly, would arrive to take her, the hilltop fire his sole guide to the correct landing place.

No doubt, she mused silently, he was well acquainted with this coast as he must surely be a smuggler, yet tonight he would carry a cargo that would attract no duty even if declared.

If she could behave nobly as a gentlewoman that was because she had aristocratic blood, a fact concealed from these peasants, these scoundrels, these bloodthirsty easily-led dolts. How she hated the rising new order in her beloved France. The fate of her mother, father and brother was unknown to her but their blood might already be on the hands of rogues just such as these.

Oh, how she longed for revenge. And vengeance could be hers to deliver.

She wrapped her shawl tighter around her shoulders, for the breeze was iced and for the first time she felt the chill reach her bones. Her two bags, containing her clothes, her 'costumes' for the times ahead, lay at her feet. Tonight she looked just as she had when she first appeared before them all those weeks ago: a poor waif, wretched, hungry, ill-clothed.

They had accepted her at face value, taken her to their hearts.

She had spirit. She had venom and she had passion, and they loved her for it.

Fools!

When she had learned what was truly afoot she wanted to be part of it and adapted her act accordingly and ensured Chastain noticed. He was a cold man, brutal and determined, and he was destined for high office when the day should come. Held in high regard he was already quite clearly one of the movement's leaders.

And now he had conceived a master plan and it had been heartily approved by the hierarchy. They had requested his work on such a subject and he had attended whole-heartedly to the matter, for he had the mind capable of such clear and strategic thought, of developing ideas with military precision.

And he had the experience, experience of the success of violence and terror. He was well used to command and brandished it like a fearsome weapon.

It had frozen her, frightened her. The extent of his scheme bewildered and horrified her.

Now she must deal with this, quash it, extinguish it.

Where is Dover, indeed!

She knew where Dover was for, unbeknown to them, she had just returned from the port. In meeting her trusted Englishman she had betrayed Chastian's cause and betrayed Chastain himself.

The man in England she had come to trust knew how to conquer Chastain's game. He would despatch the right man to match the Frenchman at every turn, and quell the design before it could gain a foothold and erupt. And in so doing cut the heart from any future plans.

The right man. She knew nothing of him and would never meet him, but she had little choice but to trust those she had put her faith in.

Veronique was confident but now eternally afraid.

Strong, self-willed and confident. But more afeared than she had ever been before.

Indeed, death might be the least of her worries.....

Chapter One

It had been an unpleasant journey. It had been a completely disagreeable day.

He was soaked through, freezing cold, and very hungry. Yet he gave no thought, not a moment's envy, for the coach's occupants. They were no better off than he, despite being inside and protected from the lashing rain on this filthy, God-forsaken February day.

A dark, miserable day. The noise of the stage as it thrashed along a road barely worthy of the title was intolerable, and if the rain was not bad enough the spray from puddles on this rutted, bedevilled highway stung his flesh. Yet he made no effort to shield his face.

In fact he stared around him seemingly absorbed in the passing Kent countryside, when in truth there was so little to see, so little to make out. His facial expression rarely changed, whatever the circumstances, and that made his moods and emotions difficult to make out.

The remaining money in his pocket had not been sufficient for the entire journey to Dover, and now he was approaching the point where he must alight, several miles short of his destination.

And night was drawing in.

Thank God, he thought, even the highwaymen do not fancy the likes of this treacherous weather!

But he knew he could not reach Dover this very day. Too far, too dark, too windswept, too wet.

None of this bothered him.

He climbed down from the coach, small bag in hand, and watched the horses make their difficult and dismal headway dragging their charge along this dreadful road.

The turnpikes had made a difference. Some roads were well maintained as a result and in truth it had not been too bad as far as Barham, south east of Canterbury. But it was winter and the dreariest and most unloved of seasons, throwing its weight behind maelstroms of bad weather and unpredictable storms, had made mess of mans best efforts to make travel reasonable or even desirable.

Within seconds he was following the coach and guessed he had an hour of daylight, if you could call this murk daylight, before night would blot out any hope of finding the road ahead.

Determinedly he strode into a small thicket and thence into a woodland, barely showing the pain of brambles clawing at his hands, occasionally plunging into muddy puddles that were now virtually small ponds, until he found what he was looking for.

An ancient tree, its branches bent double with its terrible age, one thick branch in particular curling downwards in such a way that it provided beneath it a less wet and somewhat protected haven, free from the searching wind. Neither rain nor wind could positively locate this shelter although both tried and did so with occasional success, but without troubling its occupant.

It was fine for him.

He nestled down in his sodden clothing, curled into a ball and closed his eyes. In spite of the cold, the hunger, the encircling darkness, he slept and slept well, for these were not inconveniences he couldn't cope with, and he relegated them to the role of minor issues not worthy of his concern.

Oliver Kindale had known more troublesome times.

The sounds of the night as the weather eased, the sounds of animals and birds, eerie and weird in the pitch blackness, did not disturb him or discomfort him in any way. It was a world he knew, a life he understood.

***

Kindale was on the road before sun-up.

The sun was a welcome diversion from the previous day's atrocious weather, but it rose too low in the sky to warm, let alone dry Oliver Kindale's soaking clothing which clung to him like the hug of an eager yet desperate woman.

And he had known some of them. Desperate for the warmth of a man or, in all probability, for the comfort of his money. They clung to both.

In Faversham he had wasted his money on Belo Jennie, a lady of the night. She tended to cling more than perform but still required full payment. He was well rid of her and now longed to rid himself of these dirty, sopping wet rags that dragged him back and hindered him, and emphasised the coldness that had penetrated the innermost organs of his aching body, numbing his limbs, his fingers, his joints.

He could cope with hunger and he was no stranger to pain.

About a mile from Dover he ventured a short way up a farmtrack to where he could see smoke floating lazily away from a chimney at a farmworker's cottage. It was a small building, in fact three terraced homes clustered tight together, tiny rooms, little space, and the smoke was rising from the furthest of these tumbledown hovels.

That was the property he headed for.

The man who opened the door, for all his unkempt appearance, was quite probably younger than Kindale, although it may have been hard to tell. His scruffy, unshaven face matched the rag-bag of ill-fitting and well-soiled clothes he was wearing, and his light unruly hair seemed to be growing in all directions and doing so in a loathsome maze.

The two men stared at each other.

The one at the cottage door sniffed, scratched his head, nodded and then allowed a fierce grin to form on his lips.

"Kenton said you were coming," he commented as he beckoned his visitor inside.

It was only when both were past the door and the door was closed that the two embraced.

"Been a long time Oliver, but good to have ye back. Come, let's get them wet clothes off you. God, where have you been, man, to be drenched like that?" His voice was between a deep, rasping growl and a gentler, whispered tone.

Kindale looked around him. A pigsty. Nothing changes, he thought. And yet the cramped home had a feel of hospitality about it, and Oliver knew Harry Harblow would make him welcome in any case. He spoke.

"Where's Mary?"

"Away. A week, maybe longer. Just us two, Oliver."

"I need a change of clothes and a horse...."

"No, you need food and I daresay drink, and you need sleep my friend...."

"Who do I see in Dover...?"

Harry's face hardened into strong, chiselled features that might have been easily overlooked at first sight, and he not only appeared serious but threatening, the face of a man who would brook no nonsense or argument.

"You go tomorrow. Horse out the back. And you're going to Folkestone. And there's no more till you've eaten and rested, and that's a fact my son. I'll get you clothes; mine are a sight big for you but they'll do. Get them things off while I'm away upstairs."

And he turned for the stairs leaving Oliver ready to ask more questions, but with only a retreating back to aim them at he held his tongue and did as he was bid.

Harry knew Oliver of old. Oliver's face never gave anything away. There was seldom a smile, never a grimace, no acknowledgment of surprise, no sign of fear. And not an inkling of warmth and compassion.

Harblow brought some clothes which he tossed casually in the direction of his now naked visitor.

"I'll get us some food, but first some ale, my son," and he permitted his mouth to once again melt into a grin which in its turn rendered his face friendly and appealing where it had been severe and unapproachable. He added a hearty but humourless laugh as he poured the ale and brought the poker from the fire to plunge into the drink to warm it.

He noted Oliver had a fine figure of a man, standing nearly six feet tall, looking strong and muscular, a man of power and dominance, at least from a physical perspective. His round face, expressionless as ever, was pale with a small, tight mouth, thin eyebrows and a slight shadow on his cheeks and chin where no razor had been in recent contact.

His eyes looked small and almost out of place on such a circular visage, an effect no doubt enhanced by close cropped hair which emphasised a bleak landscape, devoid of prominent cheekbones or any manly features. Even his ears were tucked neatly in at the sides, whereas, Harry considered humorously, his own stuck out even through his mop of hair!

In fact, Harry decided, Oliver looked anonymous, just how he wanted to look. It suited him and it suited his purpose. Harry wondered if women actually found him attractive. Possibly not, but then Harry wasn't a woman.

In truth, to Harry he looked a great deal better now he was dressed again.

"Ale, son," he offered, handing Kindale a mug. He knew he was the younger of the two but had always, always referred to Oliver as 'son', a mere term of friendship and affection, nothing more. It was his manner of speaking and accepted as such.

Oliver sat back, closed his eyes and drank, allowing the warm liquid to flood down his throat apace, welcome refreshment indeed.

Harry regarded his guest. Another aspect of his nakedness had been the scars. He could not have avoided seeing them yet tried to give the impression he had not. He recalled the time, some years back, when he had witnessed Oliver kill a man with his bare hands in an instant, taking a shot in the shoulder for his trouble.

It had been a highwayman, one of the rogues of the road, a hazard of travel to all and sundry.

Oliver had leaped at him, not even winced when he was shot, had disarmed the man, wrestled him to the ground where he lay lifeless, and nothing had changed his countenance. No registration of fear or pain, no anger, no ferocity.

And afterwards no expression of remorse or guilt.

A criminal executed in the execution of crime. A cold-blooded, heartless killing of a man who would've taken Oliver's life, and probably Harry's too, if he had been given the chance. He certainly was not aiming at Kindale's shoulder when he fired his pistol.

Harry had noted the mark on Oliver's shoulder, a permanent reminder that the wound might have proved fatal if the shot had found its intended mark, Oliver's head.

Harblow prepared food. It was as unattractive as it was unappetising but to a starving man it would've represented a feast, a banquet, and Kindale tackled it in the manner of a man who had not eaten for days, although the host was confident he had.

When both had eaten Harry added logs to the failing fire and they sat either side of it, glad of its warmth as the flames sprang up again.

Drinks were replenished and despatched without further conversation, whereupon Oliver Kindale sat back in his chair, closed his eyes again and this time slept.

He woke, as Harry termed it, the 'right side' of midnight having slept for hours and done so with great peace and gentle, rhythmic snores, his sleep ostensibly uninterrupted by dreams, never mind nightmares.

"Folkestone, you say?" queried Kindale, making his question sound more of an attacking statement than an interested comment. He had barely opened his eyes and his mind had turned at once to matters of importance, no yawns or civil remarks to suggest he was presently leaving the lengthy repose he had just enjoyed, no courteous discourse with Harry upon waking besides curtly asking the time.

Harry was used to the man.

"Aye. Come in on the Canterbury road. Y'looking for the premises of a lawyer, Nathaniel Ballerden. You'll need to look, maybe ask. Not easy to find. He'll give you money, answer y'questions, provide a horse. Bring mine back the day after and you can spend the night here.

He'll also tell you where to find Katherine...."

Oliver looked up suddenly and stared at Harry, but with blank eyes and a cold, unmoved face.

"Yes, Katherine's there, ministering to the needy sailors, fishermen and smugglers and a few others besides I hear tell! Reckons its safe enough these days, the pox, the smallpox they call it, been and gone in her view, taken its victims, twice over, but it's as good as gone now.

"Been working her way south, attending to sailors' needs in the Cinque Ports and harbours from Thanet to Dover! Well travelled lady.

"Stay the night with her, she'll have some tales to tell and more, praps more use than old Ballerden!

"Folkestone's her home, but you'd be knowing that, where she was born like."

Throughout his explanation and revelation Harry Harblow didn't take his eyes from those of Oliver Kindale, but remained unsurprised at the lack of any emotional response from his caller, no twinge, no change of look, not the slightest twitch to give any feelings away.

Harry nodded and smiled knowingly.

That was Oliver Kindale.

"Does your horse know his own way home? I may not have time..."

Harry guffawed at the sarcasm then was immediately serious, his face screwed in anger. The fury passed as swiftly as it had arrived.

"Make time. You'll have it," he barked, then easing into a more amiable attitude smiled and added softly, "I need to see you before you do anything. We work together, Kenton's orders, don't forget that my son."

Oliver knew better than to offer any sort of argument or protest and so, as was his wont, he remained silent and did not even try to glare or surrender any thoughts by facial changes. He was impossible to read.

Instead he sank further into his chair as if hoping it would swallow him whole.

The gloom certainly had.

There was little light in the cottage on a bright day, and today had become gloomy and wintry so candles were flickering and the fire was smouldering for want of additional fuel and a good raking, and that was all the illumination they had.

It served them well. There was nothing either man needed to see.

Conversation turned to mundane matters. Harry's employment on the farm and the fact he gave the impression to be doing so little of it at present; how his wife, Mary, was these days and where she was right now; Harry's health, which was, he explained, mostly good and hearty; Oliver's health, an issue concluded by a simple, one word curt response and almost aggressive use of the word 'fine'.

"February," Harry said in a matter-of-fact way that suggested it was a detailed answer given in full and explicit fashion. Perhaps sensing a greater explanation was in order relating to his work he added:

"Not much doing, but I get a bit of money. He's a good man, he looks after me and I take care of him. Some work on next week, he tells me."

Mary was in Deal attending to her parents, both of whom, like Mary herself, were in fine spirits and good health.

"Well, fer their age," he felt needful of pointing out, "bones an' all must be creaking a bit, but comes to us all, spose." Oliver said nothing.

They discussed politics and war, although they touched solely upon the surface of such matters, but in so doing they arrived at the subject of crime.

"They say Grey Jonnie's in Kent. Been seen around and not in circumstances anyone would want to see him in if you get me drift." Harry decorated his text with a rueful smile and a concerned frown, neither of which Oliver would've noticed in the dark even if he had been looking.

He was studying the glimmering flames in the fire as they took hold on a log and set about devouring it, licking voraciously at the wood and eating into its very being, bent on destruction.

There was a brief silence before Oliver responded.

"Grey Jonnie? That'll upset Campo and Reeves I dare say," he commented with a snort. The two highwaymen had been the scourge of the road twixt Canterbury and Dover and much of the surrounding area into the bargain, although they were supposedly sworn enemies and never worked together.

"Ah, Campo's getting too old, my son," Harry argued dismissively, "and he won't be around long and many folks agree on that. Not been seen since the autumn anyway, so maybe he's dead and gone. An' Reeves is careless, youth has made a fool of him and it'll be the hangman who corrects him I'll wager ye. And it'll be soon."

Oliver had nothing to add, or if he did he kept it to himself. Grey Jonnie a long, long way from home territory. Now why should that be?

Shortly after they retired, having taken more ale and food, and exhausted conversation, such as it was.

Harry realised Oliver wasn't going to talk about what he had to do. That was quite normal and to be expected, but Harry was worrying about Oliver discounting him in the days or weeks ahead. He wanted to be involved, *needed* to be involved, *was* involved; Mr Kenton had seen to that. And Harry's world represented a relatively safe haven for Oliver Kindale, a kind of safety and security to fall back on.

Not that Kindale gave the impression of needing anyone's help or taking advantage of any security they might offer. Both men had known betrayal and its bitter consequences. Perhaps that was why their trust was not easily obtained and maybe it was why Oliver did not put all his faith in Harry, a fact Harry knew and understood.

He himself only trusted Oliver up to a point.

For it was Oliver who had once taught him 'Trust only in yourself. Trust nobody else. Always allow that the person you trust may prove unworthy of your regard. Plan accordingly and keep an eye on your back. Don't even trust me, Harry, and I won't trust you. There is no offence in these words. We respect each other highly, and there is a kind of trust. But let it go no further.'

And so the night passed and both men were up before the dawn, preparing.

Chapter Two

The horse had a mind of its own.

Normally Oliver would've been happy to believe an animal as beautiful, graceful, powerful and elegant as a horse had intellect and intelligence and therefore a mind of its own.

But the 'old nag', as he called the mount Harry had lent him, was exercising its mind too greatly for its rider, pausing without warning to eat handy vegetation, and occasionally turning back as if it had endured enough and home was calling.

He'd never ridden a horse that so hopelessly failed to respond to the reins and to his exhortations for obedience. And the journey was taking too long.

Following Harry's directions they had been down dale, up hill and down dale again, and now up once more as they headed across country to meet the road from Canterbury to Folkestone.

Finally he could see the Channel glinting in the poor sunlight, the few slender rays that the grey, angry clouds permitted to cast their tiny shafts of sunshine upon the water. The clouds spared no thought for the land and consequently no rays, thin or otherwise, were allowed to break through the dreariness and overpowering blanket that covered most of the sky above the fields and pastures of Kent.

He had gained the right road, something that was a sight worse than the one he had travelled on to reach Harry, but at least it was downhill now. Down and down, towards the sea.

A young woman was trudging towards him with a basket on her arm and looking full weary and heavy in the leg.

"Where y'going?" he enquired in his naturally brusque style.

"Up road, another mile or more," she responded in a disinterested manner. "What's it to you?"

"Climb up, I'll take you."

It was more of a command than an invitation but, for whatever reason, she refused.

"No. Go m'own way." And after a moment's hesitation, and the resumption of her journey, "but thanks." Neither looked back.

Oliver left it at that. He was not the sort to persist let alone insist. Maybe she didn't trust him and he could hardly blame her, so he dismissed the encounter and proceeded on his way.

He found Nathaniel Ballerden with ease. At first he thought the labourer who had directed him had sent him the wrong way, for the cottage was every part as small as Harry's and probably as dingy.

In that he was wrong. It was surprisingly light and airy.

He was also wrong in his assumption about Ballerden.

Kindale expected this solicitor to be ancient, bent, thin, with a voice like a rasp being scraped across wood, and to be absent-minded, disorganised and time wasting. He was none of these.

About the same age as Oliver he was also about the same height, well built and boasting a neatly groomed moustache on a face even Oliver found remarkably attractive.

His speech was clear and precise and, unusual in a lawyer, he never used ten words where one would do. Ballerden gave the impression that time was always of the essence, that time was a gift not to be squandered or abused, and that business was there to be conducted swiftly, sensibly and with the minimum of fuss.

He spoke in the same tone, devoid of emphasis or emotion, about everything that fell within his compass as Oliver soon learned.

A great deal more money changed hands than Oliver had expected.

"My man, Whitmore, will fetch your horse. I've given orders. You'll find the animal dutiful, spirited but in a way a man may control, obedient and with stamina to spare. She's a fine mare and will do you well. Look after her Mr Kindale.

"She's yours for as long as it takes. Return her to Mr Harblow, not here. You don't come here again unless Mr Kenton advises otherwise. Confirm you understand, please."

Oliver nodded agreement. It was all that was required. He asked questions that were important to him, obtained answers to some, the ones that Ballerden could reply to, but three or four went without comment other than a shrug of the shoulders of the man of law.

"Money?"

"Ask Mr Harblow. Give him notice and he'll obtain what you require. Within reason, of course."

Within reason. Yes mused Kindale, within reason, naturally. And another means of keeping me beholden to Harry.

Finally, business finalised, he asked about Katherine.

Ballerden directed him.

"She's not a well woman, Mr Kindale." But he did not elucidate and Oliver did not pursue it. He wanted to press on and no doubt Ballerden was of the same mind.

***

In another life Katherine Downford might have been a woman Oliver Kindale would've loved, but he was not a man for attachments of any sort. And she was not the kind of woman to trust a man with anything and definitely not her heart.

She catered for their wants because to do so was valuable to her and nothing more. Her fees were modest because the purchase of pleasure was not her main commerce. Information was.

In the relaxation of inebriation and in the comfort of her bed men could be encouraged to speak, and to talk at length, often with an openness most unwise.

Information thus acquired usually had a value.

An unfaithful husband was at much at risk as a smuggler or corrupt politician.

And she had grown wealthy, at least by her own undemanding standards, on the indiscretions of others.

Her 'work' was not without danger which had led to a nomadic life, which in turn had led her back to Folkestone and 'retirement', a commitment she was pleased with given her financial security and failing health, and the need to nurse her dying mother.

Thanks to the undisclosed source of income her parents had lived in some style, that is, a style that most in Folkestone would've regarded as quality. But at that time this was little more than a substantial fishing village her parents lived in, the gradual development of the harbour and the town lying a few years ahead.

Twice ravaged by smallpox during the century Folkestone fought on.

Katherine's father had been taken by the disease, his days as a fisherman over for good. With him went a lucrative career in smuggling wool out and brandy back into his country. Death by disease may have saved him from the hangman's noose as those who worked for him were caught by the Excise men two months later.

They'd been betrayed, but not by Katherine who had, nonetheless, given up other smugglers to the law. The arrangement worked both ways. With two other girls she had once entertained five Excise men for a long night while a gang unloaded their bounty with impunity.

The financial reward from the gang had been substantial, well worth the time afforded to the lawmen, time that exceeded that which they had actually paid for.

But then Katherine had no scruples and no obvious conscience.

Oliver Kindale sat quietly, sipping the port she had given him, answering her questions with softly spoken and truthful words, just as she replied to him.

They were the superficial enquiries of old friends and contained no intimacy or demonstrated any fondness above mild affection. Both knew the questions they must never ask.

When they had met in Ramsgate those years ago Katherine had been an attractive young woman, attractive but never lovely, but with a figure envied by many women she knew, and many she didn't. And sought after by men, of course.

Clearly curvaceous then, she had now lost any such physical attributes, her face drawn and pale, her cheeks sunken, a woman old before her time. Her black hair had once beguiled him, flowing freely down her shoulders and beyond. Today it barely reached her shoulders and looked tired and matted.

She looked tired herself. Her eyes slightly reddened but not from tears, nor from the winter's weather.

"You're not in good health."

Oliver's words, possibly intended as a question, sounded like a statement and one that did not require response.

"Pains, bad pains after I've eaten. So I don't eat much. Drink doesn't trouble me; that's good, is – it - *not*?" She dragged out the words and her mouth twisted into an anguished grin. And she laughed without humour, disposed of her port and refilled her glass and immediately drank again.

"The physician? What does he say?"

"Something inside me, something he cannot get to, I don't know, *I don't know*, nothing for you to worry about. I've got medicine, leave it at that." Frustration was crawling into her utterances and manifesting itself in her facial expression, so Oliver pursued the matter no further and changed the subject.

"Your mother?"

"Dying of old age, what do you expect? Dying of a broken heart for all I know. She truly loved my father but better he should die as he did than from the full effects of the law on his head."

She emptied her glass.

And refilled it.

There was now bitterness in her voice and Oliver recognised the need to tread with care. After all, he sought information and had not called to rekindle an old fire.

He saw before him a woman eaten up by the life she had chosen, all but destroyed by the path she had travelled, and now she was staring despair, pain and anguish in the face, recompense perhaps for the unsavoury deeds undertaken all too often.

No redemption awaited her. Bitterness would accompany her to the grave. Eternal damnation would be her companion. Yet he felt no sorrow. It was not his way to feel compassion.

She proffered a decent meal, ale, tidbits of information that might or might not be useful to him, and the contentment of her bed, and he accepted all four.

And at first light he departed and rode up the steep hill out of Folkestone towards Dover.

He was riding Ballerden's horse, or rather the horse he had supplied, a fine looking animal that exuded strength and might and yet was totally within his control. Beth, by name, was all that the lawyer had promised and ideal for whatever he planned. Alongside was another mare, Harry's, the 'old nag' he had ridden the day before.

He hadn't bothered to ask the horse's name and Harry hadn't told him. But now she seemed quite happy to go wheresoever Beth led and do so without let or hindrance.

The three passed the Jolly Sailor under a scurry of thick, grey clouds and, atop the cliffs, found themselves in the force of the strong, icy wind blowing from the east. There was a possibility the sun had risen above the horizon in front of them but nothing in the way of light to confirm that fact. Nevertheless Kindale assessed there was a chance the weather would improve as the morning took hold.

And indeed it did, but not until after his arrival in Dover.

He wanted a good look round. It was some time since he had been to the Kentish port, now a well established harbour with a degree of shelter, as he observed from the cliffs above.

Yet it was far from popular with smugglers and with good reason.

He looked across the valley to the towering shape of Dover castle rising from the cliffs opposite and back down to the harbour.

Soldiers on hand to support the Customs officers.

Of course that didn't stop the smugglers, he mused. Better organised than the authorities in some cases. He knew of a gang that could summon the help of a hundred or more men when a major haul needed landing with onward shipment inland and concealment required.

It was an efficient business, a ruthless commercial enterprise, which owed much to strategic planning that would put the military to shame! The Kent coast was, for mile after mile of its length, alive with smuggling activity. Small time operations, large gangs, they were all here.

A landing would often be planned to arrive anywhere along a stretch of coast, men posted all along the way checking the movement of soldiers and other 'opponents' and giving an appropriate signal to the boatsmen to guide them to the safest beach.

The smugglers land forces would be similarly galvanised and ready to meet the sea crew.

Kindale admired the fact this was so often no haphazard arrangement, these men having a chain of effective command the envy of the army, and able to organise an event with astonishing precision, executing it with amazing skill and speed.

Not all smugglers worked in such gangs. There were what Kindale called the small fry, individuals running their own affairs but wisely keeping clear of the main forces.

Yes, he admired them, and admired them all. Too many men driven by hunger and the need to feed starving families. Some driven by greed, pure and simple. He even admired *them* but in a different way.

But that didn't mean he supported what they were doing. He knew that if caught they would probably face transportation these days and not a dance at the end of a rope. Most might prefer the executioner's halter to an all too often fatal journey to the other side of the globe.

Their deeds undermined the country's economy and financial well-being, and Kindale found no satisfaction in that.

He made his way down to the town. He found himself imagining that Ballerden was probably in the service of smugglers and was quite capable of running rings around the courts. It was not unusual for solicitors to be part of the smuggling operation for that very reason.

They should find gainful and legal employment by running the country, he thought, and laughed out loud. Do better than Pitt and all them rascals, he reasoned, and laughed all the more. The politicians, he decided, talk about what they want to do. These men simply get on and do it!

That way you get things done, he concluded.

Yes, he admired and sympathised when it came to smuggling, but loathed men engaging in acts of illegality, whatever the moral right and wrongs. In another man such conflict of thoughts might prove an ordeal too great, but Oliver could support both with equanimity.

The sun was making a determined effort to break through and there was indeed some shelter from the wind down by the harbour Oliver Kindale was now walking around. He would easily memorise details. He'd always been able to do that.

The horses were temporarily stabled and he sought food and ale at an inn. He knew where he must go next and Ballerden had given him clear directions also describing the house in fine detail.

Not that it was much more than Harry Harblow possessed, but this property was squashed in a whole street of similar unsafe looking structures that hung menacingly over the narrow road from both sides.

He just avoided a bucket of waste being emptied from an upstairs window at the neighbouring house and quickly moved to the front door of his destination. He recognised the lean, middle-aged man, surprisingly smart for this part of town, who opened the door.

"Monsieur Chastain?"

"Par-don?" Chastain's accent had given him away and put beyond reasonable doubt any question of his identity in Kindale's mind. The Frenchman had no recognition for his visitor but then he had never met him, whereas Kindale had once observed him in a crowded inn at Greenwich, and had been making the observation for the purpose of future identification.

"You are Chastain. May we speak?"

The man suddenly looked afraid.

"I am sorry, my name is .... well, I am not this Chastain. I am sorry..."

"You are Chastain, monsieur, and I will talk to you. Now may I come in?"

"No, no, I am not ... what did you say? ... Chastain. No, you may not come in. You are mistaken. There is no Chastain here. Good-day monsieur."

Kindale walked away as Chastain slammed the door. He had achieved what he wanted. He had not intended to enter the premises for he had nothing to say, that is, nothing to say at this stage. But he wanted to frighten the man, to leave him worried and fretting.

Chastain's English was excellent but his anger and fear had forced him into a basic error. In dismissing Kindale he had referred to him as 'monsieur' and no Englishman would have done that!

Oliver Kindale laughed aloud much to the consternation of those he was passing.

So Chastain was passing himself off as an Englishman and he was indeed in Dover. Very much so, for he had property here, or at least was lodging in the house. All very well, all very well, Kindale thought. Now we will see what he does, he decreed. Now we will see.

***

Chastain sat back and considered the encounter.

Was everything exposed? It could not be so. This must be a chance meeting with some ruffian, possibly a smuggler he had come across in northern France, someone Chastain had made use of and who sensed the opportunity to earn more of the Frenchman's money now he had recognised him.

Surely that must be it. Surely it posed no threat and certainly no threat to his operation.

Chastain was thorough. He had weighed up every aspect and balanced every conceivable outcome, every possible diversion, in working at his plan and assessing the chances of success. He would not, he *could* not allow the prospect of betrayal at this early stage to destroy all that laid before him. It must be coincidence.

Yes, that was it. He had used English seamen in his schemes and this man, this ragged ill-dressed wretch, had taken his pay for some particular purpose long ago and had simply observed him here in Dover and thought further remuneration might be forthcoming. Hopefully the man would accept his error and withdraw and cause no trouble.

And if he did return? Well, that would be at his peril. Chastain could deal with him as he had dealt with others who had interfered with him and his work.

The Frenchman's strength was his self-belief and he had built upon his reputation at every step. With every success, every achievement that self-belief had evolved and grown and he was now mentally awash with his own grandeur. He was indispensible to the cause, he had made himself so. At another time he might have been a great general planning campaign after campaign. But he was needed in the present in a different sphere and it pleased him for it required all his ingenuity.

21

And he knew the rewards awaiting him would be considerable.

He was invincible! Nobody could defeat him. His grand affair, planned down to the tiniest detail, would not be easily undone and certainly not by an unintelligent creature such as had confronted him at the door. Was his scheme not applauded by those who mattered, those who had commissioned its creation, development and implementation, those who knew he would not fail the cause?

Those who would promote him! Those who appreciated his talents for what they were worth and the benefits they brought.

It was a major work, the product of genius, in its way a complete work of art to be revered and treasured. He was immensely proud of it.

No, the visitor was mere coincident, and nothing to fret about. Any concerns vanished from his mind and were dusted away as one might remove crumbs from a table.

And that self-assurance, had he been humble enough to be aware of it was also his weakness, a weakness Kindale was relying on. His choice of those he worked with was as precise as his scheming, and he foresaw no possibility of betrayal amongst those he chose, those who feared him the most.

The woman he lay with at night, who acted the part he had decreed by day, was the one he trusted the most. He made love to her, beautifully, gently, passionately, cruelly, violently until his lust and his pride were satisfied. Her fear assured him of his utter dominance. But that fear was also an act on her part, an act loathed, but to be suffered at all costs.

This woman he trusted so, the one he nightly humiliated and violated, would have killed him at a moment's notice, and done so with great violence of purpose, yet knew she must not do it. It was the plan she must kill; Chastain must be alive to proceed until his project is shattered and cast before him in shreds.

***

It was later in the day when Oliver arrived back at Harblow's cottage.

He was pleased to see the back of the 'old nag' and left Harry to stable both horses while he found himself some ale in the dark, dank, yet strangely welcoming front room.

There was hardly any conversation and Oliver fell asleep aside the fire which was blazing in a glorious show of red, yellow and blue flames that made a large, damp log sizzle and spit in hopeless defiance.

After sleep there was food. After food the two men talked.

But it was very spasmodic talk, brief staccato words gingerly spoken by men who were wary of each other yet with no good reason to be so. Questions were asked almost apologetically, answers were given curtly and briefly.

There was no animosity. This was just the way their world revolved. They knew it well and understood it, so neither gave or accepted offence.

Harry would've wanted to know Oliver's plans, and Oliver was giving nothing away. Harry expected no less. It was the way it was, the way they knew.

"Ballerden must be into all sorts," Oliver commented, hoping to elicit more detail from the man opposite.

"He may be, but not my place to know, not my place to find out. But, aye, he's more than a solicitor and no mistake." A wry grin settled on Harblow's lips but even though he was looking directly at him Kindale would not have seen the smile in the darkness.

Two candles were poorly employed and might have been extinguished for the good they were doing. The fire had settled and was crackling peacefully as a man might gently snore, but possessed insufficient glow to truly illuminate either man.

"You don't cross Ballerden, that much I know. You'd do well to heed his words, my son."

"I'll do that, Harry, I'll do that. And I'll be away in the morning. I'm heading east. Deal. Can't be sure when I'll be back. Ballerden says to ask you for money when needed."

"That's it, Oliver. That's what you do. But don't turn up unexpected and want it right then. I need time to …. arrange it, that's it, time to arrange it. Deal, you say? I can give you an address if you need a room."

Oliver nodded. Harry didn't see the nod but assumed that Oliver had agreed, so proceeded to give directions.

"You ask for Jack but don't be taken aback. A lady, is Jack, a fair lady who won't take none of yer nonsense neither. Give her no trouble and she'll look after ye, for a price mind, and tell nobody you're there. You can come and go as you please. Tell her you've come from Harry Harblow and if that don't work say you're a friend of Nathaniel Ballerden.

"That opens doors, my son. Always does." And a slight, almost inaudible laugh was born in his throat and made its way with considerable alacrity to his mouth where it erupted into a lengthy and raucous guffaw.

Oliver Kindale smiled inwardly. He liked this man. He didn't trust him but that was mutual and the price of the nature of their friendship and the field in which they worked, nothing more.

Tomorrow he would meet this Jack, this fair lady Jack. Tomorrow would be the next step on his path to success, to reaching the goal of his quest. It was a good ten years since he last visited Deal. Ten long years.

So much had happened, so much had changed. He saw his life as having a defined shape where in fact it had none at all. He saw his life as a subject of natural progress, shaped by whatever fell in his way, guided not always by principles but always by determination and commitment.

His life was always about 'tomorrow'. He planned for what lay around the immediate corner, and whatever life threw at him that day he simply adjusted his tactics if necessary so that he might plan for the 'tomorrow' after that.

Although he saw life as a path of indeterminate length he was in reality caught up in the simple, uncomplicated drift from one moment to the next, and nothing in his life took him further. Never. Never once.

No long term plans, no dreams, no hopes for the future. Surviving today was all that mattered to Oliver Kindale. His targets were neatly contained by what could be accomplished in the present. If he was still alive after that he would then be planning the next moves, the ones that took him inextricably to the time immediately beyond.

Oliver's life had taught him not to dream or to wish for a future of happiness and contentment. Consequently he had formed no attachments or close friendships, choosing instead a road of mistrust devoid of a vision of later life.

In his early years he learned to check his emotions and not to be disappointed when people let him down and sometimes did so badly. It might be thought such early lessons had scarred him and provided the medium for avoiding any form of relationship, but, being of generous spirit in those formative years, he continued to let people draw close.

And suffered.

Now he was mentally and emotionally as cold as ice.

Never would anyone be allowed to melt him. Safer that way, spiritually and physically. He did not fear death for he knew he rode close to the wind and that fact may have guided his existence based solely on today and tomorrow.

It did not make him reckless. He was cautious, wary and extremely careful. His planning was meticulous. He did not fear death but he had no wish to die even though he courted his demise by virtue of the way he chose to live.

He was capable of being afraid but had learned how not to show it, least of all to an enemy.

He did indeed keep his emotions well buried. He looked inscrutable because he was. And that was the way he preferred it.

Over time he had lost the art of crying; a tearful child when things had gone wrong and usually painfully so, as they so often did, he gradually discovered he could block out the torment and that eased the mental torture and sorrow.

Never look back.

He never did. If he lived in the present and organised tomorrow he quickly forgot yesterday. It was a simple philosophy and it worked for him.

What he achieved right now was his own personal glory or displeasure, and thus it was that each and every moment was either enjoyed or disliked, and it did not go any further than that.

His sleep remained mostly untroubled, no nightmares to wake him nor bad dreams to disturb him. Sleep always came easily, as it had that recent night in the undergrowth, and it had washed over him now, so completely, so utterly.

Deal was for tomorrow, not for his sleep.

***

And after sleep came the journey.

Over the cliffs northwards until Deal hove into sight.

The transformation was instant yet steady. The pathway meandered down towards the sea as the hills and cliffs, seemingly vexed and wearied by retaining their height and magnificence, and their vain efforts to reach the sky, laid down, very gradually and very gently, in softer rolls until a degree of evenness by the shore could be obtained.

Here they rested exhausted, the flatlands extending northwards untroubled to distant Thanet.

The low hills of Ringwould and Kingsdown stood as nature's defiance to this sudden change in the dramatic landscape, a brief, almost childish and pointless attempt to stand in the way of the inevitable. A last gasp, a final challenge beyond the mighty cliffs, as the Kent coastline eased itself into the calmer, unexciting, contourless area with its pebble-ridden shores.

Here lay Walmer and Deal.

Oliver observed both castles, little changed since his previous visit, and wondered how much of a threat they might pose to Chastain's scheme. They were taking on an increasing air of the residential but he still felt they would, when fully armed, be a prodigious obstacle to French invasion or indeed any foreign incursion along these shores.

Walmer was in the hands of the Lord Warden of the Cinque Ports and looking less military than he remembered. It was already resembling something more of a grand house (befitting the home of the Lord Warden) than a base from which soldiers might pour forth on the attack or which might have to be stoutly defended. Definitely not an immediate threat to the Frenchman, he concluded, especially as the present incumbent of the post of Lord Warden was in London.

Deal appeared rather different, a military establishment ready to conduct whatsoever business might come its way, but again, to the attentive, it might seem to lean towards being a home. Which, of course, it was, just as was the case at Walmer. Kindale imagined both would rise to the challenge and be truly formidable opponents if the time should come.

But Chastain's existence was most unlikely to trouble the authorities at present as far as these two were concerned, and Oliver Kindale didn't want to involve anyone here. So the situation suited his purpose. The fewer people caught up in this affair the better.

He preferred to operate alone, and never took more than the tiniest handful into his confidence and then only if absolutely necessary.

And with those thoughts to comfort him he continued his journey in pursuit of the lady called Jack.

Chapter Three

"Jack?"

"Who wants him?" she snarled.

"Harry Harblow says Jack's a woman. You?"

She leaned against the jamb and regarded him with a mixture of disdain and dislike, folding her arms across her chest, suspicious but not afraid.

"Jack's my husband, or was. Transported, he was. Harry tell yer that?" Her voice had an air of defiance and annoyance.

She was by no means tall, but stocky with long brown hair that fell wherever it would, all around and about her. She screwed her mouth in a sarcastic gesture that challenged him to try and be clever with her. He stood silently a discreet three feet from the door and waited for her to resume her words. Her visual sarcasm manifested itself into speech.

"Lost fer words? My, I'd have expected more. You look the talkative kind and if you ain't got nothing more to say I'm busy and need to get about me work."

There was crude beauty in her face, yet it was marked with the ravages of time and undoubtedly the ravages of suffering, for so surely had she suffered. He could see all that in her eyes alone.

Still they sparkled and sparkled mischievously.

"Harry said to see Jack for some lodgings, that's all."

"You from the Revenue? Come to smile at me misfortune, come to laugh at me loss, have you? Come to tell me Jack's dead, been thrown overboard somewhere between here and hell?"

Her voice increased in strength and was overtaken by her anger and bitterness.

"Not Revenue," he replied firmly, interrupting what he felt sure was going to become a fearsome tirade against Authority, or what pain Authority could inflict, an Authority he did not represent or necessarily subscribe to. "Transported for what?" he added swiftly.

"Smuggling, what else round here? And don't tell me you didn't know...."

"I don't know, and Harry didn't say. He said speak to Jack about lodgings, and that Jack was a lady. That's all."

Her rage subsided in her face but her breathing was still sharp and frequent, her bosom throbbing, for her wrath was always within her blood and even now still racing through her body.

"Come in, we'll talk," she said at last as the fury ebbed away and hopeless resignation took its place.

A kind of laughter emitted from her lips as she took him indoors, but it was a sad, shallow laugh, a laugh of self-pity, a sombre laugh at herself.

"Me a lady? What does Harry know? He loved me once, do you know that? He did, he loved me, but I set him aside for Jack, my beautiful Jack, and now he's gone, gone somewhere over the horizon, praps to the bottom of the sea for all I know or care.

"Yes, I'm called Jack, mister, and what's you be called then, and what's your business here?"

He didn't answer directly, choosing to ask a question of his own.

"Why did you think I was Revenue just because I mentioned Harblow?" It was clear the query had stunned her a little and she was now most unsure of herself. She self-consciously brushed the hair from her face and nervously twined some around her fingers under her chin. She was weighing him up, deciding if she should be afraid, deciding if he was in any way suspicious, but knowing he couldn't be trusted.

In the silence that followed she beckoned him to a seat where he sat, crossed his legs and gave a full impression of confidence, probably because confident was what he was. But then he wasn't the one who was nervous.

Jack perched on a bench in front of the fire which itself looked lifeless and disinterested, and after a while spoke again.

"Look, who *are* you? Why so many questions? Jack's transported for his crime and I'll ne'er see him again, so what's your game? Harry never forgave me, so praps he let them know what Jack was about, revenge like. I don't know and now I don't care. There's talk y'know. Talk about Harry and the Revenue. Praps you can tell *me* if you know him so well?

"Is he helping the Excise men? No, you wouldn't tell me if you knew, would you? But there's talk hereabouts, mister, and you'd better watch your tongue in Deal if you talk about Harry Harblow. There's some here would kill if they thought he was a traitor. So what you about then and what's your name my friend?"

There was silence as the two looked steadily at each other, trying, without success, to see past the facade and to see the truth. He was warming to her.

She was a tangle! Her hair was in a tangle, her mind was in a tangle, her emotions were in a tangle. She had trouble expressing herself yet made herself plain; she was capable of intellect and rational thought but made a tangle of it!

"I'm Oliver Kindale and my business in Deal is my own and not yours. I've known Harry many long years. He's a Dover man, his wife's from Deal and is here now tending her parents. He'd no more betray himself than his own kind. I am no agent of the law and neither is he. We have no cause to side with the law. You must take my word....."

"Well, Oliver Kindale, you be minding your own business and clutch it to your heart, but be warned there's them about that hold no friendship for Harry and as likely to object to and offend any friend of his.

27

"But you can stay here the night, Oliver Kindale, and tomorrow if you've a mind. If you want to stay any longer I'll find you somewhere else. Just that some folks are, well, worried about strangers and especially strangers asking questions."

Her voice rose, roused again by memories, but this time there was more than anger, there was distress, insolence, resentment and her face became a map of her emotions as she spluttered the words.

"They came and burned the boats here, did y'know, Oliver Kindale? Came and burned the boats, try and stop the smuggling, held us back by the points of their bayonets, they did. Did you know *that*, Oliver Kindale?"

Then she was soft again, soft and cold, quiet and reflective, pitiful and sad.

"Too many womenfolk seen their men hanged or transported for trying to put food in the mouths of their chicks."

Oliver couldn't prevent the words tumbling out.

"Your chicks, Jack?"

He regretted his hasty words and saw her eyes glisten.

"Eldest taken by the pox, youngest died the moment she were born, poor mite. What Jack made smuggling he used for other families .... and me. Saved a few here, Oliver Kindale, saved a few. And they chain him up and put him in a wreck of a ship no mean smuggler would attempt to take to sea. If they'd hung him I'd know he was dead, be able to mourn."

"Pay me when you leave. I'll show you the room."

The sudden change of tack took Kindale by surprise but he recovered on the instant and followed the lady called Jack, saddened and angry at what he had heard, but only too aware it was a story that lay manifold around Kent's coasts, much as it was around the rest of England's shoreline.

He was also aware that there were many that profited and profited well from the risks taken by ordinary men. They created as much misery as they forestalled to Oliver's way of thinking.

But starving or no, greed made honest men guilty.

And in Deal there were men of wealth made just as guilty.

***

He stood on the front, a brisk easterly wind chilling his face, the spray the wind whipped off the sea stinging his cheeks, his eyes, his mouth.

The sea raced in as a relay of angry waves. Each pounded the shore in turn, roaring and rasping upon the pebbles.

He watched a fishing vessel moving away from this shore. Honest men upon the tide, risking their very lives, and he wondered which among them became dishonest when the time was right and the chance of illicit goods became an opportunity made by the gods.

His clothes had barely recovered from the night in the woods, but at least he was dry and comfortable, even if his appearance was anything but gentlemanly. But Oliver Kindale was no gentleman, and his rags, as he called them, well-matched his purpose.

Jack had been a simple, undemanding hostess. He had been given a reasonably good meal last night and something this morning and he knew he could stay at least until the morrow. There had been no more conversation of a personal nature and she had sought no answers by asking no questions, and he had probed no further, the evening passing pleasantly with each party wary of the other, but friendly for all that.

He had taken to Jack. The complexity of the woman appealed to him. A woman in turmoil, yet cogniscent of her surroundings and appreciative of her circumstances, a woman acquainted with turbulence but capable of surmounting it all, of being brave, very brave. A woman who could reason all she faced and find the right answers from the muddy quagmire presented to her.

Yes, he had taken to her.

Not quite a widow, but a widow in all but name. What an endless misery to live within. Not knowing, never knowing, unable to grieve, unable to love again should she ever wish to. What a turmoil indeed!

Oliver moved slowly along the front. Another boat prepared for sailing. More honest men set to fight the mighty ocean for its harvest and hopefully, ever hopefully, the catch that would feed honest and innocent mouths.

You could not blame these hard working men, these men whose lives were the fickle fates to decide, for seeing and grasping the chance of improved income when such opportunity arrived at their doors. These men, whose lives could be snatched upon the swirling wind, the ungainly sea, the treacherous coasts, and tossed to heaven or hell without further ado, leaving grieving widows, sad children and hopeless debt.

They risked everything in pursuit of their simple goals, and they risked even more in illicit trade.

Oliver did not envy them, but admired them.

And Deal had grown wealthy and populous on shipping related activity, from boat building and repairs to providing victuals for the fleet vessels anchored in the Downs, the waters off the town. But not everyone prospered, that was clear.

**

He entered an inn, close by the front, and partook of ale, watching all that were therein, there actually being precious few.

Watching closely, intently.

And there were one or two who quite openly observed him, a stranger among them, perhaps someone to be kept an eye on, maybe someone simply passing by. One decided to make enquiry.

"On yer way somewheres, my friend?" The speakers face was covered with the same disorderly black hair that hung from his head, a thick moustache and a thicker beard, and dense black eyebrows. Dark, black hair everywhere. His rough clothing slung about him like old sacks made it difficult to determine his size, and his age was equally difficult to assess.

Oliver considered the query very carefully. Now wasn't the time to make enemies or raise too many suspicions and he knew he was within a suspicious community; Jack had made that clear.

"Travelling from Dover to Sandwich but in no rush, friend," he eventually responded, hoping it was a neutral enough answer and the matter might be allowed to rest there.

"What's yer business, my friend, or are you a man of the road?" All conversation had ceased and attention focused on their visitor.

"Just a travelling man, friend, just a travelling man enjoying a quiet drink along the way."

The inquisitor backed away, then returned to his seat and gradually the noise of several men talking once again filled the air. It was stuffy; a fire was trying hard to provide warmth but was emitting smoke as well, ventilation being exceptionally poor, and Oliver found himself longing for the outside world away from this stale, unimaginable atmosphere.

The exchange had crackled with tension in spite of the words being gently spoken.

This was a nervous town, offering nothing but caution to greet strangers in its midst.

He knew he had done nothing to ease any doubts and worries amongst these men, but also felt that they knew he posed no immediate threat sitting where they could see him. Perhaps one would follow when he left, just to make sure he knew his way to Sandwich and was safely bound upon the road out of Deal. Perhaps. He would soon find out.

The fierce east wind continued to flow freely across the landscape and to seek reckless access throughout the town. It drove into Oliver's face yet again, but he was still able to detect footsteps behind him and he knew instinctively he was being followed. He slowed his pace deliberately and paused before turning and seeing the black-haired man closing him no more than a dozen steps away.

"My friend, I will show you the road to Sandwich," he said with undisguised menace in a low-pitched gravelly drawl.

"Friend, I know the road and I have said I have no haste."

"My friend, better you go now."

Oliver now had to weigh up a situation that he was confident he could deal with. Most importantly he had produced a reaction and that had been his intention.

"Friend, I chose my own way and my own time, and go freely as I wish."

"My friend," began the black-haired man, the menace in his voice rising with its volume as he sought to make his position clear, "Ralph, back there, he says you were at Jack's last night, and that's enough to disturb those of us who might be wondering more about ye. Better y'head for Sandwich now, my friend, before we start asking questions and wanting real answers, like."

So what did a stranger staying with Jack indicate to these people? Oliver pondered the thought for a moment, never once taking his eyes from the man's gaze. He decided he needed to pursue this, for he had indeed roused the response to his arrival he had hoped for, and now he wanted to make hay and see progress in the right direction.

It was worth taking the risk.

"Friend, I stayed at Jack's on the advice of Nathaniel Ballerden." The man's eyes widened for a brief second, and he then nodded slowly two or three times.

"Ah, y'know Ballerden, do ye?" His voice had subsided and Oliver realised his risk had been beneficial. "How well do y'know him then, my friend?"

"Well enough for him to loan me his horse. I am not on foot and will ride on when the time is right."

The man considered this very carefully then held out his hand and a barely perceptible smile appeared on his face.

"If y'know Ballerden you're welcome here. I'm Temple. Thomas Temple." Oliver took the hand.

"Kindale. Oliver Kindale." Both men continued to stare into each other's eyes as if some vital revelation would be forthcoming from the visual investigation. It wasn't.

"And yer business, Oliver Kindale?"

"None of yours." Temple's face creased at Oliver's reply and then he laughed with a deep bellow, releasing Oliver's hand.

"Aye, none of mine. None of mine. Well, does your *private* business, Oliver Kindale, keep you in Deal for a night or more or shall 'e ride on anon?"

"Here tonight, Mr Temple, and after that, who knows. But I won't be informing you."

Temple rocked with laughter again.

"I like ye, Oliver Kindale, I like ye. I wish ye well with your mysterious business, sure as I am you are here on Ballerden's business." The laughter had vanished, a look of concern and warning appearing on Temple's face in so far as it could be detected.

It was useful information for Kindale. The solicitor was held in some regard and some awe too. It would serve him well, especially if people like Temple believed him and granted respect on the very basis that he might be present in pursuit of an errand of some sort for Ballerden.

Overall he had achieved his goal. His attendance in the town had been noted and by a wider audience than he'd dared to wish for. Now to make that count.

***

"I need somewhere out of town but nearby. Can you help me?"

Kindale was responding to Jack's probing comments on his future movements with particular regard to the following night. This evening he would stay with her, but she was adamant he would not be able to stay beyond that. Her face suggested she was giving the matter a great deal of deep thought and it was some while before she spoke.

"Might be. There's a cottage just south of here. I've been asking. M'sister Charlotte lives next door and'll keep an eye for ye. It belonged to one of Jack's friends, chained up and sent off with him, maybe at the bottom with him now for all I know."

"What of Charlotte?"

"Her man's long gone. Shot by soldiers. She says you can use the cottage but she won't be feeding you. The man had no family. Place is empty. But Charlotte'll only do what's necessary. She'll be there an' that's all y'need to know, Oliver."

Jack's husband and his comrade transported, Charlotte's husband shot. At least Charlotte was a widow, her man dead and buried, and the female Jack was in an emotional no-man's-land, still fretting and unable to settle in heart and in mind. Oliver felt for her. The aching was written in her face, toned her words, oversaw her life like a dense cloud in an otherwise sunlit sky, and was a chill presence in all she did.

Yes, Oliver felt for her. A living death indeed.

The following day he paid Jack what she had asked and took directions for the cottage and Charlotte. He had tried to offer more money to Jack but she had refused.

"No charity. Nothing extra from you Oliver. You've paid what I asked. That's our business over. Pay Charlotte what she's worth to you, but no more. She won't want it, be warned."

With that he mounted Beth and the horse ambled on its way at a pace that suited its rider. He wanted to look all about him, take in the surroundings, memorise things that might help him later, become more sure of the road.

He saw hardly a soul on his short ride, save a fleeting glimpse of Thomas Temple who nonetheless returned Oliver's wave despite there being some distance between them. What nature of work did his new 'friend' engage in, that is, if he engaged in any at all? He dismissed such a passing interest from his mind as he was busy assessing the road and its environs, and everything else he could see within his range.

In a little he had arrived at Charlotte's cottage and made himself known to her.

She had a look of perpetual moroseness, which he regarded as being barely surprising, given her circumstances in life.

She had little enough hair, cut right back, and a face of sallow features. He guessed she stood no more than five feet, was desperately thin, possibly unwell, maybe badly so, and what teeth she possessed were of irregular shape and protruded from her gums at all angles. He noticed that particularly as soon as she spoke.

There was nothing to ally her to her sister in appearance. There was none of the sparkle of Jack's eyes, but then Jack's sparkle was lying dormant it was true.

Charlotte was overwhelmed by widow-hood, grief and loss unable to leave her countenance, grief and loss etched in her heart and in all she did. Her voice was one of wretchedness at every turn, her tone sombre and without expression.

"If you want feeding you'll have to give me the money before you get the food." He gave her some money.

"Food for the two of us," he said. She understood and nodded and made no argument, nor any comment, and placed the coins in a pocket in her well-worn but clean dress.

Yes, her home was clean, that had to be said, and in spite of her own appearance there was nothing to suggest she was anything less than clean herself. Pride, that had to be it.

She took him along the path to his temporary home. The wind continued to rush by and nearly blew her slender frame from the ground. Instinctively he took her arm and felt his gesture was welcome although it was not from any obvious reaction from the woman herself.

The cottage was small but the inside was not as he had assumed. Expecting him Charlotte had laid a fire which had heated the place through and which now twinkled in a kind of self satisfaction, still throwing out some warmth. Most definitely tiny, little more than one cramped room, it was immaculately kept and he knew at once Charlotte had preserved it like this.

Conceivably there was more than pride in this.

He didn't ask. Not his way.

"I'll go to town and we'll have supper at my place later."

"Take the horse, her name's Beth and she's as good as..." His words were cut short by her laughter. She rocked back, held a hand to her mouth as if she thought such laughter was a demonstration of poor manners, and laughed all the more.

"Me on a 'orse? Mercy me, not me, not me ... never ..." and she dissolved into further fits of laughter. Oliver smiled involuntarily, and believed the whole episode was somehow quite endearing but for reasons that escaped him. Regaining her composure somewhat she asked if he needed ale, for she would bring some, and asked if there was any other service he required.

She was still laughing, but in a quiet way, her hand still across her mouth almost as a signal of apology. He asked for ale, but sought nothing else, and she was gone.

Sitting in the only chair the property possessed and musing on their words and her mirth, he was conscious of the way Charlotte's eyes had indeed lit up when she had found something to her humour. The real Charlotte had risen to the surface in those pleasant moments, and the care-worn widow, embroiled in desolation, resigned to her cheerless fate, beaten down and degraded, was suddenly dispelled from his presence.

It was a transformation he couldn't explain.

She had been nothing but a miserable grieving widow, yet a few words were all it took to wipe away her distress and bring forth happiness that must, that *must* lie inside her.

He puzzled the issue for a while, decided the laughter was a separate face that could hide the pain she otherwise felt, and permitted his deliberations to move to more pressing matters.

And so Oliver Kindale set off on foot in the direction of Dover, up over the cliffs.

The wind was stronger here, or certainly felt so, and was pushing at his back as if to either aid his progress or send him across the cliff edge and to his death. With the forces of nature thus behind him he was unaware that he was being followed.

His main personal concern was that the wind would be directly in his face on his return.

He would cope. He always did, and he'd known worse.

He had intentionally left his horse behind. There were things he needed to know and things he might miss riding on horseback. No chances to be taken.

***

The ale washed down his food and as he sat beside the fire Oliver sensed a glow of satisfaction. A good day with much achieved, a small but enjoyable meal inside him, and now pleasant relaxation.

Charlotte had done well with what little he had given her. She must've been hungry for she ate ravenously and devoured her food with considerable alacrity, long before he concluded his own refreshments.

He had watched her over supper but she had not taken her own eyes from the meal.

The wind had eased but rain had come. It was a typically cold, wet February night, but in Charlotte's cottage he felt oddly at home. She'd made him welcome, but the grief stricken widow was all he saw now, hauntingly back to replace the laughter so briefly experienced earlier.

Conversation had been simple with words few and far between.

Then, as she sat opposite him, he asked the question he knew he should not.

"Why is your sister called Jack?"

"Dunno, really. She bin Jack to me since birth, an' 'er 'usband's name was Jack. Just'appened really, spose."

She didn't look at him and he knew she was lying. But no matter, it wasn't important.

They rested in silence. She had asked no questions of him and that was agreeable to him.

He studied her face, seeing her eyes were closed, and was alert to feelings stirring within him, feelings he didn't want and feelings he shouldn't have, feelings he had no time for.

It was time to go and his departure met no protest from his hostess.

On his way he made sure Beth was comfortable, at least sheltered from the weather, and that she had water. She'd been fed earlier, Charlotte had seen to that.

He settled down to sleep but feeling uneasy, feeling unusually unsure, but of what he didn't know. He was making progress in his quest, slowly, cautiously, successfully. He couldn't rush, not yet, and there was no need. Chastain was clearly in no hurry, so obviously did not have all he required for his mission.

And Oliver had to severe the supply line.

Putting doubts in Chastain's mind was not his objective. He actually wanted to encourage the Frenchman and remove worries from his opponent's mind. All part of Oliver's plan. He would strike only when the time was right and when he could eliminate Chastain's operation in entirety.

That was vital. To do otherwise would invite catastrophe.

With such thoughts he drifted into the deep sleep enjoyed by those without guilt and conscience.

A sleep enjoyed by those who can black out the horrors of life, and avoid the confrontations of their mental amblings, the waking nightmares of dread and the fears of the future.

This was how he slept. He had taught himself to sleep like that.

And he was buoyed by the thought that he would never know when his last sleep would come. His last sleep was no bother to him. When it was his time it was time to go, a straightforward philosophy. He would have no worries once he was dead.

Chapter Four

It was mid evening.

Harry Harblow had been expecting to see Oliver Kindale when he opened the door.

Instead he was confronted by a man of appreciable height, well over six feet, dressed in a long grey coat and sporting a small, neatly groomed grey beard. His blue eyes bored into Harry's. There was a sharpness, a coldness even, about his eyes.

His face was shallow and cracked, there were sores, a bruise above his right eye, and blond hair hung across his forehead from under his hat.

"I've need to stay the night. I want no food, just shelter. I'll be away before dawn."

The voice was accented, but Harry couldn't place it, well-rounded, smooth and deep. Without asking Harry knew he was looking at Grey Jonnie; it could be nobody else. The man's pistol was strapped in his belt and Harry hoped it would stay there.

He simply stood back and allowed his visitor to enter.

"I'll sit by tha' fire, if you have the mind not to object, and sleep there too. If you have some ale we can take some together. Do you know who I am?"

"No. I've no wish to know, and you don't want me to know. Sit and sleep as you wish. I'll get something to drink." Harry concluded that was the best answer in the circumstances. He had no idea what Grey Jonnie wanted beyond somewhere to sleep, but thought he might require nothing more, God willing.

He was wrong.

"If need be, do you have somewhere to conceal me, free from searching eyes, if y'understand?"

Harry nodded. "Aye, I'll show you ...."

"No, there is no need now," he snapped, as if angered by the offer.

"Do you have a horse?"

"No, I'm on foot. I can't hide a horse as easily as I can hide myself." The conversation ended there and Harry fetched the ale and two mugs before sitting opposite Grey Jonnie.

There was no more conversation at all. Both slept in their chairs.

Harblow didn't hear him go, but he had always been a heavy sleeper, and his repose had been aided by a noticeably large number of drinks the previous evening. Grey Jonnie had drunk the same but it didn't seem to have any effect whereas Harry's mind had wandered and his head had started to spin long before he succumbed to peaceful rest.

It was a bright morning but clouds were gathering in the eastern sky, gradually blotting out the sun itself. He went to the trough and threw water over his head in a bid to shake himself fully awake and rid himself of the effects of substantial drinking.

Then he was aware of feet in front of him, and horses hooves beyond them.

"Katherine's mother died day before yesterday" he said to Oliver, preferring not to bother with any customary greetings and pleasantries.

"I'll go over. Can you get me some money in a day or two?"

"Make it three and the answer's yes. Grey Jonnie was here; stayed the night. We didn't talk. Nothing to say. He just wanted shelter for the night. Gone before dawn. Asked if I could conceal him if needs be, but said no more."

Kindale considered this carefully but without comment.

"Not got much to eat, Oliver..."

"No food, thanks. I must get over to Katherine and then I'm for Dover." The two men sat and looked at each other, Harry trying to read the unreadable Oliver Kindale, and Kindale himself making a better fist of reading his host.

He deduced Harry had not so much been scared (that wouldn't have been Harry) as concerned and frustrated that he would not have been able to ask the questions, the obvious questions, of his uninvited, unwelcome visitor. And Oliver knew he hadn't asked.

You didn't ask Grey Jonnie.

"I can see no reason," Oliver decided, "why his call was any more than coincidence. Did he have a horse, anyone with him you knew of?" Harry shook his head. "Just him, putting his head down for the night, and close to the Dover road. His enquiry about concealment suggests coincidence, of that I am confident. Yes, let's say coincidence, Harry, unless you fear otherwise."

A further shake of the head.

"I'll away to Katherine. And I'll be back in three days." They exchanged knowing smiles and the warmth of a friendly handshake before Kindale was gone. He had intended to stay longer but clearly Harblow had nothing more to tell him and he wanted to see Katherine.

***

"I've not eaten for days. The pains are too bad."

Katherine looked in scarcely concealed agony, sitting hunched in a chair, clutching her stomach.

"I'll get the physician. Where is he?"

"Here yesterday. Gave me more medicine. It only works for a while. He came to see my mother when she died and he came back to see me. I'll be well, soon, Oliver, leave it be."

Her face was taut, screwed up in anguish, and the pain was painted in every expression that her face conceived. He couldn't leave her like that but she would have none of it.

"You've been, paid y'respects, Oliver. I ask nothing more of you. I need nothing more of you. The funeral will be taken care of, there's good folks and good neighbours hereabouts, and they'll see she gets buried properly, and she'll be well remembered, don't you worry."

She smothered a squeal as a stabbing pain erupted within her. Her eyes were wet. Her suffering was complete, an utter abomination.

"Where's the physician?" Oliver shouted, the venom of anxiety and distress driving his words out full force. "Where is he? I'm going for him."

Almost bent double she pleaded with him not to go, but he was determined for he could no longer bear to see her crippled in such an inhuman way. She gave him directions, it was all she could do to speak so few words, and he vanished, to return no more than ten minutes later with the doctor.

Within an hour Katherine had followed her mother from this world to the next.

The torture of her last hour on earth was almost beyond her endurance, and her squeals became screams and then terrible shrieks. It reduced Oliver to tears, weeping in a way he didn't know he was capable of, weeping to see a woman he clearly once cared for dying in such an atrocious and hideous manner.

It was as if he was sharing her unimaginable pain, and the tears fell freely.

But her release came and with it came his release.

One last morbid sigh after the screaming had receded, a ghostly sound, a weird and unfathomable noise, and she lay silent, still huddled in a ball of despair and wretchedness.

The doctor examined her and nodded to Oliver, and his tears slowly dried.

He didn't want to witness such agony again, and knew he must never get close to anyone, not that he was, or had ever been, close to Katherine. But there was something ... *something*.

Emotional involvement might easily cloud his judgement, lead to mistakes, even result in his death. And it could waste his time.

He was aware of time slipping by, time he should be spending in Dover, time he had wasted looking after Katherine, time he had wasted sobbing for her. To himself he admitted it was indeed time wasted, not that he would've confessed to such feelings to anyone else.

His heart hardened even further, greater coldness set in, and he resolved he would never shed tears and never have a soul he would ever again shed tears over. For any reason.

It had to be that way.

And in that moment he knew he had become inhuman, and resigned himself to an inhuman existence where no emotions would see the light of day, where there would be no more compassion, no depth of feeling, and where every decision would be weighed on its practical merits and nothing more.

His own feelings must never again be hostage to fortune. He must be in control.

39

He could tarry no longer.

An elderly woman from next door, two younger woman who knew Katherine, a strong, hearty fisherman who had known Katherine's mother well, an old man who seemed to understand matters but who was unknown to all present, all had gathered to help and do what they could.

Oliver Kindale slipped away. Time to go. He would return for her funeral. If he could. If it was practical.

He rode at speed across the cliffs to Dover with never so much as a backward thought for Katherine and her frightful demise. His heart had frozen over.

More time passed as he waited in the street, but this was not time wasted. He was watching the house where he had seen Chastain and wanted to be assured the Frenchman was still there.

There was also interest in the very tall, smartly dressed gentleman with the grey beard who called there but failed to gain an answer to his firm and sustained knocking on the door. Oliver noted the man appeared to have a pistol tucked in his belt beneath the dark grey coat he wore.

Interesting.

Oliver waited a full two hours, merged into the throng that seemed permanently along this road, most clad as he was in near rags, dirty and worn clothing, as they scurried or strolled about their business.

Then Chastain appeared from the direction of the harbour with a young and attractive woman and a middle-aged man who might have been a sailor, or might once have been a man of the sea. All three entered the property.

Kindale was satisfied. His man was showing no signs of panic. He could be left in peace for the time being.

The ploy of recognition, played out when he first arrived in the town, had worked enough and just enough.

Chastain might well be on edge but if he was the thoroughly professional man Oliver took him for he would not be unduly perturbed, the incident merely serving to improve the Frenchman's security and wariness. It had never been Oliver's intention to frighten as that might have accelerated Chastain's activities or caused the total curtailment.

The last factor he needed was Chastain moving away and adopting a different plan.

This thing had to be dealt with now, but dealt with in a permanent way, with no chance of resurrection should it be abandoned for the time. It had to be cut down and destroyed and left incapable of further life in any form.

His memory had captured the faces of the three visitors and their images were cast firmly in his mind for all time.

Not once had that memory or mind wasted a second's thought for Katherine.

Hapling did not tarry long. Chastain sent him on his way with a written message.

Veronique had no knowledge of the contents of the message nor for whom it was intended, and it rankled. Chastain now sat and copiously wrote various notes. He played his cards close to his chest, never discussed his business and kept his writings either about his person or, more usually, in a locked casket. She knew better than to ask.

She had to keep her anger, impotence and frustration in check. Yes, she could've broken open the casket but that would've given her away. She had used her feminine wiles with great discretion when they were abed but her probing words, mingled carefully and tenderly with words of love, had failed to gain information useful to her.

Unsurprisingly Chastain was a skilled craftsman, a man of experience dedicated to the cause, a man whose cleverness and cunning had unearthed traitors, and proved a sight too intelligent for most opponents to equal. He would have plunged a knife into 'Mrs Copwood' without further thought if he believed her to be a threat.

No, she needed to be wary and maintain her wits at all times.

But these were wearisome times. She had Ballerden's address yet Chastain was so rarely out of her sight she dared not put pen to paper. In truth there was so little to tell and it infuriated her. She felt ineffective as well she might.

Would her time yet come? She must be patient. She studied the back of the man hunched over his desk, busy at his schemes, work that must be undone but only when the time was right.

He finished writing his words, enjoyed some wine with her and engaged in pleasant conversation, and then led her to their bedchamber and her misery.

***

It was only now as Kindale rode sedately north east from Dover that he recalled the shocking and brutal way of Katherine's passing, torn apart inside by evil demons that ate her entrails and wrecked her body, torn apart mentally by the insatiable suffering that fate had deemed she should endure, perhaps recompense for the misdeeds of her life.

But if that were so then other far more evil than she should suffer worse. And the inequality worried Oliver and hurt him and left him bruised and desolate. All the more reason to kill off emotion, he reasoned.

That made him feel better. He dismissed his adverse thoughts, spurred on his mount, and galloped for the next two miles, feeling heady and relaxed as if he had crossed a great divide and was now a new man. A new man shorn of all that had been before him. A new man free to take this new life as he found it, free to unfetter his spirit, free to act as he would.

Freedom.

He recognised the figure coming towards him and reined Beth in.

"Thomas Temple! You are abroad as usual, and bound for where I wonder."

"Oliver Kindale, Oliver Kindale, wonder no more for I head to Dover from whence I would feel you have just emerged. Am I right my friend?"

Both smiled. Temple continued on his way. Oliver looked after him and then ordered Beth to trot. He was keen to return home and to sleep. There was something about Temple but it could not be assessed as it was, and Oliver wasted no more time considering the issue. The day was drawing to a close and it had been a very long day in all respects.

***

Physically Charlotte had no features that would attract the interest of a man.

Nothing at all, and yet Oliver was pleasantly disturbed in a way he did not wish to be disturbed, even less so after Katherine's means of passing. He had rejected any feelings that had squeezed into his innermost being where Charlotte was concerned right from their first meeting, and he had not approved the infection of his mind by such a woman.

But it troubled him sore.

She was set fair in his mind and he couldn't shift her, and that was bothersome.

He made his way to her cottage for their simple supper and she was politely welcoming but once again without smile or any other facial acknowledgment of him as a friend. He would've preferred it that way, of course, and sought to expel the warmth that washed through him as he joined her at the table.

Tonight there was light conversation, pleasing and devoid of depth and substance. She did not ask after him or enquired how he had spent his day, and he made no investigations of her. He certainly didn't relate the tragic, sorrowful and maddening death of Katherine. But thinking of Katherine served as a reminder of his resolve not to experience moving and affectionate sensitivity with another.

Charlotte broke the spell.

"Jess bin gone a long time. Miss me man. 'e was good to me, never done me no 'arm, an' I miss 'im. Miss the way 'e 'eld me. 'e were no more than thirty paces from me when they cut 'im down. Four bullets I counted. Always 'eld me nice and tight. Miss that."

Oliver sat stunned. He had never expected Charlotte to speak of her husband and had never intended to ask. Her few brief statements changed the whole picture.

He found he wished to speak warmly but his heart was as cold as stone. The coldness was moulded and framed in his words.

"I'll hold you, if it's a hug you miss. If you miss your man I can do nothing." And he started to eat again, removing his gaze from hers but aware she was looking right at him.

"I'd love to be 'eld, Oliver. Nothing more. One *hug*, that's all." She emphasised the word hug by stressing the h, a letter frequently omitted from her speech when it came to words starting thus. Oliver smiled inwardly and stopped eating. A singular woman, in some throws of desperation, entrapped by the need for something that four bullets ended abruptly?

Whatever her motives, however bewildered her mind, unsure of sound reason she had accepted his offer which had only ever been made scornfully and with a lack of seriousness and kindness.

They stared right into each others' eyes and slowly, cautiously moved around the table.

This was something he didn't want, but appreciated he must make the gesture even if it proved a half-hearted one. It was, to him, like giving in to a stubborn child, providing a crumb of comfort for the sake of peace and quiet.

He held his arms open and she was enveloped in his embrace. He took care not to allow any emotions to overcome his senses, even though they hammered at the door. For her part she surrendered herself completely to the moment, knowing it must pass and she must let it pass.

After the meal he went straight home, unsure if she had wished him to stay, but knowing that had he stayed it would've satisfied his desires only so much as his physical needs required. He would've used her, that was all. Perhaps she sensed that.

She drifted comfortably into a deep sleep dreaming of his embrace, their *hug* as she would've termed it in her own form of the language.

He fell straight asleep with no dreams, just a burning craving to deal with whatever tomorrow might lay before him.

And the morning came quickly to Oliver Kindale.

On his way before dawn, but on foot, he set off for Dover.

He discovered he had company.

"Oliver Kindale, my friend, Oliver Kindale, and set for Dover methinks." Kindale was conscious of steps behind him but took no notice save to be ready lest he should be attacked. Temple now matched him stride for stride and the two ventured over the cliffs in silence with a strong westerly gale now threatening ahead of them.

"Be bad today, Oliver Kindale. Storm approaching and ye have no horse. You not be going back to Deal today?" Oliver pulled up short, Temple walked on and Oliver swiftly caught him up.

"You are too interested in my movements, friend," Kindale advised, "and my movements and my business are mine alone."

"Aye, Oliver Kindale, indeed they are. But permit me to walk with you to town. I seek nothing more than company. Aye, will be a treacherous day, and wicked at sea for the poor men who must master the waves."

Kindale ignored most of this but was aggravated by comments that suggested he might be interested in certain aspects such as the sea state. He stopped suddenly and Temple drew up as well.

"My business, Thomas Temple, my business. I will accompany you to town and be grateful for your presence but I want no more of you."

It was almost as if Temple was prepared to deliberately ignore Oliver's last remark.

"Miss Charlotte looking after ye? Abed too? She's a fine lass, yes a fine lass..."

Oliver swung round and grabbed Temple by the coat collars.

"You filthy animal. Keep away from me or I'll kill you." He released his grip and walked on, this time alone. Temple made no effort to follow at once which pleased Oliver greatly. Yet this man had been watching him, knew where he was staying; it was almost as if he had gained entry to Oliver's personal sanctuary. He had to learn more.

He waited ahead until Temple drew near and made apology.

"I apologise, friend, I was hasty. Let us resume our walk." Temple smiled and then laughed, clapped Oliver on the back and then put his arm around his shoulder as they strolled.

"My friend, no offence was meant, and the lady is too much a lady for me to demean so. You must forgive me and forgive my arrogance and offence, and you must do it for her. Say your will do so." Oliver did; he needed to find out more about this man, and importantly why he always appeared to turn up in Oliver's way.

By the time they parted company not far from Dover's castle Oliver had probed enough, with subtlety and cunning, to discover Temple was one of Jess's close friends, that he regarded himself as Charlotte's guardian (even though she was in her thirties) and was interested in any newcomer lest he presented a threat to the woman.

His trade: chandler. Not much 'trade' at present, it would seem.

Innocent enough, he agreed with himself.

But he was too obvious. He was protective when there was no need to be so. This morning Oliver had been walking away from Charlotte's. Had Temple been in close attendance last night? Well, it wasn't necessarily important, and the day had more serious matters requiring attention.

Later he learned several things.

He learned that Chastain's tall visitor was probably Grey Jonnie who was plainly not afraid to dress as a gentleman and be seen in public, with no fear of being recognised let alone betrayed or taken into custody.

He learned that Chastain was living under the assumed name of Copwood.

He learned that Chastain's other male visitor was a former ship's captain called Hapling, but was unable to learn why he no longer commanded a vessel. But perhaps he did?

He learned that he could buy such information cheaply and merely by searching in the right places, and Oliver Kindale had a nose for finding such places of ready reference having honed his skills over a number of years.

He also learned the day of Katherine's funeral.

But only one woman stood in his mind.

The woman, the very striking woman, he had seen with Hapling and Chastain. She did not appear to him to be a lady engaged for entertainment or for decoration, unless it was indeed the case that she provided a more natural adornment for the Frenchman. That would make everything seem quite normal.

Perhaps she passed herself as Mrs Copwood. Was she herself French?

The image Oliver held in his head suggested that here was a vital link in whatever Chastain might be planning. She looked bright and intelligent, but looks could easily fool. Her bearing led him to believe that she was very much a lady, and self-willed and indomitable too.

Part of an act? An accomplished actor?

Possibly.

Clearly Kindale had not been informed about Veronique's presence or indeed given any reference to her part in this business.

"Have y'time for ale, my friend?" Oliver's deliberations were cut short as the voice fell over his shoulder from behind. He closed his eyes. Ye Gods, Temple again! He turned slowly and realised that here was an opportunity to make use of this intrusive person.

"Yes, but first a favour, friend. I'll take you to a house where you are to knock, and ask for Mr Chastain. I expect him to tell you that you have the wrong house, that he is not Chastain and that he's never heard of him.

"That is the sort of answer to expect, friend. Just leave it and walk away. That is all I ask of you then I will buy you a drink."

"And explain why I am doing this?"

"No. My business."

"And mine too if he dislikes my enquiry and attacks me. What of it then, my friend?"

"He will not. There is no risk. It is purely for my amusement." Temple ran his fingers through his beard as if giving the matter and Oliver's response the strongest possible consideration whereas, Oliver knew, he would carry out this task without further question. There was no need to weigh the issue so thoroughly. He knew his man.

"We will go," Temple finally conceded, and they set off accordingly.

The task complete Temple and Kindale sat together to sup their ales.

Naturally, Temple was curious and now found it peculiar that a man who was little more than a stranger had persuaded him to engage in an odd practise, and purely for juvenile delight. The door had opened and in response to his request the occupant had indeed told Temple he had the wrong address, that he knew of nobody by the name of Chastain.

And Oliver would tell him no more!

Still, that was Oliver's business and he probed no further.

But now Temple wanted to know everything he could about the man called Oliver Kindale, and he would have to find out by round-about means. It would be worth the enquiries, he decided. There was more, so much more, to the man recently arrived in Deal.

He had not been able to gain knowledge of where Kindale came from, his occupation (if he had one), much less the reason for his visit.

There was an air of suspiciousness all about him!

Thomas Temple sported a wry grin which was impossible to observe through the tangled growth of hair about his face. Oliver amused him, if only because he baffled him!

Talk was at a minimum. Oliver would give nothing away himself, and yet Temple wanted to know so much.

He would talk to Charlotte. That was it! She might have a way of extracting information from Oliver Kindale. Indeed she might. A woman's way, a way no man would possess! Yes, that is what he would do, return to Deal now and prime her.

***

Chastain dismissed his meeting with Temple.

Now totally convinced Kindale had been a smuggler he had employed in the past and who had recognised him and seen the chance of further profit, the Frenchman saw the wretched Temple as a similar villain. A simpleton, someone easily ignored.

He was immersed in his invincibility, soaked by his self-belief, and all the weaker for it had he but realised. There was no question in his mind that neither man was in any position to betray him, and he laughed at the preposterous attempts they had made to ingratiate themselves in the hope of earning a few small coins.

Veronique witnessed Temple's call, but from a distance behind Chastain. She caught the merest glimpse of the visitor before the door was abruptly shut in his face, and considered if it might be the man her Englishman had sent.

And it raised her hopes in one respect, dashed them in another.

Surely this ill-spoken, badly dressed and poorly presented man could not be such a person. And the thought tormented her. But, she reasoned more logically, she wouldn't know what to expect of him, and he might wish to appear thus in order to purely observe Chastain and subsequently merge into the background.

And she had to content herself with the latter view, and found herself praying that he was that close, a comfort to some degree in itself, and in a commanding position to act when the situation developed, as it must.

She knew a strangeness, that there was a gulf between them that might never be closed, yet they fought the same battle from the same side and were thus united in cause if not physically so. There would almost certainly never be any direct contact between them.

It pained her, yet it pleased her, for he might well have been the man sent to devastate the Frenchman's design, and he would have to be sufficient for the task. That could not prevent her worrying or suffering some distress, and she had to keep her feelings well hidden from the man in front of her.

Chapter Five

Oliver Kindale asked questions only where the answers were deemed to be important to him and therefore was not the sort of person to undertake unnecessary enquiries.

Conversation didn't come easily to him. If he lacked interest in another then conversation was time wasted, and he would thus appear rude and uncaring. He was never good company.

So Charlotte being rather talkative and extremely inquisitive was both a surprise and an irritation.

He hurried his meal and left without what had now become his customary procedure of sitting by the fire for a while afterwards. He left money for food for the next day but said he would probably not be back, but stressed she should eat anyway.

He'd decided he would stay at Harblow's the following night especially as he felt the need to put distance between himself and Charlotte if she was in danger of becoming too friendly. And he had some tasks for Harry.

If Charlotte was saddened or in any way offended she did not show it. She refused the money at first if it was only to feed herself but he insisted, saying it was also for her cleaning and the provision of his cottage; that was the agreed arrangement. She did not argue or make issue.

Oliver straightaway put her from his mind but discovered later that she would not leave his thoughts so eagerly. His sleep was punctuated with sudden arousals, nightmarish waking moments, when he would jump involuntarily and find himself fully awake, gasping and sweating. And Charlotte would be in his mind, each and every time, instantly shelved, instantly forgotten, but always there the second he shook into wakefulness.

The next day was warmer than of late, the wind had eased, no longer vigorous in its breathless pursuit of mankind, no longer destructive in its rough journey across land and shore, town and village.

Kindale rode Beth hard and aggressively, and she responded as was her wont, in full and unquestioning obedience, and gave him the power and tenacity he demanded.

He felt angry, but could not place why. The fury mounted as he rode, and Beth was obliged to perform beyond all that he thought she was capable of. But it was not the horse's fault that she should stumble in some woodlands, where the path was unclear, and throw her rider into the mud.

Oliver cried out, in frustration rather than pain, grabbed the bridle and set about whipping Beth with spite and hatred, pausing only when rational and logical thought overtook his rage. Whatever had become of him?

He nursed the animal, regretting his actions, but unable to undo what had passed, while the horse stood afeared of when the next attack might come, not comprehending the meaning of Oliver's apologies and whimpered pleas for forgiveness. He found he was weeping.

This will not do, he decided. Whatever is upon me, to behave like a madman, to so ill-treat such a willing beast, to shed tears for the result of a poor display of manliness? Why my anger, he tried to reason with himself, but no obvious answer was forthcoming.

Once again he arrived at Harry Harblow's looking the worse the wear, wet, muddy, unkempt.

The two did not speak for some time. Both knew it was unnecessary.

Again Oliver changed into some of Harry's clothes while the latter made as best he could with the task of drying and to some degree cleaning the former's.

"Horse threw me, and I had a temper on me, and I whipped her. That's not me, Harry, that's not me. I'd been riding her too hard. Something driving at me, I don't know what. But I cannot let it be, it cannot get inside my head like that.

"I must be thinking straight, clear and straight. No influences..."

From the expression on Harry's face he might have been giving the problem intelligent and productive contemplation. Oliver knew that was most unlikely!

"Well, my son, you seeing Katherine go and go the way she did, bound to affect a man, you must own that, and if you once had feelings for her ..."

"No ... no, that is not the case," Oliver snapped, almost as if he was afraid he might be hearing the truth, a truth he could not face, a truth he must not admit to, even to himself. Harry believed he was wheeling away from a fact he couldn't confront and changed the course of the exchange.

"Where now, my son? Dover again?" Glad of respite from a mental conflict that was starting to burn his mind, Oliver turned his attentions to what must be done, swearing all but subconsciously to freeze his heart across, his preferred state. He must keep his mind cold and clear. He must.

"I'm heading north but will be back tonight and will stay here, the easier to reach Katherine's burial tomorrow. You will come to Folkestone?" Harry nodded. "I have some tasks for you in Dover, Harry." His friend looked up, the warmth of excitement lighting up a face that for its hair-laden condition required much lighting up to achieve such a visible result.

"To begin with I need to know more about a man called Hapling. Former captain. I don't believe in His Majesty's service, so what *did* he command, where did he sail, what does he do now?"

Oliver Kindale explained his other enquiries, made certain Harry Harblow understood what was required of him and appreciated the need for discretion, and having obtained his money set off in the ill-fitting clothes loaned him.

He rode more easily as if to make amends to his mount and spoke to her gently and encouragingly during the journey.

Not far short of Wingham he stopped and dismounted and led Beth along a narrow track towards a barn and an outbuilding. A house stood away to his left but that was not his destination. Hearing sounds from the barn he approached and called out.

"Nicholas Telman? I seek Nicholas Telman."

A young man of about five and twenty emerged from the barn wiping his hands down his waistcoat. Strong of build yet little more than five feet tall, with a mass of light, fair hair, and a face Oliver supposed would ignite the fires of many a young woman, he looked an imposing figure for all his lack of height.

"I am he. And you sir, and your business?" His voice was as light as his hair, and flowed in mellow and attractive tones that bounced through the air. Yes, thought Kindale, a man who would please any woman.

"Oliver Kindale. Robert Kettle in Deal said to find you here. May we speak? I have some questions and will explain my business."

After some hesitation, brought about by suspicion rather than fear, Telman walked across to the rear of the small outbuilding, beckoned Kindale to follow, and sat a stone slab facing the sun. The sunlight merely accentuated his bright hair where no improvement was needed. He waited for Oliver to speak again.

***

Piece by piece Kindale was gathering information. Insignificant, seemingly unimportant morsels being locked away in his brain, there to await order and scrutiny, and added to the vital details he was unearthing, the truly serious material.

Slowly a picture would emerge in his mind and a course of action would be developed.

The pieces currently had no obvious pattern, and there were more portions missing than found.

But he was patient. His cold, calculating and fertile mind could take all this information and progressively weave a complete image upon which he could act.

His mind needed no diversions, and he had educated himself to lock out all interests that were far from relevant to his investigations, just as he had taught himself to avoid allowing unnecessary thoughts to wander through his wits. He must be clear headed at all times.

Success depended on it. He knew that and he was alive today because of it, and had achievements behind him that owed everything to that coolness of thought.

So trotting back south he was annoyed that something was nagging at him, something he couldn't recognise, something he couldn't dispel from his mental applications. It worried him, but mostly because he couldn't identify the problem that probed at him like a tiny unseen insect, causing itching and distress and prickliness. Unseen, untouchable, seeking any weakness and ready to exploit it.

He could not afford it.

Was Harry right? Had Katherine's horrible death affected him too badly? Would the burial give him peace, release from any earthly grief and torment, when he had nothing to torment himself with?

He wasn't responsible; he had no strong feelings for her in death as he'd never had strong feelings for her in life. Yes, she was part of his past, but a pleasant diversion at a time when he was free to enjoy such pleasures, and she had since offered him tidbits of information valuable to his searches. That was all.

And he hadn't seen her for years, or so it seemed.

No, he could not let this affect his judgement in any way. She was dead and that was all that mattered. He must let all memories go tomorrow. Forever.

Not once did he think of Charlotte and it would have been better for him had he identified her as a root cause of his mental wrangling. Then he could've dismissed the situation for the ridiculous folly it represented.

He would simply never have thought that she could infiltrate his mind, let alone his heart, and jeopardise his life, his very well-being, the success of his plan. It was a danger the man could not see, was totally blind to.

Neither could he realise why Katherine's death was pushing him further into Charlotte's domain.

***

Harry had enjoyed limited success.

Hapling had once commanded a small ship which had run the commerce routes to France and the Netherlands, but competition had forced the owners to lay the vessel up, and there was no evidence to suggest the man had any work at sea in the ensuing years.

Nonetheless, his skill as a skipper had probably been put to work for the free traders, the smugglers, although he had no longer seen command. Harblow could gain no information to persuade him otherwise.

And he had a reputation for knowing the northern coasts of France intimately. That was most certainly of interest to Kindale.

But what else did Hapling do to earn an income?

That line of enquiry met a wall of silence that not even money could budge, suspicious in itself.

Oliver was pleasantly happy with that outcome as he had rather thought that the case, a fact he now revealed to his friend. Harry displayed signs of aggravation but temporarily so as he then erupted into one of his throaty laughs.

"You could've told me..."

"No, no, I did not want you chasing after a notion that was firmly fixed in your mind, Harry. You had to draw your own conclusions, and demonstrate the integrity of mine. And methinks it places him within Chastain's scope...."

"Aye, my son, but we are taking note of men and not their objects..."

"All in good time Harry. Now tell me what else you have for me."

Harblow finished his mug of ale and refilled it before talking again. Oliver nodded contentedly as Harry furnished more information, disjointed and uninteresting as it appeared to the speaker who had harvested these useless details. But Oliver knew each scrap would help him paint a picture that might hopefully be quite explicit.

"And your own journey today, my son, of what use was that pray?"

"I met a man called Nicholas Telman. Do you know of him?" Harry shook his head and drank some more. "He was once occasionally called upon by a smuggler named Roger Kettle at Deal, and he could guide the men to places of safety well inland, safety for the contraband or safety for themselves, whatever was needed.

"He was reluctant to tell me more for fear I was from the Revenue. Not that he told me that. He didn't need to, it could be seen in his eyes, his face.

"Yet he indicated that he had recently been recruited, the price being very acceptable, to bring some Frenchmen north from Dover. A man called Copwood had instructed and paid him, paid him well. I only acquired that detail by deliberately leading him into a trap from which there was no escape save the truth.

"He did not speak freely, but by careful coaxing I persuaded him to loosen his tongue a little and he was pleased to earn something from his hinted words. Money can achieve so much, Harry, good and evil." Harry nodded again.

"I could not elicit where these Frenchmen went, but I had the feeling Telman left them somewhere on the road from Wingham to Canterbury waiting to be met by their next guide. He asked no questions. What wise man in such simple employment would do so and risk their lives?"

Harry looked at him from over the top of his mug and having drunk some more slowly lowered the vessel and spoke.

"We must see Katherine off. I hope it is done well. The weather has no promise for us."

"It will be done as well as can be. The weather we will cope with. I am keen to see who else attends. We must keep our eyes open, Harry. I think among any mourners we may find a surprise or two. Let us be awake and watchful.

"She was well known, but not loved by any means. She had enemies and one or so may wish to make certain she is dead and buried, if you follow my reasoning, Harry."

The next morning was cold and blustery and the wind had regained its breath but now moved to blow from the north-east, refreshed and desirous of inflicting discomfort and any possible destruction upon the people and their surroundings.

It swirled this way and that, hunting down each victim, and was no doubt a cause of disquiet to George Gordon perched, as he was, high above the sea on the cliffs north of Dover. Very high indeed. With his back to the wind, and huddled in his coat, he puffed at his pipe, a source of some comfort, yet truly very little succour in the prevailing conditions.

Some miles to the south-west, and unbeknown to Gordon, they were burying Katherine. It wasn't an event that would've either interested or concerned the Revenue man, yet it might have done.

Oliver Kindale sat by the body for some while and stared at a face he could remember from an earlier time, not the face of agony or the face worn down by the trials of life that had come to epitomise her before death released her.

Death had done that. Spared her further torture, spared her face and returned it to a vision of true womanhood, that of a woman who had pleased men in a most agreeable way, that of a woman that had brought brightness into a dark world. But at what cost?

How much of a facade was her life? What was the real Katherine? Was she never to be found and now left to perish amongst the wreckage about to be buried?

Kindale was grateful some of her handsome looks has been restored with the passing of earthly pain. Not a religious man or a man of religious understanding he still wished her spirit well. And happiness in death.

What a rotten path she had chosen! But she had done well from it, and he consoled himself with the thought.

The wind, having no respect or sense of duty, howled around the churchyard as she was buried and drowned out the parson's words, much to Harry's pleasure. There were a few mourners, all heads bowed except those of Oliver Kindale and Harry Harblow. Both recognised one man, one they had not expected.

He arrived late and departed early. Oliver followed him at a discreet distance. The man might have known Harry but not Oliver.

Kindale had the sense to lead Beth knowing he might need his horse at any moment.

The man went into a small building, a house that was both meagre home and a workshop although it was not immediately obvious what work was done there. He did not appear again.

Harry arrived with his own mare and Kindale spoke.

"I must wait. Take Beth and stable her then return home. I'll ride back later."

"What's William Tydeman doing here? What's Katherine to him?"

"He's out of Ramsgate, probably knew her once, but why bother with her burial? Well, I would be willing to wager the outcome is in that house. He went straight in, so he must be known, or he's taking lodgings there."

"Perhaps he was here by chance, learned of Katherine's loss and decided to pay his respects to an old friend."

Harry looked at him. Oliver returned his glance and explained.

"I jest, Harry, I no more believe that than you!"

If there was one thing that displeased Harry Harblow it was being removed from the area of immediate attention, and Oliver wanted him to go home when he sought nothing but involvement.

There would be no arguing, he knew that, and set off to stable Beth as required of him. Then he rode back to his cottage to find himself more involved than he wished to be.

***

"We have word. Hythe tonight. We can take some soldiers. But watch for yourselves, my lads, they may be expecting us."

Down in Dover town George Gordon addressed the three men with him, still drawing on his pipe and finding blessed sympathy from it.

"That pirate Tydeman's the one I want. Get him, my lads, but get him alive."

In Folkestone Kindale had been asking questions but without the need for anything to slacken tongues. He learned the house belonged to Daniel Copwood, a skilled maker of domestic furniture who also fashioned inexpensive coffins when needed, an important provider of additional income as it would seem.

He had made Katherine's coffin.

Kindale discovered that by calling at the house and asking directly, sensing it might be the case.

He also asked if William Tydeman was there. The colour drained from Copwood's face and was replaced in its pallor by fear.

"I know of no one by that name. William Tydeman, you say? No, I do not know of him."

Oliver weighed up the situation and decided it was worth the chance. Tydeman had to be there, possibly watching him now from within, but would not want the risk attached to being seen particularly if he was in Folkestone on business.

"He entered here not an hour ago having attended the burial of Katherine for whom you made the coffin"

Copwood took on all the appearance of a man who knows his last hour has come, and was sweating and shaking and stuttering. He had no idea who was facing him but he was only too aware who was behind him, around a door, pistol in hand. The foe in front might be as deadly as the foe to the rear.

"A m-m-m-man, came here, I don't know his name, he paid for the coffin, that was all, but he is long gone, sir, long gone. I do not know who it w-w-w-was, I swear I do not. The p-p-parson told me someone would come to pay me. I would not have made the coffin if there had been no payment...."

"His name is William Tydeman and he is still here."

Copwood was close to collapse. Kindale acknowledged the man was scared witless, and unwilling to see retribution hurled upon a man who might be innocent or at least unknowingly guilty, he withdrew without further word.

Chastain was using this man's name, there could be no coincidence. And there was no coincidence Tydeman was here. Kindale contented himself with the intelligence and went to find Beth, there being no advancement of his cause in bringing about difficulties in Folkestone.

He returned to Harry's cottage to find a worried and distressed Harblow sitting outside, full of anxiety and fidgeting accordingly.

"Thank God you're here, my son. Grey Jonnie's been here again. Wants me to hide someone for a night or two. Paid me." Oliver clapped a hand on his shoulder.

"Harry, Harry, just do as he asks. But keep your eyes and ears open. Think carefully and give attention to all that takes place and all that is said, if anything is. It may be useful to us. And I will tell you where to find me if you must make haste away from here. I am returning to Deal for the time being but anticipate moving on, I know not where, possibly Folkestone. Wheels are turning, Harry."

And Kindale disclosed the incident at Daniel Copwood's, and all that he had gleaned from the carpenter and the meeting.

Harblow sensed a vibrancy, an eagerness and an excitement about Kindale's comportment, and felt a nervous pang in the pit of his own stomach. His friend had been unhappily morose and withdrawn, aggressive and cold these last days, but now he had been lifted and was more like the Oliver Kindale of old.

Yes indeed, Harry concluded, wheels must be turning, just like he says.

But, Harry knew, he realised that wasn't necessarily good news from his own personal point of view.

His heart sank, for he believed for certain that he would be left outside once Kindale was on the move. But there was nothing he could say or do, except dare to hope that his contribution might yet be the greater. And first he had to cope with a night or more with a person Grey Jonnie wanted hidden.

"Quite simply," Kindale explained, "his previous visit was establish you had somewhere to hide a man, that you were not inclined to work with the authorities, and that you would do as you were told, forgetting the matter in the moment it was over. I am pleased, though not for you, Harry, as you have to bear this inconvenience, but I am pleased for the occasion as you may yet learn something of interest and value to us."

If his comments were designed to improve his friend's humour and to imply that such a contribution was vital to Kindale's progress, essential to their mutual work and benefit, then it failed to achieve its aim.

Harry was downhearted and, even through his mass of facial hair, managed to look it.

Kindale took his leave and headed for his own cottage.

He needed to disentangle his thoughts, there being many speeding through his mind. Chastain using Copwood as his alias; Copwood himself visited by Tydeman; Grey Jonnie calls on Chastain;

Tydeman allegedly paid for Katherine's coffin; Telman escorting some Frenchies to Wingham; Grey Jonnie needing to hide someone, who? for a night or two; Hapling, a master who knows the seas off the Kent coast and the French shores besides .... many thoughts indeed.

Wheels turning and too many for someone's scheme to be lying idle!

Kenton was right. This is imminent, he deduced.

Chapter Six

"You're quiet tonight."

Charlotte spoke with the damning voice of a careworn wife who knows her husband has something to hide, and would actually prefer it remain hidden.

Oliver Kindale looked up, his spoon poised in mid-air dripping broth from its sides. He stared at Charlotte, and even in the dim candlelight could make out the spare features of her face, all of them, there being no hair to hide any part of them. Her hair had been cut further back so her head was little adorned.

The sadness in her eyes, allied to the grave and resigned appearance in her face, made him feel sorry for her, almost protective, as if he wanted to shield her and comfort her in some way. That did not prevent him making himself clear.

"My business in mine. Keep to your own. Temple has seen you, wants you to find out about me. He must mind his own business." She was about to reply when he barked:

"Tell him!" and then calming, "tell him, and keep your nose out of it too." She looked as if she might cry but took only two deep breaths before responding.

"Aye, I will. He is only concerned for you. He's a good man, Oliver, and 'e thinks you are too. He thinks you ..... well, 'e thinks you're into .... something ... and he doesn't know what and he wants to know."

"He cares 'bout me ... not like that .... but 'e don't want me coming to no 'arm." Her voice, sweet and mellow, was all but pleading, and Oliver did not mistrust her sincerity, or for that matter Thomas Temple's.

Here was a man who saw a stranger in town who might be on either side of the law and who might pose a threat to Charlotte. Of course, he was her guardian angel, even though she might not want his attention. 'Not like that' she had stressed, so she sought no personal comforts from him, or perhaps he had not suggested any.

"He's just a nice man, he's looked after me since ..... since me 'usband was shot .... 'e keeps an eye out for me. Think Jack put him to it. She don't want no 'arm coming to me." Charlotte was now looking down at her lap, he own broth unfinished. Oliver had drunk every drop.

"Miss Jess," she continued, "Thomas don't 'old me, not fer 'im." She looked up again and searched out Oliver's gaze. "You 'eld me though, you *held* me, Oliver Kindale. You want to *hold* me again?" There was cold desire in her voice. Tiredness, bleakness, emptiness.

He spoke as softly and calmly as he could.

"Finish your meal. I've not had all my bread. Here take some of mine. You need food."

She gingerly took the offered bread and slowly sipped her remaining broth, but without removing her eyes from his. Between spoonfuls she spoke but once and in that brief interlude Oliver saw a shimmer in her eyes, a kind of sparkle that her sister's eyes could glow with.

"Then you *hold* me, Oliver Kindale?"

He recognised this as the invitation he least wanted; it was quite possibly an invitation to a greater feast, a much longer dance than implied by the intimation that an embrace was all that was sought.

"I'm going to be moving on in a day or two, Charlotte. I will see Jack before I go. And I do not want Temple following me when I depart." He felt stronger in character now, powerful of mind, determined and able to dominate the situation to his own advantage. He yearned to share Charlotte's bed but knew he could not.

That was a natural craving, the desire of a hungry man starved of such pleasures. She was nothing to look at, thin and gaunt, but he had no misgivings that she was capable of giving and of making it mutually worthwhile. He was the man in control.

Take and enjoy. Share no emotions beyond the passions of the moment.

He could have what he wanted and that would be it, done. Ride away without a backward look.

Forget in an instant, as she must do.

Instead he rose and took his leave. She spoke not a word, nor showed any sign of disappointment, of sorrow or desperation.

Shortly he was lying in his bed but he could not sleep. He knew he had let Charlotte into his private sanctuary for reasons he could not explain. Now she was stuck in his head and he was an unwilling prisoner at the very time he needed to be free.

In the morning he took her the money for their food that day and it was as if nothing had passed between them the evening before.

He had slept badly and he did not like that.

His sleep was usually untroubled, unfettered by conscience or concern, yet Charlotte held on to his dreams and nightmares alike, and he could not shake her off.

Suddenly his mind was cluttered and that was not his natural state, most certainly not the state he appreciated when there was much to dissect and assess.

He rode back to Folkestone and sought out the parson.

It was true a man of Tydeman's description had paid for the coffin, which was as well as, even with contributions from one or two others (the parson named them) there was not enough to make it a good burial.

Kindale was touched by the man's lack of humanity and lack of Christianity, and with a wry grin told the parson so.

"These things must be paid for, and that is all," he said dismissively, and Oliver turned, slammed the door behind him and set off for Copwood's home.

Not far from where he strode another man rested and looked across the sea, unaware of the wind that thrashed against his face and tore the smoke from his pipe and raced away with it, a demented elopement.

George Gordon was rueing a lost night, a fruitless expedition along the coast, the word spreading amongst the local people as the wind now hurtled apace, their well accounted signalling giving intelligence of where danger lay before those at sea.

Gordon had been unable to gain knowledge of this process and was consequently left undone in every respect. Unreliable sources had deliberately led him astray, taken his money but given dishonesty in return, and while he and his men and soldiers took up their positions south at Hythe, the contraband was landed at Folkestone.

And of it now there was no sign, nor any sign of the men who had partaken in such illegal activity.

He had learned of the disaster the same way he had allowed himself to be taken in, by buying information from those who gladly gave it knowing they would come to no harm, either from the law or from the law breakers, and that the goods were well away, safe and sound.

There had been a suggestion carrier pigeons had been used to warn those along the coast. It would not have been the first time.

George Gordon was facing a period of mixed emotions.

There was anger: anger at being thwarted, anger at being lied to, anger he had missed Tydeman, if indeed Tydeman had been there.

There was bitterness: the King's money had been used to buy information that ultimately led to wrongdoers avoiding paying their taxes to the King. Free trade? He scoffed. There was bitterness that he was impotent against such organisation.

There was resolve: he would not abandon his task, he would work harder still, he would see Tydeman yet hang from the gibbet, some recompense to his Majesty for money spent on his behalf!

There was sorrowfulness: a wasted venture, a pointless duty executed well but to no effect. He wished he had half the organisation these smugglers had.

There was some little joy: no shots had been fired, no knives and swords drawn, no cudgels swung, and he and his men were safe and had been at no risk.

He took the pipe from his mouth to laugh out loud. A hollow, limp bellow, a rueful appreciation of his failure.

Had he but known it William Tydeman was less than a furlong from him, safe inside Copwood's workshop, for Daniel Copwood had managed to make a disguised place of concealment such were his carpentry skills, and the soldiers had not located it, let alone its occupant, upon a thorough search of the premises.

Oliver Kindale was not aware of any of this, but he wanted to frighten Copwood again, especially if Tydeman was there.

Copwood's reaction told him he was. The man was as white as a sheet and anxious to deny knowledge and close the door in Oliver's face.

Achieving his desired aim, Kindale regained his mount and rode out to Harry's cottage, quite clear that Tydeman would've observed him and would now be keen to learn of his interest. The visitor to Copwood's home was a threat of some sort.

The parson had something to hide, Copwood had something to hide, and Tydeman was a common factor, almost certainly, Kindale decided. So did Katherine's grave have a part to play, with maybe something to hide?

***

Harry Harblow received his own visitor the night before.

There was no evidence he'd come with Grey Jonnie or indeed anyone else, and he had no horse.

The man simply introduced himself by saying he was expected. No other dialogue passed between them. Harry indicated a chair where he might sit and offered ale by gesture, an offer that was refused by the shake of the head.

"Food?" Harry then enquired. The man gave another shake of the head and then placed his gaze into the glowing embers of the fire.

"Your wet cloak, sir?" Harry ventured but gathered no response beyond a slight dismissive wave of the left hand.

Unwilling to been seen to be too curious Harry made do with a short, firm glance at his guest, trying to take in all that he could observe and committing the results to memory.

Thin, medium height and build, possibly forty or more, black hair that hung on his shoulders, drawn in cheeks, prominent and pointed nose, the look of a worried man, the look of a man with the weight of the world upon those shoulders.

A damp coat that would soon dry without the wearer removing it.

Boots. Mmmm.... boots that might be of military origin, he mused. Now what of the voice when he'd spoken those precious few words? Harry decided the sound was English but accented, not unlike Grey Jonnie's in fact.

Oliver would be pleased. He'd gathered much information, but for whatever it was worth and that might well be nothing at all.

The man slept in the chair, again refusing food and drink, and was gone in the morning, way before sunrise. There was no way of knowing if he'd be back but at least nobody had come looking for him.

Oliver Kindale arrived anon.

The two men talked convivially for a while and drank off plenty of ale for both had acquired an unseemly thirst, Harry through vexation, Oliver through elation.

"Forget the words, Harry, think carefully. Was there anything that might hint your guest was a foreign gentleman. Bearing? Gestures? Attitude?" Harry was crestfallen. He had not made any such detailed observations and was angry with himself for failing to do so, for indeed he might've seen something to indicate the man was not as English as he sounded. That might account for the accent.

"His skin was not dark and he looked starved yet he refused food."

It was all Harry could add and he knew it was woefully inadequate.

"To take food, Harry, would've meant engaging in conversation and our man was determined not to give himself away. A foreigner, Harry, mark my words. The less he spoke the less the chance of revealing more about himself from his voice.

"Military boots. Perhaps a man recruited from the army. But whose?"

In silence the men washed down a mug of ale apiece before Oliver spoke again.

"I'm back to Deal today then I'm bound for Ramsgate. Katherine spoke of a woman there who will be interested to meet me, and I fancy she knows William Tydeman. The pieces in this puzzle are manifold and well spread wide.

"Do I reach Kenton through you?"

"Aye, son, I go to Ballerden and I'll report all if ye wish it."

"Yes, Harry, tell him what we know, and ask him about Copwood and Copwood's business, and about the parson too. Many a parson has dirtied his hands in free trade, if you understand me!

"And see if he has any contacts in the Revenue I can use if needed. Good ones, you know what I'm after, Harry, not the ones that want to uphold the law at all costs. Reliable ones, people who talk our language, Harry."

Harry understood and knew what was expected of him.

He was lively and exhilarated, in part due to the ale and in part due to the fact he felt he was now on the front line of an important mission and not to be discarded or left to fester while Oliver careered around the county on his own.

"And some money if you're seeing Ballerden. I'll be back as soon as may be, be assured of that my dear friend." Even Oliver was merry and light, but he refused further refreshment knowing the ale was taking its toll. The chill wind, still north-easterly, would sober him up on the ride home, and he could sleep the rest off at his leisure.

After making sure Harry was fully acquainted with all the information necessary to pass on to the solicitor, and all the questions to ask, he took Beth and they rode to Deal where he went straight to his cottage and collapsed in a dead sleep, snoring heartily.

And this time his sleep was without issue.

He did not realise that Charlotte looked in on him, made up the fire and threw a rug across his prostrate form. She would have his meal for him, whatever time he awoke. She would leave a candle burning in the window he could see from his cottage so he would know she was still awake should it be late at night.

But it was very late when he arrived.

The candle was nearly burned out and Charlotte was asleep in a chair. He considered not disturbing her but his heavy tread upon the floor rendered such thoughts unnecessary, for she was suddenly awake, and eager to attend to him.

Later he sat by her fire and saw a rare smile on her lips. It was a tender, bittersweet smile, and her face betrayed no emotions to add to it.

How he wanted her. Her ugliness was her beauty, her repulsiveness her attraction, her untempting body her appeal. It was only for the next few hours. Then he would be gone. Forever, probably, as far as she was concerned.

Did she recognise that? Was that what drove her towards his arms? Or was she hoping, dreaming that she might detain him and that something deeper and more enduring be their combined destiny?

If that was the case, she would lose. He could offer nothing but himself for the pleasure of the night and then be away. Either way, he ached for her. Belo Jennie he had paid for, Katherine was from old friendship and nothing beyond, but what did Charlotte represent?

Nothing, he gave himself in answer, and that resolution gave strength to his longing. For he would not hurt her as they would share nothing other than their bodies. His meditations gave credence to his belief that here was an experience, magnificent and delightful, but with its own limitations and without sentiment or magnitude of commitment.

He would ride on, suffer some minor disgust, and forget.

But tonight he could leave the world and sample a paradise of sorts, a paradise of their own making, and it need mean nothing more than that.

Satisfied his mental examination had arrived at the right journey's end having evaluated every known aspect and potential outcomes, and finding himself pleased with the result, he opened his smile to return hers in anticipation of joys to follow.

"Time you returned to bed, Oliver Kindale, you have a journey later, I know, and you must sleep. Bless you for your company, but you go now."

Unsure of his ground he asked if she would like him to hold her. As he spoke the words the folly and nonsense of his question bewildered him. His words sounded false. His words were childish and empty and he felt he had cheapened himself in pursuit of his desires. He wanted her desperately but was she dismissing him or encouraging him?

Did he expect her to surrender and be as lustful as he was?

"No. I thank you, but you must go. In the morning you will be out of my life and I would not want anything to stain my memories. My memories are for me and no one else. If you hold me you will want more and they are not memories I need. Please understand, Oliver Kindale, and leave me be."

He left her cottage, returned to his own and threw himself on the bed.

He had not read her well, not read her well at all.

And now he was angry, with her and with himself. She had denied him. Why, why, why?

The rage infected his mind and kept his sleep at bay. Her memories? What memories? What had he brought to her that gave her memories worth saving? Excuses more like!

And he allowed such thoughts to calm his fury until sleep overcame him, but his repose was wracked with demonic dreams, fierce and dreadful, fiery and vicious, and he awoke with a scream hurled from deep within his bosom.

He sat on the bed, his head in his hands and realised he was crying. Then came the sudden comprehension that it was daylight. Struggling to his feet, his whole body aching, he saw a thick frost from the window, a white covering everywhere his eyes could see, yet he was warm.

Turning he saw the fire, freshly made and burning comfortably, and knew she had been in and silently prepared it for him while he slept. But had she also witnessed his torments, for his sleep had been visited by the devil himself, of that he was certain?

No matter. He would call on the way past and immediately dispensed with the notion. No, he would not. No good to come of it. It was all over. She was right.

And he felt irritation rising in his blood and swiftly quelled it. That would not do. He must let the coldness return to his heart and emptiness return to his emotions.

Save his anger for anyone who deserved it.

Shortly he rode through Deal, a frozen land today, and tried to eliminate Charlotte from his own memories. He was shaken from his attempts by a cry from a familiar voice.

"My friend, off early today, and bound for where?"

Thomas Temple was still the incurable rash that infected him mercilessly. Charlotte could be easily despatched, or so he thought, but Temple? Annoyingly he appeared as if by a witch's spell, an act of magic, and Oliver at once likened him to the devil who had tormented him in his nightmares. That made him smile, and his temper was stilled.

"Good-day to ye, Thomas Temple. Do not wait for me, for I will not be back." And he spurred Beth and galloped along the frosted road, his breath like thick smoke trailing behind him, and made his way north to Ramsgate.

If Katherine's suggestion was to prove a sound one it might well be a profitable visit, profitable in terms of what could be vital information.

***

Ursula Wellfern was going about her daily business.

Ramsgate was a busy and successful town, self-governing and a major port, garrisoned, alive with soldiers sailing to and from battles on foreign soils, and wealthy from its trade.

Roads were good and lit. The town's success and wealth were manifest everywhere.

Mrs Wellfern had benefited by marrying 'above' herself, for she possessed only the dressmaker's trade, but had made herself thus invaluable to the society of the area. Her creations were well sought after and brought in a pretty income.

Her marriage to a shipwright had come about by a circuitous route.

He had commissioned her to make a ballgown for the woman he was courting. The disadvantage lay in that Ursula was unable to measure or fit the garment as it had been intended as a surprise.

She was obliged to make observations of the lady and use her judgement accordingly.

For this she would be paid handsomely.

It was nevertheless an appreciable task.

And the gift was not appreciated for the work of art and emblem of achievement that is was. It fitted well, but the lady refused to believe that it had not been modelled by Mr Wellfern's mistress, assuming he had one. He did not, but the hand of suspicion had cast its shadow, and he was doomed.

He returned the gown to Ursula and confessed that he was no longer engaged to the recipient.

In his misery he found solace in the dressmaker's arms.

Such solace subsequently left her with child, and Mr Wellfern decided to undertake 'the honourable thing' and marry Ursula, not an act he would've contemplated otherwise.

The child was born whereupon Mr Wellfern expired.

His widow inherited the family home in the town and a noticeable sum of money to provide her with sufficient solace for her own loss.

And Ursula discovered she liked being able to solve other people's problems by appropriate intervention in discreet and gentle ways. This extended itself to intrusion into matters that might be seen to stand either side of the law and, in a few cases, very much the wrong side of it.

She ingratiated herself with the high-born, and high ranking. She put herself in a position where she could glean information more useful to felons than to the upholders of the law, and therefore improved her income at every turn.

And Mrs Wellfern of Ramsgate was where Oliver Kindale was heading.

He was not dressed for Ramsgate society, but no matter.

The place had changed since his time there with Katherine and, he assumed, it had improved to the liking and with the blessing of the people. But it had little appeal. It wasn't the sort of place he could settle in. Too busy, too many people, too many houses.

But they cleaned the streets! A changing world.

He preferred the countryside where they didn't need streets, and certainly did not need to light and clean the roads and byways they had.

He preferred the countryside where the work of men was not destroying all that nature could provide, where mankind worked in harmony with the surroundings, and both benefited mutually.

He preferred the countryside where a man may walk in peace and be alone with his thoughts, undisturbed by his fellow man, unchallenged by social development.

Yes, the countryside was his haven, both an escape and a home, and something to be cherished, possibly even worshipped. He did indeed prefer the countryside, and preferred it to the hellish bustle and cramped conditions of towns, confining, breathless and restrictive places that they were in his eyes.

The world was changing and he wasn't persuaded he wanted it so, or that he could abide it.

His first attempt to see Mrs Wellfern was rebuffed by a servant who assumed him a vagrant.

So he took a room and wrote a brief letter, and a day after it was delivered he gained admittance.

Ursula stared at the crudely dressed man in front of her. To him she looked a perfect lady regardless of her years. She invited him into her withdrawing room with some reluctance, and with even greater reluctance offered him a seat.

Her disgust and depression was all too plain on her face, a face that was showing its age despite her substantial attempts to repair or at least hide the damage with lotions and feminine additives. And it was a round, jolly face, with plump cheeks, plumpness being applicable to all parts of her body.

Nonetheless she dressed impeccably, walked with grace and majesty and was by all accounts elegant and decorous.

Oliver wasted no time explaining the reasons for his call. He did not look to social niceties, or respect protocol or etiquette. He knew what he wanted and that was all he asked.

"How is Katherine?" she enquired, taking him completely by surprise.

"I am afraid Katherine is dead, ma'am. She died but a few days ago in terrible pain. I was there and attended her funeral." She nodded appreciatively. Oliver made no explanation for her illness and demise and Ursula asked no further.

"I am glad she was well attended and well buried, Mr Kindale. I knew her well, many years ago. Now as to your questions. I knew Katherine but I do not know you, and I will not place myself in ... shall we say .... *not* place myself in a *difficult* position by helping you.

"There are enquiries to be made about you. That will take time. Tell me where I can find you."

Kindale knew this could not be rushed. In her position he would've been taking the same precautions, but he also knew there was little she would discover and might jeopardise his pursuit of information. He explained that.

"Do not fret, Mr Kindale. I am not going to leave myself open to later problems by telling a complete stranger all he wants to know. But there are people here who remember Katherine and may even recall you, I daresay.

"Tell me who you know and I will enquire."

Oliver thought about that and decided on the following:

"A solicitor in Folkestone, Nathaniel Ballerden. I have no wish to disclose anything further for much the same reasons that you are reticent with me."

She smiled.

"I will let you know. Good-day to you."

He was on the street almost before he realised.

Unwilling to waste any time Kindale elected to carry out some investigations of his own and headed for the bustling harbour.

***

Another man heading for a harbour, elegantly dressed as a gentleman and accompanied by an equally elegant wife, was Chastain, who was neither a gentleman nor a husband.

It was one of the rare occasions 'Mrs Copwood' was allowed out of the house, and then simply for show so that 'Mr Copwood' might be seen as the Englishman he pretended to be. They sought out Hapling who was handed a pouch of documents and letters Chastain had written and which were clearly destined for France.

How Mlle Descoteaux wished to read the contents! But she could guess at the nature of the communications. And she had learned that at least one other Frenchman was in town, probably a spy, who had come to their home the day before. He and Chastain spoke quietly in a corner before his brief visit was over but although she could make out so few words all she heard were in French.

None of Chastain's other visitors spoke in such a tongue; they were all English, of that she was positive.

Her fear mounted. Not that she was afraid of death but that she might perish before Chastain's plan could be ruined. And she yearned for knowledge, an understanding of what was going on around her that might lead to her enemy's downfall and the destruction of his scheme.

Where was the man sent to battle with Chastain? What was he about? Oh, the annoyance that ripped through her emotions time and again, the frustration of not knowing and not being able to find out, and even more frustration at not being as directly involved as she wished to be. The frustration of having to be patient.

She knew it would be like this but that patience was now sore tested.

Chapter Seven

"We came from Norfolk, Mr Kindale. Do you know where Norfolk is?"

A small nod from her guest sufficed to confirm his knowledge. He ignored her obvious sarcasm.

"My father was a fisherman, my mother a seamstress. As all reasonable hope of a fair income diminished my parents decided to move here in search of improved wealth. Yarmouth and Ramsgate have not been, may I say, good friends.

"They knew this town by reputation alone. I was about six or seven but swiftly learned the ways of prosperity. My father was, to put it simply, something of an expert. Indeed, I believe he may also have left Norfolk before the law was about him, if you understand me, and not just for a better life.

"My older brother followed him well, but is now overseas for much the same reasons.

"I live well and comfortably, admired and respected, and do not intend to have my life shortened by succumbing to errors of judgement."

Oliver Kindale understood this, just as he had from the moment he met Mrs Wellfern. And now he perceived she was preparing the ground to advise him that she would disclose little or nothing to him.

"I will not be questioned," she continued, "and I'll tell you what I may, but will not talk further and will remain unchallenged. On this we must agree, sir, as I am confident you would behave in such a manner if our roles were reversed, and indeed I suspect you would cherish secrecy and diplomacy in a far greater way than I.

"I do not think I have underestimated you, sir, have I?"

Again, a slight nod.

"William Tydeman. He is south of here but not active. It therefore follows that if he has abandoned, albeit temporarily, his hunting grounds, and not from fear of apprehension, he has found some lucrative measure to involve himself in. It will be a worthwhile venture, you may be assured of that, Mr Kindale.

"Clearly he has been encouraged to leave here and I believe it is because of his skills and crafts, if we may call them that, that he has been sought. That the scheme is of *mighty* benefit to him is all too obvious. He considers it worthwhile and worth any risks.

"And I fancy he feels the risks have been reduced to the minimum.

"There are French spies everywhere, sir, and here in Ramsgate. Why, only a week ago a gentleman thought to be making too great an observation of the harbour and the navy ships, and having an accent that betrayed him, was persuaded to join a fishing vessel across the Goodwins. He went believing he would learn something to his value.

"The boat returned without him. A sad loss.

68

"A man, possibly Chastain as you describe him, took ale with Tydeman some time ago.

"A word of caution. Tangle with Tydeman at your peril. You may not lose your life but you may lose all you hold dear. A man who crossed him just last year returned home to find his wife and child murdered, and brutally killed at that."

"I have no such connections, Mrs Wellfern. I have taken care to ensure there are no such attachments...."

"Please do not interrupt. Be wary, not adventurous. Think before you act. That is all I caution.

There is intelligence that something is planned, and it will require reliable men. By reliable, I am sure you comprehend my words.

"It may be a French project, but it will require English .... *expertise*."

Oliver had questions but knew they must not leave his lips. It was frustrating but he must make do with what he had learned, and it was good enough, it had to be. The rest was up to him.

"That is all. Before you leave I wish you to make the acquaintance of Lieutenant Dugald of His Majesty's ship .... well, that does not matter. He is .... *reliable* ... in our sense. I will tell you where to meet him tonight. I will send a note to your lodgings.

"Good-day Mr Kindale. Do not return, there will be no welcome for you. But I am grateful for anything you did for Katherine, please know that. And I wish you luck, every good fortune."

His meeting with Lt Dugald was of limited outcome as both men were suspicious of each other and neither was prepared to yield any ground and be in any way forthcoming. Nevertheless Oliver learned Dugald had come across Hapling and was concerned about his loyalties to King and country, to put it in the realms of courtesy and politeness.

Oliver closely observed Dugald's expression as the Lieutenant talked briefly and guardedly about his fears with respect to Hapling, and that exercise revealed he had a strong contempt for the man. Reading facial expressions had been valuable to Kindale and had often put him at an advantage as it did now. Dugald said more with his face than his words ever could.

There were other matters about which the navy's Lt Dugald chose not to speak, especially when an enquiry about Tydeman was made, yet he gave himself away with the way he looked.

As a result Dover and Folkestone beckoned.

But first his journey must mean a visit to Harry Harblow.

Mary Harblow was home and most pleased to see Kindale who she welcomed with a smile and a laugh and a wholehearted embrace, releasing him swiftly as she had all manner of questions to ask him. Good cheer aplenty and a mug of ale besides. And questions, questions.

Oliver took it all in good stead, smiled affectionately in return, and replied to those harmless questions where they were of no great consequence to him, ignoring those that were, or where to answer would've given more away than he wished. This didn't bother Mary; she was simply delighted he was there. Harry was still in Dover, she explained.

Harry's wife was rotund, with a head of curly black hair, and a happy sort of round face, with a full mouth set in a permanent grin, and eyes that sizzled with excitement and a degree of sauciness. Oliver had never known her to look anything other than content and had never seen her beset by sorrow, although he was sure she had known sadness. In truth she had been grief-stricken by a failure to bear children but was now completely resigned to life without them, not that Oliver was aware of her loss and suffering or its reason.

***

Harry's arrival was greeted by muted little shrieks of happiness and pleasure as Mary took hold of him, hugged and kissed him, and allowed him to lift her and to twirl her around, admittedly half a twirl only.

This was no surprise to Kindale either on account of the open show of love and affection, or the cavorting that involved lifting her off her feet, for he knew they loved each other beyond any known words. She was a substantial woman but Harry was strong enough, and Mary adored the attempt and revelled in being lofted high, even if the gesture was for a brief moment.

Kindale wanted to get down to business and Mary realised that would be the situation as she had known Oliver long enough, so went off to prepare some food, singing and skipping like a young girl, the young girl she might have been many, many years before.

"Have you been away long, Harry?"

Oliver's question was based on the knowledge it could've been no more than a day or so, and that he was incredulous about Mary's extreme reaction. In fact he shook his head as he asked.

"No, you forget, Oliver, she's been in Deal and is just returned." Of course, and Oliver had indeed forgotten. That troubled him. Now was not the time to be losing the powers of recall.

The friends sat either side of the fire and drank. Harry began.

"Revenue. George Gordon. Mention Ballerden first or you'll get nowhere. Gordon's on the coast and rumour has it he's after Tydeman in partic'lar.

"Ballerden will look into the parson. He knows him well, but no suspicions. But ... well .... he'll get looked into, my son," and Harry chuckled at the thought.

"Copwood. Ballerden fished him out of a problem with the law over some stolen wood. Been beholden to Ballerden since and that suits our solicitor friend. Shall we say 'friends' of Copwood supplied a bit of timber in exchange for a hiding place for one of their number and they paid his ... shall we say ... legal costs, as it were.

"Daniel Copwood has built a permanent hiding place at his workshop. It's a treat, my son. Been searched twice, soldiers and revenue, and they never found it.

"But, here's the thing. Copwood's afraid. He's got a wife and a new baby. Ballerden reckons he's been persuaded, if you know what I mean by persuaded, to act unlawfully against his will. So tread carefully, my son, don't let him or his family come to harm."

Oliver listened intently.

More and more it made sense and the pieces were starting to lock together.

Chastain might be in Dover but Kindale was now sure his tentacles spread to neighbouring Folkestone, and not just to Daniel Copwood either.

Harry had one other piece of information obtained from Nathaniel Ballerden.

Grey Jonnie, whose grey coat, grey hair and beard earned him his popular name, was actually Will Cosney, born near Huddersfield and in trouble with the law before he was ten. His exploits as a criminal had been noted primarily in Yorkshire but also in Derbyshire and Lincolnshire.

If all the dubious evidence was to be believed he'd robbed as far afield as Cornwall, south Wales, and Cumberland, as well as Lancashire and Northumberland. There were other stories too. It was not unusual for conflicting accounts to arise relating to raids that occurred about the same time but at places many miles apart.

Grey Jonnie had always aroused public interest and romantic notions, but his most credible hunting grounds of the past lay in his native county and those immediately surrounding it.

And now he was in Kent, and in league with Chastain.

"I won't stay, Harry. I think Mary wishes to have you to herself after such a long absence, and I can return to Deal." The friends smiled knowingly and Harry offered no debate.

So Oliver Kindale returned to Deal.

Wishing to avoid Charlotte he went first to Jack, but Jack had a guest and a fair twinkle in her eye. There being no obvious alternative and the time pressing on with darkness approaching he rode down to Charlotte's where, Jack informed him, her sister would be pleased to see him.

If she was she didn't show it.

She escorted him to his own accommodation, made up the fire, spoke very little, asked no questions of his time away, and enquired only as to his health and his requirements during his present stay.

He admitted he didn't know if he would be back the following night, such was the nature of his trade, and she simply added he could come any time. Nobody else would be staying there.

The cottage was still all but immaculate and Kindale couldn't quite believe that she would want to keep it so clean and tidy when it was customarily unoccupied. Perhaps it wasn't.

She had no food. It didn't perturb him but he could see she was hungry.

"I'll take you to an inn," he offered, but she shook her head and declined, and left him with no further words. Was she upset about their previous meeting and his departure? It wasn't a matter he needed to perplex himself about and he resolved not to do so and dismiss the thoughts completely.

But that night the thoughts returned to haunt him and keep him awake. He couldn't shake them clear but eventually the toil of fighting such mental wrangling overtook him and he slept till morning.

***

"Nathaniel Ballerden suggested speaking to you."

Kindale looked at George Gordon as a master tailor might visually assess the measurements of a client, and accurately so, and Gordon himself felt conscious of Kindale's precise observations, whereas he had no need to make a similar study, beyond placing his visitor's face firmly and neatly in his memory. That would do the Revenue man.

"Tydeman," Oliver continued, as if one word was sufficient to unveil his entire meaning, while continuing his scrutiny of the man sitting opposite him in the inn.

"Hapling," he added when Gordon made no facial acknowledgement of Tydeman's name. The name Hapling similarly produced no response whatsoever past a concentrated and steady gaze directly into Kindale's eyes.

Gordon sat unmoved. But for the smoke from his pipe drifting lazily away from his mouth Kindale might well have thought the man had died in front of him. However, he realised Gordon was weighing him up just as he was weighing up the Revenue man.

Eventually Gordon removed his pipe and smiled. But that was all he did.

He was short and stocky with a substantial beard, now well grey, that ran from ear to ear and under his chin, but did not incorporate his mouth, almost as if such an omission was by design to keep his mouth free for speech, food, ale and pipe-smoking.

There was a ruggedness Kindale admired at once. No nonsense. Practical. Determined. It was all in his face. And Kindale liked what he saw. Finally Gordon spoke.

"You wanted this meeting, Kindale. You do the talking. I'll decide if I wish to make answer."

Oliver considered this carefully.

If Ballerden 'recommended' Gordon he must be approachable and 'flexible' in his outlook.

"If I deliver Tydeman and Hapling to you, but when the time is right for me, and bring you a good few smugglers into the bargain, I'll be looking for help from you in the meantime.

"Means sharing information, Mr Gordon. And you don't move till I send word. That's vital. What I am after is a deal more serious than the evasion of duties due on exports and imports. Much more serious.

"I am asking much of you, and for your part I will share nothing with you and expect a great deal in return. Not much of a bargain, my friend. But talk to Ballerden. Hear him, then let me have your answer.

"But you get the catches you want most. With your help I can all but guarantee it."

Gordon's eyes had widened slightly, and now he returned to pipe-smoking as he thought about this extraordinary meeting and the words of a man he didn't know and knew nothing about.

"I'll talk to Ballerden. Meet me here tomorrow. G'day Mr Kindale."

***

Charlotte exuded sorrow and hopeless resignation, much as she had done the first time they had met, and, Oliver had to admit in all frankness, much as she appeared on most occasions they spent together.

Even her gaunt, withdrawn, pallid and sombre facial expression rarely submitted itself to anything remotely more lively, and never to anything ambitious and uplifting such as unbounded joy, optimism or hope.

He studied her as she sewed at the other side of the fire. It had been a fine meal. There had been little enough money but she had done well on it, with some ale besides, but had not been able to include conversation as an addition to pleasurable repast or as an aid to digestion. His words now took her completely by surprise. He watched her face for the reaction he knew would come.

"Where's Jack's husband?"

"Y'know. Y'know full well, transported," she replied with all the indignation she could muster.

"No. Never apprehended. Still at large." He deliberately spoke with calm softness.

Charlotte, wide-eyed and clearly stunned, made several small movements driven by the fluster of confusion she felt within her, her eyes darting everywhere exploring the darkness, the glow of the fire, the light of the candles. Only once did she look at Kindale and he was staring straight at her, unblinking.

It was he who ended the momentary silence between them.

"He's here, probably in Kent. Maybe even in Deal. I know, Charlotte, I know. I am not an officer of the law, not the revenue. He is of no concern to me. But I have learned more of the man and I am interested, that's all."

Charlotte was shaking, though from rage or fear Oliver could not discern.

"Where d'you hear such nonsense?" she blurted out, full of defence, irritation and worry. He could see it all in her face.

"Charlotte, I *know*. I *know*. I am no threat to him or any of you. No word of this will ever leave my lips, I assure you.

"Oliver, y'know nothing. Nothing of the sort. Nothing." Her words now lacked body and conviction and he knew his information was correct.

"We will not speak of it again. My apologies for my impertinence. Now I'll go."

"No, wait Oliver, wait." She now spoke with the voice of surrender and reconciliation, the voice of despair and submission.

"Don't go. I'll tell you. H-h-h-have some more ale, keep me company, and I'll tell." Oliver recognised the edge of desperation as she swiftly spluttered out her plea, her words as shaken as she was. He sat and she quickly refilled his mug, seemingly anxious he should not depart. Ideal, he thought. He had no desire to leave now.

Charlotte slowly explained that Jack had been identified as a leader and there had been a price on his head. Gradually it had emerged that he was innocent of that charge and that his involvement in one particular smuggling enterprise had been achieved at pistol point, his assistance obtained as an alternative to instant death.

Unfortunately the authorities never cleared him completely, largely as they believed he was a smuggler anyway, which was quite true, Charlotte stressed. So he simply merged into the background, became invisible to view.

Oliver realised that the sparkle in the female Jack's eyes, not easily perceived, was a flame that burned for a love that was very real and very alive, and a frequent visitor.

"What does Thomas Temple know of this?" he asked.

"Thought it was 'e who told you." It was her turn to look right into his eyes to seek the truth, and earned an honest smile in response, for Oliver saw the gaze for what it was.

"No, not Temple. But he knows?" She nodded in reply. "And what's Temple to you?"

Charlotte knew it was pointless fighting. This man who wouldn't explain his cause, this man who wouldn't reveal his trade, this man who had eyes and ears everywhere, but for what purpose? He had invaded her being, infiltrated her world, and in her bewildered state she wondered if Oliver Kindale knew more about her than she herself did. It was a fearsome thought and one that left her cold.

"Temple's Jess's step-brother," she conceded, "so 'e takes it 'pon himself to watch over me, if y'must know, Oliver Kindale, but it's not what I need, don't want minding like. But he keeps an eye for me, so was suspicious of you and you done nothing to ease his worries that way, nor mine I'll tell ye.

"He'd like to do more to look after Jess's widow, mind, but I won't let 'im. He's not fer me. Have to be a really fine gent to take Jess's place and Thomas Temple ain't that, I know."

"And who does my cottage belong to?" It was a quite natural development of the questions Kindale had been asking, and Charlotte had been dreading it, but dreading it because she knew she could only be truthful and the telling would be painful.

"Jess's sister. His sister Martha." Charlotte, defeated, sunk further into her chair, her eyes glistening as the memories swarmed across her mind and savaged her heart. "His sister, that's who." The defiance and aggression, the defensive nature and firmness of her voice, all vanished as she recalled the loss, the bitterness and the torment.

There was no resentment or hostility now. Her speech was calmed, tender and smooth, devoid of any emotion except acute wretchedness.

"I loved 'er like me own. She was *my* sister you could say. They lived in *your* cottage, Oliver Kindale. Their parents' home. When I was wed to Jess we had this place. Both belonged to their father, see, that's how we came by them. The old man's long gone now. At least 'e never saw 'is son shot.

"Martha, she were with child. Would've been their first. She tried to protect Jess when 'e was shot. She tried to stop 'em soldiers, so they shot 'er too. That's what they did. Innocent woman, in front of my eyes, Oliver Kindale. Shot clean through 'er loving heart. Killed 'er, killed the baby, poor mite.

"That's what you wanted to know, Oliver Kindale, for what it's worth. Yes, I saw me man and me sister and 'er unborn baby murdered in front of me."

Kindale sat motionless, understanding yet not understanding. He could not imagine the agony, but he could appreciate the suffering. He could not conceive the horror, but he knew the aftermath bore utter desolation.

"Jess and Martha, when the old man died, their mother married again, gave birth to Thomas then the pox took 'er. Where old man Temple went I don't know, an' I don't think Thomas knows. Heartbroke, 'e was, that Thomas.

"Tell you about Thomas. He came late upon the scene, but in time to see Jess and Martha killed, and thinking I was going to get the same fired on the soldiers, wounded two and was away. An' they forget all about killing innocent women, left me alone and set off to chase 'im.

"But he's good, too good, knows every way, and Thomas leads them off of me and gets away himself. He was never known to 'em, they don't know whats he looks like and that. So he got away. Probably saved my life.

"But in that moment I wanted to die. Wanted to be dead. I had nothing to thank him for then. He'd done me wrong, by my way of thinking, saving me from being shot when I wanted to die and be with me man and with Martha." At last the silvery tears that had been kept in check slipped slowly and gracefully down her cheeks and dripped, one by one, into her lap as her head rolled forward and the pain thrust from her heart and shook her entire body.

The weeping increased its intensity, the sobs became an audible moan, and then an anguished wailing as Charlotte began to rock backwards and forwards, her memories, her nightmares all that remained in the acquaintance of her mind.

Oliver put his mug down and moved slowly to her side.

His understanding was limited by his coldness of heart, and yet his own experiences of such atrocious emotional grief that had long ago helped freeze his feelings now warmed his soul. And he felt for her, and he knew in that instant he should not let it happen.

But he could not prevent it. And for the moment he would not let it trouble him.

He placed a comforting arm around her shoulder and as the tears fell more easily and swiftly and the wailing became squeals and distressed cries, she nestled into his chest and accepted his comfort.

Now he knew why she kept his cottage so well, and why she seemed sullen and beaten by life.

Now he knew.

And he now knew he wasn't comforting her simply from human compassion.

***

"I need a sign from you, Kindale.

"It's all very well, but I'm an officer of the law, and I won't let Tydeman and his sort go just to suit the schemes and whim of a man I don't know and who, for all I know, may be leading me astray and away from my quarry.

"You must tell me more of your scheme, Kindale, or we go no further."

George Gordon, having said his piece, allowed himself a few generous pulls on his pipe and diverted his eyes from the man seated opposite to observe the smoke spiralling upwards. Kindale had been expecting these sort of words. He had to play his man carefully, but he had to win, had to get Gordon to stand resolutely by his side if this plan was to succeed.

He decided to wait and perhaps encourage the Revenue man to speak a little further. Gordon acknowledged the course of the game, nodded, withdrew his pipe and added:

"Ballerden. He's the only reason we're talking and talking like this. Who *are* you, Kindale?"

Oliver knew he needed to distract him from this latest quest. It was time to back his own hunch and Gordon, he reasoned, was just the man. Making sure there were no obvious ears to hear their conversation Kindale spoke:

"Dig up the grave of Katherine Downford, recently buried. You'll find contraband at least, maybe more."

The look of surprise and dread on Gordon's face was all but astonishing, but his expression was enhanced when he bit the end off his pipe, his shock complete. Kindale knew he was winning.

He could piece together snippets of information, make thoughtful analysis, make wise assumptions, and come to well-reasoned conclusions. In suggesting a course of action to Gordon he had given much consideration to what he knew himself, and to what he'd been told. He was confident the result of Gordon's search would be valuable to both of them and make the exercise (and law breaking) worthwhile.

But first he had a pressing matter to deal with.

"There's a carpenter called Copwood. Young wife and baby. Get them away first, get them to safety far from here, I implore you. His family will be the ones murdered if you do not. His involvement was not from choice, and I am certain you understand me in that. Do this for me, and do this before you dig.

"Gordon, do not have the blood of innocents on your hands."

The Revenue man's look of amazement had now surpassed all reasonable description.

"I cannot dig up a grave, Kindale."

"It must be done, Gordon, it *must* be. You will see I am right."

"How do you know what's there? You must have some part in this. You must have some knowledge. I won't be taken astray here, Kindale. Be warned. Try to fool me and you'll regret it."

"That I know, Gordon, but I am convinced my summation is correct and my assessment of certain occurrences and involvements tells me you will be successful. I do not seek smugglers because they are smugglers. There is something far more serious afoot.

"I have to deal with that, but I need your help and I will deliver what I have promised. Ballerden has your confidence and he'll have endorsed that." Gordon nodded and Kindale knew he had his man.

"Do not cross me, Kindale. You'll not make a fool of me and ruin me, I do so assure you."

No further words were spoken. Kindale rose and offered his hand which, after a moment's hesitation, was taken by Gordon. Both men smiled knowingly. It was a bloody business and they knew it, and it could not possibly end peaceably, but it was a task they had to undertake.

Mary Harblow welcomed Oliver as her husband was engaged in farm work which was his true trade and therefore his true means of employment. It was necessary for him to attend to it from time to time even if he appeared to regret and resent the intrusion in his life.

"But he'll be in soon, Oliver," she advised.

Always cheerful, Oliver thought; Harry must be a happy man with such a woman. And those thoughts took him immediately to Charlotte and her great sadness. A pang of deflation came upon him. He was hurting for her but determined he must keep his feelings under control, and not let her sway him from his course.

It was a difficult time for him. He had privately confessed to himself that he had feelings he couldn't afford and was doing his best to drive them from his mind. But now he was finding it hard to drive them from his heart and that was what worried him.

Best not to return to Charlotte he had resolved, and thought so time and again, yet he was infested with a desire to be with her when he could and yearned for her when he was away.

His mind was twisted and knotted and he could make no sense of it. He *must* put her out of his life. He must leave the cottage. That was the only way. But why had he allowed her safe passage into his mind and why was she so difficult to expel?

Had he wished to acknowledge it the answer lay in his heart for that was where she now resided and was not about to surrender occupation. Until he could accept that he would never find a solution to his mental ordeal.

The one thing he was certain of was that he could not for one moment permit anything, *anything* at all, to intervene in the processes of his mind and the execution of his task. And thoughts of Charlotte were interfering, a matter he could not let rest and unaddressed. But for a man who had taught himself to be free of the warmth of heart he was now faced with the inconceivable notion that a thaw had set in at a time he least needed it.

And Oliver Kindale needed clarity of thought, coldness of temperament, and precision of judgement now more than ever.

Now more than ever, as he was certain action was imminent.

Chapter Eight

George Gordon was not the sort of man to worry unduly about rights and wrongs, and thus was appropriate to Kindale's task much as Kindale had hoped in securing the services of such a person.

And Gordon was therefore unlikely to concern himself with legalities if it suited his purpose, despite being regarded as an upholder of law and order. He was a Revenue officer but knew the guilty could escape while the correct procedures were followed. He was not averse to moving just slightly to the wrong side of the law if he believed such a manoeuvre would produce results.

Act now, answer later.

He knew Ballerden well. The solicitor would give nothing away about Kindale, but supported the man at every turn, so Gordon, having wrestled with his conscience and sanctioned the view of his intuition, decided on two courses of immediate action.

Men were despatched to warn Copwood and to take him and his family away.

The carpenter was shaking with fear but knew he must go, and was duly escorted from Folkestone across the marshes and into the weald with no knowledge of the destination chosen for him.

Allowing a safe time to pass before commencing their next assignment Gordon and two of his men eventually arrived at the graveyard. Once Gordon decided Copwood must be well away from the area the small group went to work with their shovels.

The soil was easy to work as the grave was a recent creation.

Such activity must arouse local interest and people began to gather in ones and twos to watch the process they found deplorable. Desecration! An abomination! And by Revenue officers too! They watched from a distance, shocked by such abhorrent and ungodly work, angered by such disgraceful goings on, and managing to enjoy something so dreadful without confessing to themselves that the event was exciting and pleasurable.

Heaven forbid!

The parson flew upon the scene in great uproar, waving his arms furiously and damning the three men to purgatory and eternal suffering.

"Oh dear," muttered Gordon under his breath, "I appear to have overlooked the courtesy of advising the parson of our intentions." He caught sight of Nathaniel Ballerden but swiftly returned to his digging which was about to prove rewarding.

If the small crowd of onlookers had been invigorated by the mens' obscene practices, whilst publicly condemning them and agreeing with all the oaths sworn by the parson, they were about to be enlivened by the results of the digging.

It was not the first time a grave had been used to conceal goods, but this one had a spectacular yield.

A man's body was unearthed. A rapier wound suggested he had been 'run through'.

Then came the gold, the coins, then tobacco and cloth.

Gordon then made a decision that enraged the parson beyond the bounds of his ability to cope with the situation. Katherine's coffin was opened but there was nothing to be found there and it was sealed promptly.

With similar alacrity the three men filled in the grave as if anxious to restore the woman to her rest.

In amongst the commotion of the onlookers another interested party took note and turned his back to make haste to those who must be told.

Within an hour Copwood's cottage and workshop was ablaze.

Gordon had his haul but not the perpetrators. There was also a document in a foreign hand and he fancied Kindale would be more than interested. It was wrapped in a piece of cloth to protect it from its immersion in the soil.

He guessed the words were French but neither he nor the two men with him could read them.

Kindale was now of great value to him. He could be used much as Oliver had used *him*. The two could work together, but trust was still the barrier, still the loose shingle they walked upon where a footing could be lost with the suddenness of surprise. But trust must make its birth somewhere, and Gordon was prepared to move closer to Kindale, whilst at the same time making sure he did not slip on those pebbles.

Yes, this was a relationship that might do very nicely.

But for the moment he needed to placate the parson while his men gathered together the treasures of their work. For an experienced man he needed no telling of the value of their haul and he needed no telling that its previous owners would be raised to violent curses and insatiable rage by their loss!

***

Mary Harblow delighted in having Harry and Oliver about her.

Tonight the three yarned while the fire, seemingly entertained, applauded vigorously with vivid flames and crackling wood, and kept them warm on another bleak, cold February evening.

The fire was the main source of light and the three candles that burned added nothing of value to the illumination of the room. Small, this night very cosy, the room hugged them all in and made them welcome and comfortable.

A meal taken, ale was now following, and the men in particular were in joyous mood, apparently divorced from Oliver's undertakings, and prepared to share a pleasant intercourse on matters of little importance. They talked about times a-past, shared their humour and their experiences, sad as well as cheerful, yet never ventured into any realms that did not concern Mary.

Oliver had already taken Harry aside to ask for more money.

He was also anxious for more information from Ballerden. He wanted to go directly to the solicitor's but knew he must not. The situation annoyed him, but he long ago learned the way of things, and had to accept them and allow them to proceed at their own pace. It was bound to irritate a man like Kindale, always keen to keep on the move, always impatient if he thought he needed to be more active in one direction or other.

And that was now.

Somehow he swallowed his anxiety and made his company pleasurable to Harry and Mary.

But they retired early, just as the rains came, sweeping in on a strong north-easterly. Kindale would be on his way long before there was any hope of a dawn to herald another day.

That night he once more found his thoughts awash with Charlotte. How he hated it. He longed to be free of it, free in mind, free in heart. He could not at any price afford to find his thoughts clouded in this way.

To do so could cost him his life.

So he fought to expunge them and the more he fought the more they refused to recede. In the finish he had a bad night, with little sleep, and too much torment, and was pleased when he reasoned it was time to go.

***

"One of my clients in Greenwich is paying me for a number of services, Mr Gordon, and that includes looking after Mr Kindale in whatever line of work that man pursues. I will tell you no more than that, but be aware that he is known in high regard by those in authority and his work here is, I believe, of the utmost importance.

"I cannot say if everything he does is legal, but then digging up a grave without proper authorisation certainly isn't."

Gordon lowered his eyes from Nathaniel Ballerden's gaze, almost in embarrassment, sensing the solicitor was toying with him and making a point.

"Please do what is necessary, Mr Gordon, and if it pleases you then offer Mr Kindale every assistance." Ballerden sat back in his chair, upright and with his hands palms down on the desk, and continued staring at his visitor.

George Gordon felt hemmed in. He had co-operated with Kindale and left himself in some measure of difficulty. Ballerden was right, of course. He was now implicated in an area of illegal activity, regardless of the successful outcome of the dig, and therefore now felt obliged to continue this odd association with a man of dubious methods and an unknown background.

And above that here was a man of law clearly prepared to endorse if not participate in such illegality!

Revenue or Excise. Solicitors. We're all men of law, he mused as he strolled down along the steep approach to the sea at Folkestone, to the few fishing vessels and the handful of men still ashore. There he looked out across the sea and along the coast as far as he could make out, which in truth was not far either way.

Ashore peace. Calm.

But a fairly rough sea, as grey as the disdainful, ugly masses of clouds overhead. Two fishing boats heading for shore, their crews no doubt tired and weary but hopefully looking upon a decent catch.

How many, Gordon wondered, found illegal ways of improving their income?

And he puffed at his broken pipe and smiled ruefully. Ballerden! Not at all forthcoming about Kindale, but he hadn't expected him to be. A client in Greenwich indeed! What an upright gentleman, Gordon thought sneeringly, a lawman like me, yet he twists the rules.

Yes, just like me, he concluded, allowing his smile to spread to his whole face which was now pleasantly alight with good humour and understanding.

In that moment he decided he would work with Kindale and do so without question. And the prospect of landing a large catch of his own warmed his thoughts.

"Snow later." The disembodied voice growled and rasped like a man walking over stones.

"Snow," it intoned again, lest Gordon had not heard the first intimation of a change in weather.

"You Excise?" it asked, and then the voice was joined by an ancient looking body that emerged from where it had been concealed.

"Excise, revenue, bastards, call us what you will, aye, that's me." Gordon continued with his pipe and paid no heed to the newcomer who then stood in front of him and occupied his entire field of vision.

The man was rotund by any means of definition, with a fat, red face and an untidy crop of grey hair that hung where it pleased, much of it about his face. Gordon now took in the figure and realised this man was old enough to be living on borrowed time, and despite his corpulence, or maybe because of it, posed no serious threat.

"Y'not welcome 'ere," he was advised, but before he could reply the man had shuffled away from whence he came.

George Gordon resolved to buy a new pipe. I don't expect to be loved, he thought, but at least I have a wife and children who love me. Then perhaps they don't! Maybe my profession does not lend itself to me being much liked. And my wife hardly sees me, so then that's why she loves me. My rare appearances at home and the money I bring must be very welcome, mainly because I'll be going away again soon, and to earn more money!

The retreating elderly lump turned to hurl one last comment.

"Jeremiah Hundash. The body you dug up, if y'need to know."

***

"Oliver. Oliver Kindale! Abroad again."

Kindale stared in disbelief. Thomas Temple, it had to be. The man appeared as by some magician's spell.

"Have y'nothing better to do than be in Folkestone, friend, or are there riches enough for you here?" Temple rocked backwards and forwards as laughter roared up his throat and thrust its way into the air beyond his mouth. "And Charlotte told me about you, and about Jess, Martha, and all that happened."

"Did she now," Temple returned, "well, yes, that's it my friend, and I do keep a good eye for her."

Kindale dismounted and tethered Beth to an overhanging branch before offering Temple his hand. The gesture took the man by surprise but with a glint in his eye he took the hand and did so as a welcome sign he had been accepted.

"Good to see yer, Oliver, good to see yer. Bit of a do here, you might say. Excise men dug up a lass's grave, fresh dead she was too, and found all manner of things they shouldn't have, if you know what I mean. Then there's a fire, carpenter's place burned to the ground. Folk say he helped smugglers, but he's long gone, Oliver, long gone. Nobody knows where master Copwood's gone.

"An' there's a body too. A dead body. No, not the woman, I can see what y'thinking, Oliver. No, not her. Some man, nobody knows who. Buried. Been run through. Sword through his heart and out the other side. Now what d'you make of that, Oliver Kindale?"

"Let me buy you a drink, Thomas Temple, and we'll talk some more."

They strolled in silence, Temple looking decidedly pleased with himself. Over a drink Oliver enquired again.

"Why are you here, friend?"

Temple, although it was always difficult to tell through his facial hair, managed a weak smile and then turned his head slightly as if to exaggerate a conspiratorial expression. Kindale recognised the truth and smiled across the table, a smile of ruthlessness and cunning, a smile that patronised the man opposite.

"Slept in Dover and came over the cliffs this morning. There was talk in Dover of the Revenue digging up a grave here, and quite a to-do about it, I can tell 'e. So I took it upon myself to come and have a look, ask some questions and what did I find? Why, my friend Oliver Kindale."

Kindale considered this. Some was nonsense, but what had driven Temple to take a long and risky walk to Folkestone? Not quite all he had revealed, that was for sure, but no man would surely make such a journey simply to verify gossip?

"Temple. What trade are you in, man, where does y'money come from? Speak plainly."

Temple looked hurt and scratched his hairy chin as he tried to work Kindale out. How should he answer? The man would know a lie, yet he wanted to know more of Kindale. Mysterious about his own business, so why should he tell Kindale all?

"A chandler by trade, my friend, but I do anything I can turn my hand to. And if that means buying and selling things what I shouldn't, so be it. The law hasn't caught up with Thomas Temple yet, nor will it." And he added another mighty guffaw as Kindale sipped at his ale and never removed his eyes from the man's face.

"That do ye, Oliver Kindale? And I've found it pays to know what's about along this coast. So I am making enquiries of my own, y'might say, into recent events here. Difficult to learn things in a big place like Dover. Folkestone's a bit quieter, in a manner of speaking. People talk to you and you can talk back and that way you learn things."

He was studying his friend's face all the while, hoping to see some reaction that might suggest Oliver's true feelings, but he learned nothing at all. Trying to be clever he changed the subject.

"Charlotte's missing you, Oliver Kindale." Again, no obvious reaction. Kindale spoke and ignored the last comment.

"And what have you learned about events here, Thomas Temple?"

"Ah, now, would it be worth anything to tell you, Oliver Kindale?"

"Then let me tell you. A revenue officer called George Gordon dug up a grave, found a dead body in addition to the one in the coffin, and all manner of riches some scoundrels had buried there. The carpenter who made the coffin, Daniel Copwood, has fled with his wife and child and the people who thought they owned the riches in the grave set fire to his home and workshop, believing Copwood had betrayed them."

Temple's eyes had widened and he was holding his mug at such an angle a few slops of ale made good their escape from it, and avoided his notice. His words were spluttered when he eventually found the power of speech.

"Oliver Kindale, my friend, you learn as good as I do. And do you also know the body had a name, Jeremiah Hundash?"

"No, I didn't know that, but you have shared such intelligence freely, so therefore there is no value to all else you have learned, at least not as far as I am concerned."

Temple replaced his mug on the table and permitted a maddening tangle of thoughts to run amok in his mind. He had been taken completely by surprise. Kindale had left him trailing in his wake.

And the man had even deprived him of the opportunity of earning a coin or two with the one piece of information Kindale did not have. He had walked into the man's trap. A clever one, this Oliver Kindale, and with such a consideration allowed a smile of surrender to decorate his face.

Once more Kindale knew what he had achieved. He could read Temple and that pleased him, especially as so much of Temple's face seemed hidden from view!

"A shave would do you no harm," Kindale suggested, "for I can read your face just as well fully covered. Here is the money, friend, spend it wisely."

Temple roared with laughter.

"You have done me well and proper, Oliver Kindale, and I will do as you say and buy a shave, and do so here in Folkestone. I know the very place." He fingered the growth as he spoke. "You will not recognise me, my friend." And he laughed heartily again.

"Very well, Thomas Temple, very well. And I do buy information that is of interest to me, but will not waste money on what I already know. Perhaps you can obtain information I have no knowledge of, rather than scratching around in the dirt wasting your own time."

"Tell me what you'd have me do, my friend, for I am willing to learn and to earn."

"I'll let you know if I need you and tell you what I expect of you. Now I must be on my way, and I would prefer that you did not chance upon me wherever I may tread." Both men smiled and then laughed, and Temple offered his hand across the table.

Kindale knew his friend would be useful and on matters that needed examination that would devour too much of his own time. An idea had formed in his mind. Temple could be despatched to dig in his own way and search through dense webs covering issues Kindale might otherwise have to ignore. If, of course, such issues existed, and there was no guarantee Temple might find employment in such a field.

But if it kept Temple at bay for the time being so much the better!

As he strode towards the tree where he had left Beth he suddenly recalled Temple had mentioned Charlotte, but obliterated the thought as quickly as it had appeared. He had work to do, and urgent work at that.

***

And the snow came.

The cold north-easterly blowing in squalls brought with it snow, tender, gentle flakes at first, an overture to a freezing and deadly symphony, full of drama and passion.

The flurries on the biting wind were bad enough but then came the blizzard. It was the last turn of events Oliver Kindale wanted.

It might hinder Chastain or it might provide just the cover the Frenchman needed to make good on his plans. Chastain was just one part of the problem as he knew full well, but he was the main part, the central focal point around which all other activities radiated.

And Kindale was horribly aware Chastain's plans were well advanced.

The business in the churchyard would neither bother nor hamper him, but he would be interested if only because Tydeman's affairs were linked to it, and he would wonder if Chastain's association with Tydeman was as secure as he thought it was.

Either Tydeman's work was betrayed, as seemed most likely, and by the carpenter, or something more sinister was afoot. It would be just enough to worry him, to sow seeds of mistrust, and that was exactly what Oliver wanted. An uneasy ingredient in the savage and vulgar plan the Frenchman was hatching.

The fact Chastain was masquerading as Copwood suited Kindale's purpose, for news of events at Folkestone would carry to Dover, as indeed they had done, and the name of Daniel Copwood mentioned widely. Someone, somewhere, might relate Daniel to another Copwood!

A hint of local suspicion was always an unwanted irritation to a man trying to maintain a low profile, Kindale reasoned. And he smiled at the thought. Yes, things were working out well.

His brief meeting with Gordon had gone well.

He was Kindale's man now. He, his men, and the soldiers would be vital at the right moment.

The snow was another matter entirely and a troublesome one. But it might yet be of greater assistance to Kindale than to Chastain.

He'd asked Gordon to search into Jeremiah Hundash. There had to be more to the subject than the need to hide a dead man. Not Tydeman's style by any stretch of the imagination! He would leave a body as a medium to gloat over, as a warning to others, and as a source of his own vile humour.

No, there had to be a reason Hundash was left where it was assumed nobody would ever find him. Gordon agreed, and puffed cheerily on his new pipe although it was yet to give him the pleasure he was used to. A new pipe was like that, like a new pony. You had to work at it, break it in, nurture it, and train it to serve you.

The two men discussed one or two other things, but the most important aspect from Kindale's point of view was that Gordon was prepared to yield to his venture in order to gain the prizes he most sought. Neither man trusted each other completely, but they were speaking the same language and in agreement on central questions.

Both had their own desires, their own paths, but the route was now interwoven and both could benefit from this liaison.

Oliver had wanted to return to Deal but the weather was too atrocious and he rode instead to Harblow's cottage, and as he pulled up his clothes around his head, the wind thrashing into the right side of his head, the snow stinging his ear, he found himself thinking of Charlotte.

Why, oh why, did she impinge on his mind with such ease? Why did he let her do so? Temple's words haunted him. Charlotte missing him? Why? There was no attachment of any sort between them.

Beth was making little progress in the conditions, and, with the light failing, Oliver dismounted and led the horse keeping to her left side so as to shelter from the worst of it. He was so absorbed in trying to erase thoughts of Charlotte that he gave no consideration whatsoever for the willing beast, and it was only when he arrived at Harry's that he felt pangs of guilt at such negligence and perceived cruelty.

So he looked after her, stabled her, fed and watered her, and spoke as a lover might woo his sweetest and dearest companion. Here at least she was warm for the night. Oliver thought she appeared happy, but then he realised that was how he wanted to feel about her.

And with that thoughts of Charlotte flooded him as he made his way through the sodden, clinging and deepening snow to the cottage.

Mary welcomed him and took him straight to the fire.

"You must get out of those clothes, Oliver. Come let's get this business attended to."

Harry positively beamed as he looked up at Oliver and Mary, sensing the man's embarrassment at his wife's request.

"It's alright, my son, Mary's seen a naked man before. Take y'clothes off, man, and she'll get them done for you." He had never seen such a look of horror on Oliver's face and for all he knew he didn't think his friend was capable. This was a revelation all by itself and Harry laughed at the scene.

"Go get some of my clothes then, my son, change out of Mary's gaze if that's whats a-bothering you," and he laughed all the more.

That is what Oliver did, not quite sure whether the idea of stripping in front of Mary had any concern for her, or even some appeal! It clearly didn't worry Harry.

He returned feeling far more comfortable and handed his own clothes to Mary who informed him food was on the table. Harry had built up the fire so that it raged in a gentle fury and warmed the room appreciably so, and indeed threw light upon it, for, as ever, the candles added no light worthy of the name.

They ate, drank and settled by the fire which was now sizzling raucously. The three of them. Warm together. Comfortable. Happy in their way.

There was little conversation as little was needed.

Harry would've liked to ask Oliver many questions but knew he could not, for in any case his friend would not answer, and the topics were not for Mary's ears.

The next morning seemed brighter than usual but that was because of the whiteness of the snow.

The wind had eased very much and although the clouds swept by, thick and dreary, grey and angry, they deposited nothing more. Perhaps their supply had been exhausted. The quantity on the ground suggested that. For it was full, particularly deep, and where it could do so the wind had piled it up in drifts.

Harry's cottage faced east and the snow was halfway up the door and most of the way up that wall, only the heat from the fire, which had somehow penetrated through the stone walls, keeping it from swamping the place entirely that side.

Oliver and Harry set to clearing the path, and Harry went to see to the horses while Mary prepared some food. The other adjoining cottages were no longer occupied there being no work for those who had lived there. Oliver was impatient; he had work to do and wasn't at all clear about how he could make progress in the present conditions.

But he assumed it was much the same everywhere in this south-eastern corner of Kent, and probably a lot further afield too. So he was surprised when a horse hove into view and its rider called out a greeting.

Chapter Nine

The news was half expected.

In fact, Kindale had left money on account, with more promised, so sure was he of the outcome.

Nicholas Telman had been visited by two men. From the description Telman now gave him they appeared to be Grey Jonnie and William Tydeman. He was being asked to conceal several men on their way to London in a few days time, keep them until they were fetched and led away.

Telman asked no questions. He showed Kindale the money he was given in advance which, like Kindale's, would be added to, come the time. And he had wasted no time setting off south from Wingham, despite the desperate weather, Kindale's financial reward being well above Grey Jonnie's.

There was another factor.

Kindale wasn't a threat, whereas Grey Jonnie gave clear warning as to the consequences of betrayal, Tydeman delivering a sudden and violent blow to Telman's midriff as a means of supporting the caution.

Telman trusted Kindale and believed that anything he could do to rid the county of such oppression and fear was of vital importance. Yes, he could be bought but by those he considered to be worthy of his attentions and involvement, usually the free-traders and those escaping the Revenue and the soldiers.

It was a conformity, a relationship of sorts, with his fellow man, something he had been raised to understand. Them and us, his father had said. You work with and within your community, we are as one together and we will not be put asunder. His father's very words. We act as one, always.

We act and defend, we support.

So Nicholas Telman knew where his loyalties lay, even when that meant siding with those engaged in illegal work, if they were local people, people he knew and trusted.

But he abhorred violence for violence's sake.

He detested those who proposed violence as the first and most simple way of overcoming a problem, especially when the problem was the law.

Nicholas and Harry recognised that community philosophy in each other from the start, a common bond that provided the basis for friendship from the outset, and they were obviously at ease together. That helped Oliver's cause. The visitor was less likely to try and fool or betray as he was now as one with Harry.

Besides, Oliver knew this man, had appreciated his integrity from the first meeting, and could see safety in the man's face, his expression and the way he spoke. He had studied people since childhood and found the study fascinating and usually revealing.

Some such education had been necessary in order to avoid annoying the wrong folks, and to gain the advantage by using the traits of others to his benefit. It also told him where his trust might be misplaced.

He learned how people deceived others, with or without intention, and he did all this by reading those he met. It sometimes made him prosperous in thought as he could foresee recklessness, stupidity, cunning, wickedness. He could assess those easily led, and those who were the leaders.

By the same token he could see genuine kindness and good desire.

Mary Harblow exuded genuine kindness and a very real cheerfulness, and he loved her for it. She and Harry were happy and he felt a sharp pang of concern, worry that he should come to grief helping him.

And in that moment resolved to keep Harry at arms length in his mission.

He realised he could not bear to see Mary bestruck by the heartbreak of losing her man, and indeed he would not let it happen.

Oliver wanted to know when Tydeman was putting to sea; that was now central to all that might yet happen. Tydeman had no ship of his own and neither did Hapling. So he would set Harry to work in Folkestone, Thomas Temple in Dover and he would be bound for Deal, for he remained convinced that was where Tydeman's eventual landfall would be.

And he certainly didn't want Gordon or any soldiers there to spoil it!

Telman was to come to Harry's as agreed as soon as he had word.

But today the snow had added a nasty dimension to his plans. The snow's beauty confounded him, for in that beauty was nature's treachery, an exquisite and delightful siren ready to lure admirers to misery and possibly even death.

The loveliness of the snow was as deceitful and misleading as a thick fog, and beyond trust.

Mary, being Mary, made sure all had eaten and eaten well, before seeing them all on their various ways, Telman northwards, Kindale to the east, and her beloved Harry south-westwards. All faced the terrors of the splendour of the snow, evil, slowing, cold, wet, dragging as it was, as they trudged up and down hill.

All three led their horses.

It was pointless riding them until they could make out better roads and pathways.

It consumed their time, ate into their determination, irritated their souls and added to their immediate melancholy. And in all this Oliver Kindale had not spared a thought for Charlotte; it was as if he had finally removed her from his inner being.

But his heart was not to be so easily defeated.

***

George Gordon had been wasting his time.

To a lesser man it might have been disheartening for it happened so often.

But for Gordon tackling the smugglers was all he cared about; it absorbed him totally, and he was prepared for failures as long as he enjoyed occasional success.

He had paid handsomely for a tip that goods were coming ashore south of Deal, and well they might have been, but the heavy covering of snow had thwarted his attempts to conceal his own activities and local people duly warned off the boat. Now he had no option but to send the troops back to Dover empty-handed.

The contraband did not remain at sea, he was sure of that. But where did it make landfall?

In the snow lying around and about in such terrible quantities, and with movement severely restricted, it was hopeless and pointless trying to search elsewhere. He himself decided to spend the morning in the area.

For one thing he was cold and wet through, and for another travel was sickeningly slow amid the fields of white. On another day he might've admired the prettiness of it all but today he cursed it, loathed it, and saw it as nature's attempt to surmount his authority and ruin his calling.

It didn't seem to ail those who chose to break the law.

So he struggled into the town in search of warmth and refreshment and there chanced upon Thomas Temple who, as ever, was interested in any stranger coming to Deal, especially in such atrocious conditions as the snow presented.

In the meantime Oliver Kindale had also arrived and made straight for his cottage.

It was freezing cold inside and no fire waiting to be lit. This did not bother him for he was used to hardship and to suffering the worst aspects of the weather regardless of where he was.

He had seen to Beth and made himself as comfortable as he could while he contemplated his next move. And that was to be into town.

Within a few minutes Charlotte appeared at the door, sticks and logs in her arms. Oliver rose at once to take the firewood from her. Despite his entering the cottage, noting the lack of a warming fire, and sitting quietly by the fireplace, Charlotte had never troubled his mind once, but now she did by her presence.

They made the fire together and did so without accompanying words.

It was only when there was a decent blaze that she spoke.

"Not 'specting you, Oliver. I'll get some logs in. Not got any food, mind."

He followed her to get the logs and asked when she'd last eaten. She hesitated and then made no answer. That was good enough for Oliver.

"Come into town and we'll get something. You look warm, well wrapped up, Charlotte, you'll do. We'll go now, the fire can await our return." She looked ready to protest but thought better of doing so and allowed him to lead her out.

"Here, you ride Beth and I'll lead her." Again Charlotte tried to intervene but her few muttered words failed to reach Oliver's ears. He collected Beth, took hold of Charlotte and lifted her onto the animal's bare back, bridled the horse and led them through the snow.

The wind was stilled, but the sea was dark and rushing in vehemence at the shingled shore, wave after wave battering all before it. The sky was at one with the sea; a mixture of furious black and grey clouds lingering mercilessly above as if observing the wretchedness the snow had wreaked on the land. And being dissatisfied with the outcome.

A little later and Charlotte was attacking her food like a scavenging bird, clawing at the meat, tearing off mouthfuls, chewing and spluttering, choking slightly when she tried to swallow too much, and Oliver looked on with amazement and knew she hadn't eaten at all since they were last together.

He was not disgusted by the sight in front of him. In truth he was upset and saddened by the spectacle, or rather what it represented in terms of real hunger and desperation, and knew feelings were astir, those same dread feelings he knew he shouldn't have and could not afford.

She was nothing to him. An ugly creature, poor, hungry, unattractive in every respect. Yet he knew such thoughts were masking his true feelings.

There was something there and Oliver grew angry with himself because there was no time to be like this, no time to pity a fellow human being, no time for a distraction no matter how his innermost feelings tugged at him, no, *begged* him think otherwise.

And there was no time to suffer and to face such inconvenient sentiments. No time at all. It was wrong, and he knew he must extricate himself from the problem at once. No more thoughts, no sensitivity, no concern. Be rid of them all, stop them battering down the door of his mind. Let them be gone, don't let them back in.

Charlotte finished and wiped the back of her greasy hand across her mouth. And she smiled at him. Not a simple smile, but a smile that spoke a thousand words or so it seemed to him. Her lips parted just a little, her misshapen teeth glistened beyond, and there was an inexplicable charm, an impossible lure to her smile, indeed her whole face.

Oliver studied her face. He couldn't look away, or even in that instant find anything else to think of to divert his thoughts. He was emotionally paralysed. Shocked. Stunned. This will not do, he reprimanded himself.

Shortly they were away, Charlotte astride Beth, Oliver leading the horse.

His thoughts were placing various matters of intelligence into their appropriate mental boxes, arranging known facts in sensible order, weighing up hearsay, the possibilities, the probabilities, and ensuring order existed in such widespread knowledge.

And Charlotte persisted in imposing herself on those thoughts.

She said not a word, was behind him, and yet as he struggled to compose rational prospects in a brain teeming with information Charlotte deflected his mind at vital moments and concentration was lost.

The sky was still angry, the clouds a mixture of filthy grey colours idly biding their time, making slight adjustments to their positions, but always, always threatening. The snow's whiteness was obscene in an otherwise dark, cold and unpleasant landscape.

"I like you, Oliver Kindale."

The voice from just behind him destroyed all he was trying to reason, with essential conclusions, intentions and planning evaporating as Charlotte's tiny voice thudded into ears more atuned to the natural silence around him. He gritted his teeth, then pursed his lips and knew she was under his skin and she was making him livid with himself.

She was also jeopardising his mission, or at least her presence was.

He would have to move on, leave this woman forever. He had to free his mind.

They had paused to buy some provisions. Just basic essentials, food for the next meal, candles. Nothing that wasn't important or expensive.

"Where d'you get the firewood from?" he'd asked.

"Thomas. *He* looks after me like that. Looks after you, Oliver Kindale, cos 'e likes you, so 'e leaves enough wood for both of us. O'course 'e wants me all the time but I don't want 'im.

"Want you though, Oliver Kindale."

He'd said nothing in reply and was now leading Beth through the snow, still believing he could rid himself of this unnecessary imposition, and that the way forward was to remove himself from her closeness. Yet he needed to be in Deal. He'd ask Jack. Yes, that's what he'd do.

Charlotte hadn't wanted him that time before. Perhaps her pride had intervened. And at that point he knew he would've used her and cast her aside without hindrance. But now? It nagged at his mind and occupied space he needed for his own thoughts and mental deliberations.

Time. When the 'time' came there would be precious little of it, none to waste, and he would need to act quickly. He wasn't used to having someone he might have to explain his actions to. Certainly not a woman who might question his motives and worse still know when he was being untruthful (as he probably would be) and probe deeper for the truth.

No, he had to be alone.

"Do you want me, Oliver Kindale?"

Again, the voice of sweetness, the voice of affection, the voice of the siren. He had to resist.

"'Tis not for me, Charlotte." He did not look back and hoped his answer would suffice and explain everything. The annoyance rose within him and his breathing increased in intensity as he clenched his fists in defiance, and silently, wordlessly begged her to speak no more on the subject.

There were no more words. He left her at her cottage, stabled Beth and returned to remake the fire. He was unaware of the cold. His anger was keeping him warm.

It had to be done, do it now, he decided. Then go and see Jack.

He marched, enraged and full of determination, towards the neighbouring cottage and burst through the door. She looked startled as well she might. His face was awake with fury and she was suddenly afraid. He stared at her and found he had no words.

There she was, unlovely, her eyes bulging with terror, her thin fingers clutching at her collar, a portrait of horror and repulsiveness, her lips quivering as she shook violently with dread, awaiting whatever terrible fate was now going to be visited upon her.

Kindale could no longer put his feelings into any sensible order, arrange his thoughts in a manner that might produce the right words, and speech was rendered impossible.

Charlotte let out a short squeal, and in that instant Oliver was furious with himself for subjecting her to his acrimony, for letting her witness his loss of control, for letting the issue reach this ridiculous stage. It was his fault, not hers.

And as he allowed his emotions to ease and felt his breathing return to a steady pace he saw a very different woman before him. He stepped forward and stopped as she backed into a wall and stifled a shriek, covering her mouth with her arm, sweat forming on her forehead.

He was sick he had frightened her so, horrified now by his own actions.

Instinctively he held his arms open in submission and as a gesture of reconciliation.

Tears ran down her cheeks but he moved not an inch, for he knew to move in her direction would frighten her more and he had to wait for her, if she wanted to come, if she would come.

And so he stood still and waited.

The tension gradually drained from her face but her breathing was still fierce. Then she dashed across the small room and into his arms. He gathered his arms around her and wept with her.

Her own thin, weak arms were around him and holding him tight. He felt her face against his and knew he had surrendered, knew he wanted her, and knew nothing else mattered. The surrender was complete. His mission lay asunder in that precious moment. All other thoughts deserted him as his heart took control of his destiny.

He could smell her and the fragrance intoxicated him. He could feel her slender, throbbing body and it awoke his long dormant passions. He could feel her breathing, rapid and exciting, and it was exhilarating and enflaming. He could sense every slight movement of her body, of her limbs, of her head and it delivered him to an enchanting paradise.

How he wanted her. Needed her. Ached for her.

And he yearned for those lips, those tender, beautiful loving lips, the kindness of those moist, desirable lips. Yes, she was desirable. She was a princess and he was her prince. It was a dream but it was living dream. Then their lips met and he was lost. Lost because he wished to be so. Lost because she was all that mattered.

Lost, because he wanted the lovers' heaven that now awaited them both. Lost because he must sample the nectar of love, something he had never known, never understood, never craved.

And it was all about him and in every part of him.

As if to bless this act of beauty some of the clouds relented and gently parted to permit the sun to shine upon the union. Where there had been only darkness and despair there was something so feverishly bright and full of hope, so alive, so radiant and dazzling.

For Oliver and Charlotte there was each other. And that was all, all that mattered, all that existed, all that engulfed them, all that overcame their senses.

And they became one with such enthralling beauty, one with nature, one with love.

Outside the snow glistened in the brief sunlight and the day smiled upon the blissful pleasures of their love, enjoyed in the warmth of the cottage and of each other. Their haven, their castle, their den, their diversion from the real world and the pain it bore.

***

George Gordon had wasted his time again.

Initially he believed Temple might be useful, a man who could come by information and be willing to sell it, for Temple, quite deliberately, gave him that impression. But as time slipped by Gordon recognised that Temple would never have anything of value to negotiate with and dismissed the notion from his mind.

Temple was being clever.

He'd intentionally led the Revenue man on and then left him in no doubt that he was as close to an imbecile as it is possible to be without actually being one. Gordon was disappointed, but that was his lot in life. Failure after failure with a success, an accomplishment, occasionally added to his normal diet of failure, as salt might be added to a meal in the vain hope of improving flavour and digestion and making an overall wretched feast palatable.

Achievement was a rarity. But now Oliver Kindale had offered him the opportunity to land two mighty fish, and probably others besides, and hand them to him on a plate as the main course.

All he had to do was trust Kindale, and he could see no reason why he should, despite the implorations of Ballerden who, it had to be agreed, was never wrong.

And his concern was not lifted by discovering Temple claimed to know Kindale and to be a close associate.

Temple? This ignorant rascal? In league with Kindale?

It made no sense. Yet with Kindale anything was possible.

Having gained nothing from his brief stay in Deal Gordon reluctantly began the trudge south, leading his own horse towards Dover. Temple watched him go, convinced he had won the duel and that the man considered him a fool, a person of no significance and definitely outside the confidence of the smugglers. Even in Deal!

In fact Thomas Temple was as yet unaware Oliver Kindale was about to cast him in a drama that might cost him his life, and equally unaware Oliver Kindale had lost his heart to the widow Charlotte, a woman Temple himself wanted.

He felt that time would be a healer and that in the years ahead she would come to see him as the pathway to happiness, for he was sure she could make him happy and content once warm memories of her husband became the treasured possessions that overtook grief.

Gordon endured a miserable journey back to Dover, his mind wandering far and wide and retracing its steps countless times, and presenting him with much too much for a man of his mental capabilities to deal with comfortably. Consequently a headache was now upon him, although whether it was a real pain or an imagined one he couldn't be sure.

Harry Harblow was little known in Folkestone and able to pass about almost unnoticed. Nathaniel Ballerden obviously saw him as the solicitor returned from the front but chose to ignore him; it wouldn't do for the man of law to acknowledge him on the street, Harry realised that.

He wandered into the graveyard and to Katherine's much disturbed grave. He knelt and said what he assumed would be accepted by the Almighty as a prayer, although its form and its wording were unlikely to find their way into a prayer book or a vicar's sermon. But it had to do. He wasn't religious yet had a certain worry that God could exist and might be all too easily offended, and that he might well face a judgement day of his own before the good Lord.

The outcome of that might depend on how he behaved in circumstances like this. So he put his hands together, closed his eyes and whispered words for Katherine and for her soul, and more words of sorrow that her eternal rest had been disturbed.

He felt sufficiently moved, concerned for his own safety in the sight of God, if there was truly a God, to absolve himself of all blame for the actions of the Revenue men, and sought forgiveness even though he had no hand in it.

Unsure as to whether he had succeeded or not he spent some time in complete silence, eyes closed, until he realised his knees were aching. Once more he apologised to God as he climbed to his feet and started backing away from the grave as if departing from the presence of some gracious all-powerful monarch, whereupon he tripped over another grave and fell on his back, gasping.

The parson appeared and chased him from the graveyard. He was pleased to be away.

Now to the task in hand. And where to begin?

***

For once it was Kindale who sought out Temple.

And it took the local man by surprise.

He looked as if he might have had something approaching a shave, but his mass of hair was so unruly it was quite impossible to tell. So much for telling Kindale he would be unrecognisable!

Oliver allowed himself to be directed into the sorry looking dwelling that passed for Temple's home. No fire, colder within than without. Positively damp.

"Come, I'll show you my goods and chattels as it were." Oliver followed him through the dire cottage and into an adjoining building that, at first sight, might have once been a barn.

It was even colder than Temple's hovel.

But it was well stocked and with all manner of maritime bits and pieces.

"Chandler you see, Oliver my friend. Supplies all kinds o' people for their boats. Just not a lot of trade as we speak, if you understand me.

"Revenue raids me now and then. Think I've got something to hide! Not me, not that stupid. Not in here leastways!"

Oliver remained unmoved but was wondering why, with so many ships and boats on the Downs, there should be so little business. No matter, it suited him. A man who would welcome an improvement to his income, and clearly a man without scruples, possibly without conscience.

"Temple I seek your help and will pay well. But I must trust you and have no thoughts you will betray me. It is more important than you could begin to imagine. You must resist all temptation to betray me, and to that end I will match whatever you might be offered.

"But, betray me and I will kill you. If I am not in a position to administer the fatal blow it will be done for me, I do promise you so.

"And what I ask of you will be dangerous. My threats to your safety will be the least of your concerns. Others may take it upon themselves to relieve you of your life, friend."

It was hard to tell if Temple was making any facial expressions beneath the thick mass of hair, some of which must surely have perished had he been properly shaved, but inside he was in turmoil. Whatever was Oliver Kindale about for a man to speak thus?

"Oliver, for Charlotte's sake I will not betray you. My hand offered to you is the hand of friendship, and there is no betrayal in such friendship. Not for me, Oliver. I will be true to whatever is your cause. But these *risks* you speak of. They worry me, not that they would detract from my purpose, and I will help you, my friend."

Kindale gave one brief nod, just a small movement of his head. Temple continued.

"Tell 'e what, my friend. Withdraw your threats knowing I will not betray you or your cause to any man. I'll do that for you, and I'll do it for Charlotte. Then we work together as friends."

Oliver discerned a look of pleasure and of warm-heartedness in Temple's manner, for it was quite impossible to tell from his face, and nodded again, knowing the man was speaking the truth as a matter of honour, and speaking *of* the truth for the same reason.

"Here's my hand, Thomas, my threats withdrawn. But know your life will be in danger if you work for me. I will tell you no more."

Temple eyed his man first with suspicion then with great humour before he burst forth into one of his prodigious guffaws. He took Oliver's hand and shook it vigorously, then clasping his shoulders and pulling him into a mighty hug, slapping Oliver's back as he did do.

Fortunately the embrace lasted a few seconds only and Oliver was relieved as it had been as if all the breath in him had been ferociously squeezed out. Temple spoke.

"I'll take the chance, my friend. Now, let's have some drink and you can tell me what you want."

***

"Two things, Kindale."

George Gordon had decided to show him the letter he had found in Katherine's grave.

"Jeremiah Hundash. Metal worker from the weald. Into all manner of illegal employment. Mainly, of late, owling and that probably ties him in with a gang on the marshes, or perhaps even from Hawkhurst way.

"By the by I cannot learn more of him or how he came to be killed, or why his body should be concealed. But this letter was in the grave. I was going to show it to the authorities at Dover but thought it might be of greater value to you. Do you read French, Kindale?"

Kindale's face remained cold and untroubled, and he made no movement other than to hold out his hand, and spoke no word in answer to Gordon. It wasn't necessary.

Oliver read the document, for he knew at once it was no letter.

It was a list of the movements of certain persons although the names appeared to have been shrouded in code. But there were dates and real place names. The substance seemed to surround visits and meetings and all were in the near future.

He needed to get this information to Kenton.

It had to go through Ballerden. There was now no choice.

If the forthcoming arrangements of important personages could be allied to dates and places in the list then it should be possible to decide who was actually involved, to whom the coded names referred, and then to seek out any relevance to Chastain.

Later, and after a long wait at his premises, for Ballerden had a client with him, he was shown into the solicitor's room. Ballerden's eyes were wide with anger, but his fury was under complete control, and somehow he spoke with a softness that was alien to his expression and his manner.

"You have done what was forbidden, Kindale. This will not do."

Ignoring his words Kindale handed over the letter and explained his theory.

Ballerden read the words and slumped noisily into his chair.

"Why bury it?" he snapped, showing the first real signs of his anger and vexation.

"Wouldn't do to be apprehended with that in someone's possession. Copwood's place was fired, as you well know, so it must be Tydeman's doing or he has a hand in it. And for that matter, find out more of Jeremiah Hundash, from the weald, for it may provide a valuable link.

"If Tydeman buried that document then this scheme with Chastain is involved. I've come to you, Ballerden, because now time is more vital than ever. You must do as I ask."

The solicitor's anger was subsiding and after a moment's hesitation and contemplation he reached his decision.

"Right. Leave this with me. You were right to come, I'll grant you that. I'll get word to you, don't return here. This will be done, Kindale, you may rely on it. Now go."

Chapter Ten

Harry Harblow, by virtue of being all but unknown in Folkestone, and therefore in the advantageous position of recognition now or in the future being most unlikely, decided to pay a call on the parson.

With the knowledge that he would be in little danger from the authorities to add to his feeling of personal security he elected to ask his questions with his fingers on the trigger of his pistol. The parson would be able to look down the other end of the gun and, Harry hoped, be thus encouraged to speak freely and honestly.

After all, he was a man of God. Surely truthful in all things?

It was an interesting meeting.

The parson made prayers for Harry's salvation in between squeals for mercy, all the time mopping his sweating brow and waving his arms about in exaggerated fashion. A nervous man indeed, thought Harry, just what I want!

Harry watched and listened in mild amusement, quietly repeating a question when he received no answer and pointing the pistol at arms length when he felt a greater degree of persuasion was called for.

Eventually the parson collapsed in a chair, sobbing bitterly, sweating profusely, stuttering endlessly, choking occasionally. Harry warmed to his examination, the parson's response only fuelling his conviction that he was travelling the right road.

The interrogation complete, a very self-satisfied Harry Harblow left a donation 'for the poor of the parish', assuming the parson would see himself as one of those, and set off sporting a mischievous grin and emitting a chuckle from time to time. Oliver would be pleased, he was sure.

He hoped his 'donation' would ensure no further action would be taken against him.

It had been a worthwhile venture. The man was implicated in crime, most especially smuggling, and knew Katherine's grave had been desecrated by those acting on Tydeman's orders.

Harry roared with laughter. The parson had pleaded with God to save Harry's soul, and to forgive his terrible transgressions. It appeared to Harry that his mission had in some way been blessed by the Almighty!

But Jeremiah Hundash was a mystery. Never mind. There was more work for him to do, more enquiries to be made, and he was suddenly conscious of the fact that discretion was eluding him, that his attempts at maintaining an insignificant presence in the place were being jeopardised.

Time to rethink his strategy, his whole approach. Keep the pistol out of sight, he concluded. Move silently without disturbing the waters. He had made progress with the parson because he believed what he had done was right in the circumstances, but it would not work elsewhere and it would not do to draw attention to himself in that way.

People would lose their tongues, be disinclined to yield information even for money. He might possibly be attacked, probably killed, if he started asking the wrong questions of the people who knew the answers.

On the basis of intelligence shared by the parson Harry trudged, happily and free from weariness, towards the north and East Wear Bay, the Warren, a forbidding place at the best of times as he recalled it.

High and steep wooded cliffs dropping almost straight into the sea, and a favoured landing place for the free traders. Harry knew there was more than one way up. The smugglers valued this uninviting stretch of coast as it was easy to evade the authorities here.

He felt comforted by such knowledge, and amused by the fact Excise men and the military believed this area was perfect for penning in their opponents, trapping them helplessly between the sea and the cliffs soaring above them. Nowhere to run, nowhere to hide. And he laughed out loud.

The smugglers outwitted the law all but freely here! And nobody on the side of the law thought it was worth venturing here on a rough night with heavy seas running, for they believed nature's elements were against illegal operations.

Harry himself had, just a year ago, been part of a well organised event that involved both export and import each component free of tax, free of duty.

It had been a filthy, stormy February night, high winds, flurries of sleet and snow, and waves cascading onto the front one after the other in relentless assault. Brandy and other delights had been landed and the owlers had loaded their wool for the return to France.

He'd supervised the movement inland of a quantity of brandy casks which, together with three other members of the gang, had been concealed at his home until it was clear the project had gone unnoticed by the authorities. Mary, with her usual good cheer, had made everyone welcome and satisfied them with a decent meal every day and enjoyed a handsome reward from one of the casks.

In fact, that particular cask made no further journey as it was as good as empty, and what was left was consumed swiftly by Mr and Mrs Harblow.

Consequently there was a convivial atmosphere at the cottage for some time with Harry and Mary frequently engaged in raucous but pleasurable activity.

He was well paid.

It had been a useful experience as it gave him an insight into the organisation the smugglers went to, and provided him with new friendships that he felt could be valuable if the chance presented itself. Oliver had frowned but said nothing.

The man might have disapproved of law breaking but accepted that being inside or on the boundaries of crime could have recompense in the form of the ultimate apprehension of wrong-doers. An acceptable means to and end.

And Oliver accepted that Harry, as an insider, had access to information he himself could not acquire.

Information was what was needed now and urgently so.

Gradually such information was being harvested, but it was not to be only in East Wear Bay that a life and death situation was about to be faced.

***

Kindale in his journeys between Dover and Deal had tended to follow the cliff tops and skirt inland above St Margaret's Bay, but today his curiosity got the better of him and he determined to pay a visit. South through Walmer and a steady climb onto the clifftops, made all the more treacherous by the snow and the murky, ill-tempered weather, followed by a rapid descent to the front.

Used by smugglers, it wasn't a popular choice with those breaking the law as there was limited and steep access and here they did run the risk of being trapped.

By the same degree the soldiers and Excisemen found it both difficult to approach without being seen (which always resulted in boatmen being warned), and a point where they themselves could be easily picked off and attacked.

Oliver appreciated all of this as he looked around him, and tried to assess if, for those reasons, it might be the proposed landing site, or at least one of them.

"Hang the snow," he grumbled out loud and was surprised when a woman's voice replied.

"You not from here, snow or not, you're away from home. What's y'business?"

He turned and was astonished to see a young woman, fully six feet tall, brandishing a pistol and waving it at his head.

Little more than arms length from the less agreeable end of the pistol Kindale considered his options.

He could be upon her and disarm her before she could pull the trigger. But she might not be alone and another's weapon might be similarly aimed at him. If not, her scream, and she was sure to scream, would fetch help.

She was not unattractive, with bold green eyes that did not blink or sway from staring into his own eyes. Her face possessed a maturity, perhaps weather-beaten, with firm, high cheekbones, and a look of uncompromising capability, confidence and determination. Yet she was almost smiling, but maybe that was because she had the situation under her complete control.

"My name is Oliver Kindale, from Deal, and I had it in mind to call into St Margaret's on my way to Dover. But my business is my own."

102

His voice had a challenge about it, a defiance that the woman was quick to realise. Her mouth screwed slightly to one side as if she was contemplating the matter and finding she wasn't hearing the truth.

"You don't look like anyone. You working for them soldiers? For the Excise?"

The gun was still waving in front of his face. He knew of women (Katherine had been one) who could fire a pistol accurately and without conscience.

"I am not 'anyone' as I have given you my name. I am a friend of Thomas Temple and I am no friend of the law. And now I wish to continue my journey."

"Your story, Oliver Kindale, is not true. Why visit here in this weather and just on a whim? Temple I know and I doubt he knows you." Still the pistol pointed at his head. Her face now looked ferocious without being obviously angry. She had a full and pleasant figure, Kindale observed, and his observations were instantly recognised. She laughed in a hollow fashion and just for a brief second or two. It was mocking laugh.

"Think you can buy me, do you? You like what you see, Oliver Kindale, but I do not like what I see, and if I kill you here you will be buried here and nobody will know, nobody will ever find you." Now she chuckled more heartily.

"On y'way, Oliver Kindale, but I'll be asking about you. Don't come back here. You've seen here, there's no more. Go, and mind I don't shoot you in the back."

He trudged away, confident she would not shoot, and took pains to make further sightings of the lie of the land as he went. He had seen no other person yet was conscious he was being watched by more than the girl.

After a short distance he turned but she had vanished.

An interesting place, this, he decided, worthy of a great deal more attention. He would talk to Temple, find out who the woman was, investigate further. It was almost as if the settlement was expecting some major occurrence. It might simply be a smuggling run, an unwelcome visit from the soldiers, or possibly the landing Kindale was sure was close to imminent.

He threw himself behind a tree as a shot rang out.

A warning perhaps? Quite possibly.

He could see no one. After a pause he resumed his journey and without further incident. It was likely he might be followed but concluded he would at least be allowed to reach Dover and then it was certain nobody would fire at him. It being pointless trying to lose a follower he resolved to vanish from view once he arrived in the town.

Meanwhile Harry Harblow had reached his own destination and also found himself confronted by the wrong end of a pistol.

"Harry! Harry Harblow!" The man wielding the gun lowered his weapon and smiled pleasantly and welcomingly at Harblow. He was just short of five feet in all probability, had a round, ruddy face with ginger whiskers hanging lamely about his ears. A strange sort of hat otherwise covered his hair which Harry assumed was also ginger. In any event he didn't recognise the man.

"Just the person, just the person. Harry Harblow! Could do with your help tonight. The snow has meant not everyone we might be able to call upon can be here, and now you land here as if by providence. Archie, Archie Blackwell, my old friend. Come and join us."

This was an unwelcome distraction.

He remembered Archie from a year before, but he had added considerable weight especially around the middle and, if Harry recalled correctly, he sported short blond hair at the time.

Kindale would not thank him for getting involved and, frankly, he was far from keen.

"I cannot stay, Archie, for all that I would. My wife is sick and I must return."

Archie's pleasant countenance vanished and his face hardened to one of anger, and he raised the pistol again.

"Y'wife will wait, and I hope she recovers, but you stay here and help or try and leave and die anyway." That settled the issue. It was beyond Harry's choice. The parson had suggested a mission might be running this very night, and along East Wear Bay, but Harry had reckoned without chancing upon the gang at such close quarters.

Nevertheless, he reasoned, Archie might divulge useful intelligence if he stayed to help and therefore offered his services freely.

"Mary'll be fine, Archie, to tell the truth she renders me annoyed and frustrated, fetch this, fetch that, and she nags me too well. She'll be fine." Archie lowered the pistol and laughed, clapping his hand on Harry's shoulder by way of better greeting.

"You poor man, Harry. My wife, Agnes, she's the same. Does us good to find a rewarding diversion, eh?" And Harry readily agreed as he was led through the snow to the water's edge.

The snow was already melting and in places turning into a dreadful grey slush.

Kindale found he did not need to worry about anyone following him, or indeed the state of the road as the snow began its long melt for as soon as he arrived in Dover he was cornered and taken by a press gang.

In itself it wasn't a problem but it was a nuisance for it was time consuming and he had no time to waste. He had exemption but it was necessary for the naval authorities to clear the matter with Ballerden. It was an agonising delay when he felt there was so much to do.

The wind had found its purpose again and sent the fierce, cantankerous, ugly clouds scattering westwards, not that Kindale could see for it was pitch dark when he emerged onto the streets and a cold, blustery night was all that greeted him.

He found accommodation for the night and in the morning, a softer, gentler morning, headed for Harry's cottage. The wind was icy, but now not too strong, and the sun was making a feeble effort to gain a height in the sky, but no effort whatsoever to warm. The snow was unsure, unsure whether it should retreat and continue the thaw that assaulted it the night before, unsure as to whether or not it should freeze over and present icy footfalls.

A very tired and weary Harry Harblow was returning to his cottage.

He had been worked hard and been fired upon by the men in the Revenue cutter that pursued to boat carrying the contraband to shore. He worked hard unloading and then carrying and he was quite out of breath.

Nonetheless he stuck to his tasks, much to Archie's pleasure, and earned the favour of information that he otherwise would not have gained. He was wise enough to know that had he been shot such information would be useless to him, and even less use to Oliver. But it was a risk worth taking, he knew that full well.

But now he was exhausted.

Freed from any further obligation to Archie he was now on his way home, his travels made heavier by the slush. It was a long journey on foot at the best of times, but the winter's weather was against him. If God had preserved him from a Revenue bullet, all saintly intervention had been withdrawn, and he cursed with an energy he barely possessed.

He praised God for sparing his life, and raged at the Almighty for the worst effects of the climate.

Once or twice, submerged in the darkness that was nonetheless illuminated by the ghostly sparkle of the snow covered ground, he tripped and fell over some unseen obstacle, cursed anew and wanted to die where he lay. Each time he dragged himself to his feet and continued with his wretched and ungainly struggle.

With no idea of the time, or when dawn might approach, he was only too aware of the biting wind, yet he knew it was easing, and it gave him renewed strength for the trials ahead, of which he feared there would be all too many.

He gashed his leg but not badly and collapsed wailing and cursing in equal measures.

On he went again, his circumstances sapping not just his stamina but dragging remorselessly at his life itself. Then thoughts of Mary sprang into his mind, and he cherished such thoughts and allowed his heart to devour a feast of pleasurable anticipation, and it drove him on, on and on to the warm welcome he knew he would receive.

***

The new day blossomed with sunshine.

But there was no warmth and little joy. The sun had no real impact on the snow which had lain thick everywhere it could land and everywhere it could be driven by the wind. A thaw of sorts was taking place but managing to make poor headway.

Oliver Kindale threw himself into the chair by the fire offered by Mary, and sank the mug of ale she proffered without hesitation. He rubbed his eyes and then his face. She could see he was all in, and wasn't surprised when he refused food. He needed to sleep, and moments later there were loud snores as he slipped into repose and a very deep sleep indeed.

It was not long before Mary's worries were relieved.

Harry stumbled through the door, kissed and hugged his wife, took one look at Kindale, still in a dead sleep, and collapsed into the other chair and was swiftly snoring in unison with his friend.

Later they talked.

They discussed what had befallen them, leading Kindale to a conclusion.

"The entire coast is nervous, Harry, worried, fretting. Could be people are being forced into behaving as they are. Threats, swords, pistols, cudgels ... very persuasive. Or there's money to be earned, or earned anyway."

"Aye, my son, looks that way. There's more wariness than usual, and strangers are not merely not welcome, they're seen as an enemy. Something's a-brewing, mark my words. Ask someone the wrong question and y'more likely to get yer throat cut than be given an uncivil reply!"

Harry had swiftly realised that Archie was far more nervous than you would expect a man to be who was merely going about his normal if dishonest ventures. And that merely confirmed Kindale's verdict. The coast was alive and vibrant with anticipation, excitement, nervousness and fear. It made the very air sizzle and spark.

Something was about to happen.

"Harry, I need you to see Ballerden. He may have some answers for me. And I want to know why Jeremiah Hundash met his death. I think that's important.

"You see, my friend, you may be right. Hundash asked the wrong person the wrong question. If that is so then I want to know why he was asking, if you follow my thoughts, Harry."

"Aye, that I do, my son. Leave it to me. Where do I find you?"

The two agreed to meet in Dover and not far from Chastian's abode. Oliver had more to think about, and knew the event was close. What worried him most of all was the prospect that the scheme was more likely to be executed by a much larger force than had hitherto been anticipated, and that would take any hope of action out of his hands.

Gordon and the military might have to be rather more involved than he'd hoped, and he found that disagreeable.

Too many people. Too many opportunities for mistakes.

Too many people not sure where their loyalties lay, or all too certain about them!

He *had* to be able to control the impending situation with regard to the authorities. He felt confident Gordon would respect the pact between them. But supposing he now had to approach the army? Or the navy?

Perhaps he could talk to Lt. Dugald again? Maybe.

Was he like George Gordon and 'flexible'? He could not afford to misread the man.

The crux of the matter was more knowledge than he presently held, and he decided it was now imperative Ballerden, Harry Harblow and Thomas Temple, and he himself, Oliver Kindale, had to reach the answers with great alacrity.

He believed Ballerden to be steadfast, Harry was as trustworthy as could be, but Temple might be the weak link. Then there was himself. And things had not looked simple anymore from the moment he became involved with Charlotte.

Damn her! No, he didn't mean that.

And it dawned on him, in that moment, that perhaps this was what extreme fondness felt like, and he knew he had to shake it off or jeopardise the whole issue, his entire purpose. He also knew his feelings for Charlotte would not be so easily shaken free.

And it troubled him and plagued his otherwise well ordered and disciplined mind.

***

They sat together away from ears that might be too keen to listen and Harry relayed what he had learned from Nathaniel Ballerden.

"Hundash, Jeremiah Hundash. Some sort of officer of the crown it seems. Got in with a gang on the marshes, worked as one of 'em, y'know, undercover and that. Ballerden reckons he made a mistake and betrayed himself or, more likely, got betrayed.

"An' Ballerden thinks there could a traitor closer to home, if you get me meaning, Oliver.

"The man was hoping to lead them all into a trap and get most of 'em caught, so it seems, Oliver, but it went wrong. This gang, I'm told no known association with Tydeman but that don't mean a thing right now.

"Anyway, your letter. Ballerden said to tell you two coded names might, *might* tie up with two prominent people, you'd know who he said. And he also said to say it's soon, Oliver, it's soon.

"I'm to go tomorrow and collect a sealed letter for you. More information, he says.

"Destroy the letter, share nothing with nobody, and that includes me, don't it?"

Harry Harblow looked horribly disconsolate as if he was being excluded from some childish prank and adventure which all the other children were looking forward to. Oliver spoke.

"Listen Harry, your part in this in vital. I need you to be my ears, my eyes. But it is essential that we do not discuss matters. If you don't know you can't tell. And it's best not to know, believe me. Harry, my friend, you have Mary to think of. Now trust me in this.

"And I need you to move down the coast now we know more of Jeremiah Hundash. Get along to Hythe and further south if need be. If Tydeman is involved with this gang on the marshes knowledge may be more likely available nearer their territory.

"Work your way into the marshes if you can.

"It's dangerous Harry. But don't take any more risk than you need to. Mary doesn't deserve to be a widow."

"Oliver, that much I know, and respect you for your concern. Aye, I know what you mean and I'll play it with care, my son. Mary knows I walk a perilous line especially when I work with you, and she accepts that, Oliver, she accepts that. But, you're right, the less I know the better."

The two old friends shared another drink and Harry, being friends with the landlord, ordered brandy that he hoped he wouldn't have to pay for just yet. The landlord disappointed and it was left to Oliver to fund the spirit, but he did so in good humour, a knowing grin stretching across his face.

Although no words were spoken Harry wanted to toast their friendship conscious that this might be one of the last times they could do so. He also wanted to toast the mission, whatever it was all about, and how he wished he knew!

He felt fear.

It was unusual in the man, but he felt some great dread that this was going to be more serious than anything he'd previously encountered. More lethal. Deadly for both of them perhaps?

And he felt the fear spread as he drank brandy with Oliver and he could do nothing to reverse it. Fear, he knew, could help keep you alive, prevent you making silly mistakes, keep you on the edge so you were always ready.

To Harry that justified the feeling of fear and excused it.

So he found he could welcome it, and that allowed him to relax. But he feared for Oliver too. Could Oliver be killed just as Jeremiah Hundash was? Who could betray them? Anyone who wanted a handsome reward for so doing!

That was the way of things.

And if by betraying someone else you made your own life safer, well, that cleared your conscience as you pocketed the money.

Oliver was right. The less you knew the less you could tell someone who might sell such a disclosure. But that didn't stop the fear mounting. And Harry started to wonder how much more he might see of Oliver Kindale, and whether his friend was already a marked man.

All this, and the intake of strong brandy, played a heavy game in Harry's mind, and he found a mixture of fear, resignation and worry repulsive bedfellows in his thoughts.

Kindale recognised all of this but said nothing, for there was nothing to say.

He could not calm Harry's thoughts, could not quell his disquiet, for the danger was now ever present. Let him know some fear. It might save his life. Let him worry, for that was what such men did, and it was better they should worry than try and subdue their concerns.

Leave them on the surface where Harry could deal with them.

Oliver had a worry of his own. Charlotte. Harry must take care of his own, and Oliver must take care of his, Charlotte being a trouble of his own making, a difficulty he now had to sort out before it endangered his life and imperilled the work he was doing.

Even as he resolved to clear this issue from his mind his heart told him it would not be so easily accomplished.

Charlotte was there, whatever he thought of it.

And part of him liked it, regardless of the risks.

Chapter Eleven

Gordon puffed contentedly at his pipe and watched as the smoke obscured his view across the Channel.

He was sitting on a low rock, not looking at all comfortable, and from time to time using his right hand to hold the stem of his pipe firmly in his mouth. His right leg was raised as the structure of the rock dictated he be in such a position.

When he removed the pipe from his mouth he rested his elbow on his raised knee and used his pipe to point out certain vessels about their business at sea.

Kindale watched and listened.

George Gordon knew exactly which vessels might be engaged in illegal activity.

"Any ten-shilling men work for you?" Kindale enquired, interested in what he had learned of Jeremiah Hundash and the prospect there might be a traitor amongst the Revenue men.

The 'ten-shilling men' were former smugglers now finding a living on the other side of the law.

There was no great flight of fancy to believe such a man might easily have a foot in both camps.

"Aye," replied Gordon, "Edmund Whardley. Saw the errors of his ways, y'might say. I keep my eye on him, can't ever trust a man like that. But he's good and strong. Powerful man, that. Fearless. Like having him alongside me when we're confronting 'em.

"Can frighten the most hardened adventurer! But I wouldn't turn m'back on him, not for a moment. Why d'you ask, Kindale?"

"Curiosity. Something that's kept me alive, Gordon. Perhaps the same reason you like Whardley where you can see him." Gordon chuckled and drew on his pipe without removing his gaze from the water. Having considered the man's answer from every angle he sighed heavily and retorted softly.

"You'd not tell me, you'd not tell me, Oliver Kindale. But there's more to this, I'll be bound, sir."

Kindale let the words slip quickly away together with the pipe smoke, both abandoned to the whim of the breeze. The Revenue man changed the subject.

"Pleased the snow's not staying or getting worse. Old man down the harbour, old fisherman, he says the weather's set fair for a while now, and I rely on him. Just all this ... this *muck* ... it's got to melt and make wide nuisance of itself in its going." He turned slowly and looked directly at his companion.

"Better seas too. Good weather for mischief, Mr Kindale, and I dare say that's of interest to you. And we have .... an *arrangement* Mr Kindale. One that makes me nervous. Makes me shake if you follow me.

"I don't like having to trust a man I know nothing about...."

"You don't have to trust me, Gordon. Just believe that we fight from the same side and that I will deliver what I promise. Ballerden has assured you of that.

"You told me you were only speaking to me because of Ballerden. You have faith there, Gordon, so keep faith with me, and be sure of this. I'll not cross you, I will achieve my aim and with it I will make certain I pay my price to you."

Gordon nodded, looked away and sucked his pipe only to find it was no longer alight being devoid of tobacco.

"I pay well for my baccy, and that includes the duty," he said in a voice laden with a subtle and unusual blend of weariness and anger, "and the men I chase get it for free. Altogether free. No tax."

"Never mind Gordon, it must make it more worthwhile when you catch up with them!"

The two men shook hands and departed.

Kindale could see in Gordon's eyes and his very open face a degree of respect and trust, and knew he had truly won over his man.

Back at Harry's cottage he read the letter Ballerden had sent as soon as it was handed to him.

It sent a shudder down his spine.

It also gave him a limited range of dates, dates that were all too close.

But it confirmed his worse fears. Two men, identified only by code in the document found in Katherine's grave, were revealed by those dates. It might be coincidence, but it was improbable in the circumstances.

And they were, by any definition, two men of great prominence. Kindale had dreaded the possibility it was them, yet knowing that he would not be here now if it had been anything much less. No, none of this was coincidence. The substance of the document suggested that.

He screwed up the letter and threw it into the fire, raking the flaring embers as the paper was consumed and utterly destroyed.

He felt frustration and rage well up within him, and he knew he must intensify his quest for information.

That which he had come by had merely confirmed what was afoot, and he now knew the time was bearing down upon him. Next, he needed to speak to Temple, and that meant returning to Charlotte's. And he found the thought agreeable.

Very agreeable.

***

The weather was indeed turning mild.

Milder compared to the freezing winter conditions the snowfall had imposed, but still cold and now blustery.

The sea state was certainly not calm but could not be described as rough, and no real seaman would have done so.

Oliver Kindale dragged himself down the slope away from St Margaret's, through the mud and slush, the snow that determined to linger and in great piles, mostly no longer white and no longer in any way beautiful, and melt waters that searched with accumulated violence as they tried to find their way to the sea below.

Underfoot lay a treacherous path, with no surety of safe passage.

The mess of the snow covered landscape made hard work of travel, and wore bitterly into Kindale's every step and scratched away at his resolve and purpose.

Northwards he went, through Walmer and to Charlotte's cottage.

Charlotte waited until he was ready to embrace her, and he appreciated her all the more for that.

Undemanding. Intimate when it was right to be so, a companionable talker and listener when the time was appropriate, quiet and unobtrusive when she knew she needed to be.

Never inquisitive. Never asking questions she knew she should not, even when she yearned for and inwardly cried out for the answers.

She could read her man well enough. She understood the rules of their friendship.

And at the moment Oliver was largely unaware, or at least unable to comprehend that she was set on pleasing him by knowing him and knowing what was expected of her. It would've concerned him if he had, and it would come to worry him in times ahead.

For the time being he was happy to be in front of a roaring fire, mug of ale in hand, physically relaxing while his mind digested, analysed and categorised all the intelligence that had been placed before it.

He must forget nothing, overlook nothing, take every aspect at face value and dig down deep beyond that facade and consider, carefully, what it all might represent.

Charlotte prepared food and spoke no word. She recognised his mood and let him be.

There was no conversation over their meal, precious few words exchanged save about the quality of the food, which was excellent, and praise for her cooking. Thence he took himself back to the fire and to blessed sleep, the sleep that had been calling him for hours.

Much later he awoke to find Thomas Temple in attendance. Good!

He shook the slumber from his body, and accepted Temple's invitation to go into town. Both knew Temple's words were not for Charlotte's ears. Perhaps she realised that, hated it, felt degraded and frustrated by it, but she didn't show it. Not her way.

Temple's news was important and the man was aware of it. He could barely wait to explain.

"Oliver, Oliver, friend, there's movement on the marshes and, word is, Grey Jonnie has enlisted some local villains. Ruthless men, Oliver. But men not readily recognised in Dover, and Dover is where they're headed."

Temple was becoming quite breathless in the telling of his story being also overcome by the effort needed to plough through the snow whilst speaking. Kindale stopped him and placed his hands on his shoulders at armslength.

"My friend, you will die here from exhaustion. I am keen to hear you but not to be present at your death. Let us proceed slowly, and you proceed slowly with what you have to tell me."

They smiled at each other. Temple nodded and they returned to their trudge.

"Tydeman has been on the marshes, directly west of Hythe, been seen at Dymchurch, been seen with Grey Jonnie. And I seen the pair of them with ... guess who, Oliver, guess who?"

"Hapling, and in Dover."

Temple stopped in his tracks, and insofar as it was possible to discern, looked positively deflated. He looked sideways at Kindale, as if he was now suspicious.

"Were you there Oliver? Were you there?"

"No, my friend. But that is the way I knew it would fall out, for, believe me, Thomas, all is gathering pace. And we have milder weather, so I am told, for a few days, and a good sea into the bargain.

"Thomas, we must find out where Hapling will set sail. He will go to France and return at once. And I have to be ready for his return."

"Oliver, Oliver, he has no boat, friend!"

"Maybe not, but he will have one. Perhaps that's where Tydeman has a part to play. Do you understand me, Thomas?"

Thomas did.

They walked on in silence until they found their favourite inn.

"Charlotte likes you, Oliver Kindale."

As they located seats away from the raucous noise of sailors and landsmen engaged in making merry, not always amiably, Temple took his friend completely by surprise.

"I know she likes me. But that is that, Thomas."

"No, Mr Kindale, that is not all that. Far away from it. Take my word. She wants you as her man, and she could do no better unless she took me instead."

"Take her, Mr Temple, and be welcome."

"And that would not pain ye, Oliver Kindale? It would too, I'll be bound." There were no more words, but plenty more drinking as both men eyed each other unblinking.

"Right, Thomas, your story. Think back, tell me all and omit Charlotte, *if* you please." Temple roared with laughter and nodded his approval. But Oliver knew that Thomas was correct, it would pain him if Charlotte had another man now.

It still was not right, not how it was to be. He had to free himself, this distraction might yet cost him dear, and certainly his life was a price he was not prepared to pay. He must end this nonsense this night. He must.

As a diversion he sought information about the woman he had encountered at St. Margaret's. Temple bellowed with laughter as Oliver recounted his tale of events although the latter could see no humour in the way matters had unfolded.

"Oh, Lord, help us," exclaimed Temple amidst great mirth, "Why, that be Nancy Gild, and I have known her many a year, and known her well as you might say. I *have* too, let it be said. A woman from head to toe, be they some appreciable length apart, with plenty to entertain a man betwixt!" And he laughed all the more heartily. "She is of no matter," was all he added.

Oliver decided it was of no consequence and spoke again.

"Thomas, I have to remain in Deal. This is where it starts, this I know. Yet I have no way of proving what I say!

"Thomas, Thomas, oh Thomas! Y'must keep your vigil in Dover for me, my good friend, and I must be wide awake here. Deal; this is the heart and soul of all this, despite Chastain being in Dover. This is where it will start. But we must have all the pieces to put together a good picture.

Temple gave a slight chuckle.

"Y'talk in riddles, man. I don't understand you." He laughed some more, a brief, ironic chuckle. "You'll ne'er tell me what y'on about, Oliver, but I like you and I'll follow you on this, count on me, my friend. Dover it is for me then, is it? Well, so be it. Good luck to ye, Oliver Kindale."

"Good luck to you, Thomas. Be careful. Be safe. I'm away to find master Kettle. He may have a new road I can explore."

***

Robert Kettle had been prepared to disclose knowledge at a price.

But he would not divulge anything that might hinder his business interests, as he called them, damage his personal prospects, especially of living a long and happy life, or come between him and those who knew him or had come to rely on him.

So he dispensed information with great care.

He assessed the person asking rather than the amount being offered, the former being a better guarantor of his own safety and the continued well-being of his day to day life. Nothing was ever revealed that might hurt an associate, regardless of whether that associate was in legitimate business or employed in something darker.

Kettle had exchanged all that he was prepared to tell Kindale at their earlier encounter, and earned a pretty shilling or two by so doing. But was not so keen to part with more detailed explanations, conscious that Kindale was asking questions no man should ask of another when it came to less than legal operations.

The only thing that impressed him was that Kindale was not offering an improved rate of pay or any additional funds. He therefore decided the man was not desperate and probably not a representative of the Preventive forces that had so dogged his existence and his ability to make a small fortune.

Kindale had decided a more leisurely and unconcerned approach might win him over and learned to his pleasure he was correct. Kettle spoke guardedly and in general terms, avoiding names and specific places, but raised an eyebrow in passing when Kindale mentioned Tydeman and the possibility of a man looking for boat he could borrow, but do so initially without the owner's knowledge or agreement.

Tydeman, he assured Kettle (who would've known anyway), would not be above violence and threats to ensure the owner's co-operation. He stated it as a fact and let his words permeate Kettle's mind. He thus avoided making it a question, whereas he hoped for some acknowledgement from the smuggler and an unintentional surrender of certain intelligence.

And he knew from Kettle's expression that he was well acquainted with the Ramsgate man's intentions. He just wasn't saying, nor could he bought on the subject. It didn't matter. Kindale felt he had further confirmation the story would start right there in Deal.

Now to despatch the only obstacle that prevented clarity of mind in what was likely to prove a totally absorbing piece of work.

He needed no distractions, for the work was going to be difficult enough, fraught with danger and with the added ingredient of treachery. After all, if he could buy information then so too could others. And Robert Kettle claimed to have given a Revenue man (matching the description of Gordon) a tall story about Kindale himself!

Oliver gave him some additional coins so that he might further perpetrate deceit on his behalf. He realised Kettle was probably lying and upon receipt of any monies exceeding that given by Kindale would most likely divert himself from deceiving his paymaster.

It was the way of the world, it was the way of life.

Of course Gordon would've been asking about a man he had struck a bargain with! A man he was unfamiliar with, someone he'd never met who nevertheless had Nathaniel Ballerden's trust.

Charlotte was learning how to play her man. If Kindale had skill and craftsmanship in reading people and the ability to gently direct them to do his bidding by whatever means were appropriate, then Charlotte unwittingly had the same arts dealing with the man she now wanted.

She weighed up his present situation as soon as he walked through the door.

His business was going well but he was laden with a great deal to think about. And she was in the way. She would have to go.

As he accepted his mug of ale and sat by the fire, deep in thought, she instinctively knew the lie of the land and how she must deal with it. He was not getting away from her. He was the man for her and she needed him desperately.

He was good for her. More importantly, she was good for him, and she believed she could encourage his feelings until she couldn't be flung by the wayside. This she knew.

No escape, Oliver Kindale, she told herself. I will win because we need each other and I will be your woman, Oliver Kindale, and I will take care of you as a woman should. Then a pang of fear shot through her slender body.

What if he should die in this project of his?

Well, she resolved, I shall make sure he does not. I will use Thomas Temple, he will do as I say, and Thomas will watch over you, Oliver Kindale, and bring you home to my bed.

"Do you want food or rest?" she asked in a firm but sensitive voice.

"My bed, Charlotte. Just for a brief while. I'll go now. Something to eat when I wake, perhaps."

"Do you want me, Oliver?" Her voice had softened and was sweet and tender in his ears.

She stood right before him, arms at her sides, her lips quivering as he looked up. Her eyes were pleading, her face full of the pleasures she now offered him, and she herself desired.

The aching wrenched at his heart. He had to leave her, to end all this. And he wanted her, not simply as a woman, or as a man wants a woman, but because he knew that, for the first time in his life, he held something so beautifully special in his hands.

This wasn't just a woman, taken because she was a woman, flesh and passion, this was enchanting and deep, delightful and exhilarating. This was love.

And so they went to bed and he was lost, lost forever.

***

It was a different Oliver Kindale that arose later.

He had never had any time for the future, but now he wanted a future, *how* he wanted a future. It pulled him asunder, tearing at his soul, for he had work to do, a task to complete, yet he wanted Charlotte and the future she represented.

Well wrapped, they ventured towards the pebbles and the sea and sat together looking aimlessly across the spluttering waves breaking ahead of them. She instinctively allowed her head to slide onto his shoulder and smiled warmly as she felt him that close.

"I came to tell you I had to go, Charlotte. But now I know I will never leave."

"Dear Oliver, I knew what you had to say, but not why. But I want you, Oliver, and if you want me, well, we'll make the best of it together."

And so they sat side by side, snuggled closely, both knowing a pact had been made between them, an arrangement for now and for the future, fondness and affection melting their hearts.

No more words at that moment.

Still he allowed thoughts of separation to infiltrate his mental considerations.

There was no way of preventing them. He had let her into his life in the most extreme and permanent way possible and no part of him wanted release. He simply had to find a measure of determination to carry on with his mission and exclude Charlotte when he needed to give his all in pursuit of his goals.

Kindale felt he could do this.

He had the resolve, the cold edge, the ruthlessness. Yes, he could and would carry on exactly as before, moving thoughts of Charlotte into a safe and enclosed part of his mind, away from his work, when it was essential to do so.

In no circumstances would he permit her to be at the forefront when his work came first. He felt a new confidence surge through him. Yes, he could love her, dream with her, but he was more than capable of giving her no thought when his mind must attend to more important matters.

Having determined how he would deal with the situation, and having no knowledge of how the heart can leave one unprepared, or catch one out in an unguarded second, Oliver Kindale decided to enjoy his new arrangement.

And he decided to dream and think about tomorrow and the year beyond.

No sooner had he warmed to his theme than a cold wind stiffened his backbone. He was advancing into one of the most dangerous activities he had known, and he had known many. He might be killed or badly maimed. Did he not owe it to Charlotte to warn her and only proceed with her if she accepted the peril he faced?

Would she endeavour to dissuade him from further involvement? He acknowledged her womanly wiles had led him this far, captured him, bound him and left him a hostage to her whims. Then again he had nothing to offer but himself; she wasn't trying to better herself, take a man because of his wealth and position, or because he could offer a future worth investing in.

There was him, there was Charlotte and there was the cottage, and this was it. He had no income beyond what Ballerden gave him and once this matter was concluded no income at all. What could he turn his hand to?

Many ideas raked through his mind as he studied the low grey rollers cascading up the shingle as they shattered into so many foaming pieces, their energy spent.

"I have no trade, Charlotte. When I am finished here, if I settle here, with you, I have no work, no means to put food on the table."

"You'll find work in Deal, Oliver. Thomas will help you. And I have always lived poorly and all the better for it. No expectations. We'll be the better for it. Just every day as every day comes, and we'll work at it and make it as good as we want it to be, Oliver."

Once again silence stood between them as there were no words necessary, for what Charlotte had uttered appealed to Oliver Kindale in a manner he had never experienced. He was learning that any man may have a future if he wishes it, and he knew he had never wished it, nor wanted it.

And now he wished for it, and it was new and bright, a beacon in a dreary existence that had ruled his life since beyond a childhood he preferred to forget, a childhood he wished he could expunge from memory, but a childhood that would not disappear from his waking nightmares.

He wondered if it would always be there.

Did it matter? Would it always disturb him or could he now ride across it whenever it surfaced? Charlotte might have that power, the power to sweep the darkness out into the sunlight, the power to wake him from the slumber of eternal depression and gather him up into something mystical and astonishing.

Something beauteous and stimulating, something to live for, something to dream for. A future there for the taking.

It was Charlotte's inner loveliness he sought; even now he could see no attractiveness in her features yet he craved sight of them and longed for the touch of her body.

Here was promise, here was delight. Here was happiness.

He needed nothing more and that united him with the vision of contentment that swam across his mind and absorbed his soul. There was more than what he was doing now, much more.

Kindale had always seen his work as everything today was about, and he had simply never wanted a job with prospects tomorrow. Now Charlotte was presenting him with a future he had never contemplated and never dared to dream of.

And yet, and yet....

She stood in the way of his success insomuch as thoughts of her, and thoughts of the future, might blind him at the most vital of moments. He just had to find a way of dealing with this. And in that minute realised how much he wanted to protect their future.

He put an arm around her shoulder and pulled her tighter, and she responded by nestling further into him. This was perfect, but so new, so fresh, so clean, and nothing should sully it or make it unbearable. This was so desirable, such a vision of completeness.

I must finish this job, he said to himself, and free myself for Charlotte. That is how I will do it.

Devote myself to what must be done and then give myself freely to this woman.

Their lips met again, gently, tenderly. Their kiss spoke a thousand words, illuminated every grey patch in their lives, liberated their senses and stirred their hearts fervently.

Presently they stood and, arm in arm, returned to her cottage.

And there it was that Thomas Temple found them.

Chapter Twelve

"Came straightway, Oliver."

Temple looked agitated, anxious, excited.

"Tydeman, Hapling, Grey Jonnie, all come to Chastain's. And another. Don't know him, but I saw him later with the Revenue man, Gordon. Strange that, I thought. Seemed to be deep in talk but it was like Gordon was giving him orders. Might be wrong..."

Probably not, thought Kindale, but he kept his thoughts silent.

"Describe him," he said instead.

"Tall, scrawny looking if truth be told, shallow cheeks, eyes set deep, if you know what I mean. Walked a bit strange, like he limped a bit, praps one leg a bit bent. I don't know, just didn't walk quite right. Do y'know him, Oliver?"

"No, but I'll see what I can find. You've done well, Thomas, but we need to do more. Are you ready? This is all going to happen soon. I still need you as my eyes and ears and I need you now more than ever."

Thomas looked across at Charlotte who looked away.

She had been excluded from all this but the mystery of what she was hearing now sickened her, as at once she realised her man might be in danger, was clearly deeply involved in something and some activity she knew she would not like. Knowing Temple she thought it was probably illegal. But Charlotte was not a woman to ask questions.

You upset a man like that, and she didn't want to upset Oliver. She must hide her cares and concerns and be there when she was needed most, but in the background at times like these.

"Enough for now," ordered Kindale, sweeping his eyes from Temple to the girl. Temple immediately understood and besides there was nothing to add.

The conversation falling to more general matters Charlotte felt she was on safe ground asking about employment.

"Thomas, could a man find some work here, some honest work, if he had the mind."

Temple's eyes swung across to meet Oliver's gaze, and he noticed the man looked shocked, the first time he had seen any recognisable expression in Kindale's face. In an instant he knew that Oliver and Charlotte had become close.

It pleased him for Charlotte's sake, but he worried that perhaps she had said more than she should, and Oliver was not planning an alternative to his current pursuit. He let it ride in the air and replied in wider terms.

"Aye, Charlotte, that he may, if he be willing, and if work be about. There's precious little in my game but I hear the fleet may have need of my services before long. Old Thomas Temple will make a good penny from the navy!"

There being no more discourse on any subject, and a small meal to be eaten, the three sat at the table and enjoyed their food together before Temple set off south again, Dover bound. It had been Kindale's intention to follow later but his plans were overtaken when he noticed Gordon riding into Deal, accompanied by two men.

His eyesight had never let him down and even though they were on the road in some distance Kindale knew one was the Revenue officer, and just the man he needed to see.

Taking his leave of Charlotte he set off towards town.

Close up he realised that one of Gordon's companions matched Temple's description. He caught Gordon's eye and indicated with a glance and a slight movement of his head that a discreet meeting was required.

Gordon understood and despatched his men on a mission to the front. He knew that would give him time enough.

Moments later he and Kindale met away from eyes that might see too much.

"Soon, Gordon. And it starts here, I'll swear to it. I'll send word and instructions, and I'll not let you down you may be sure. But I ask with all I hold dear that you be ready but do not act until you hear. Then act as you see fit and I'll deliver my promise, you have my word."

"I'll be at Dover Castle, unless you wish me to be here."

"No, Dover will suit my purpose. I will not come myself. Harry Harblow or Thomas Temple."

"Good. Tell your man to ask for Major Wendle and to say they have an urgent message for me. Wendle would appeal to you, Oliver Kindale, the sort of man you could work with. And I know you understand me well."

Gordon smiled and set about lighting his pipe.

"Whardley. He is with you?" Gordon nodded once and produced a cloud of dense smoke that caught on the wind and drifted into their faces. "Gordon, don't trust him, and don't speak of our arrangement nor engage him on this mission. Can you move him away from here, give him gainful employment further south?"

"Would look suspicious, Kindale. But I'll find a way of diverting him when I hear from you. Trust me on that. Better to have him with me in the meantime where I can keep an eye in his direction."

Kindale decided to take a chance.

"He's been seen with Tydeman and Hapling in Dover. Are you aware? Is that your doing?"

George Gordon looked stunned and stopped puffing at his pipe.

"Ye Gods! Has he now? No, not my doing. I have no intelligence as to where those scoundrels are and wish I did! I keep my silence with Whardley on that matter I take it?"

Kindale nodded slowly, then moved away and returned to the cottage without further intercourse. It would not do to spend too long with Gordon especially with Whardley so close to hand. There was no handshake, just a mutual understanding, and Kindale swiftly vanished from the Revenue man's view.

But not from the sight of Edmund Whardley, even now heading back to report to Gordon.

And Edmund Whardley was accomplished at noting all that went on around him. His given purpose, instructed by Gordon, had proved a fruitless task and was sufficiently pointless, now Whardley came to consider it, to be dubious.

Sure enough, Gordon had wanted quiet words with someone. But who?

Leaving his companion on some insignificant excuse he darted swiftly around the streets, sensing the other man was walking southwards, and came upon Kindale face to face.

They walked past each other in opposite directions, Whardley making a clear observation of Kindale, and storing the picture in his mind.

For his part Kindale recognised Whardley and knew too well what the man was doing there, and that his meeting with Gordon had not gone unnoticed. It confirmed his own suspicions. Whardley did indeed limp but it was not an inconvenience, that was certain.

Whardley's companion had since met up with the Revenue man and explained that Whardley had been temporarily detained for 'personal reasons' and would be with them shortly. In its turn this now aroused Gordon's qualms particularly when Whardley approached from the south and in a state of some breathlessness, as if he had been running.

George Gordon puffed at his pipe but it gave him no pleasure and no comfort.

He now had a problem and he alone had to come to terms with it.

Not being a conventional officer of the law by any means he began to muse on how he could mislead the man and ultimately put him out of the picture altogether. And as he considered the more extreme measures the more it amused him, and so it came to pass that he once again enjoyed his pipe, and permitted a broad grin to open his face. He could deal with this.

But he must do so without performing any action that might alert the wrongdoers and send them off their track. Kindale wouldn't welcome that!

He was a resourceful man and set about conceiving his own plan, one that would not hinder Kindale and not directly interfere with Tydeman and Hapling. Certainly not anything that would cause them to change their arrangements!

And at that very time he realised he would not like to face Oliver Kindale if he proceeded incorrectly and ruined the scheme! Yes, there was a man who would kill, he concluded. A man who could kill if crossed.

***

Harry Harblow had spent a couple of days wending his way south along the coast, past Hythe and Dymchurch, engaging in conversation with whoever would speak.

He pieced together shreds of hearsay and opinion and was lucky to come by them, for people were loathe to talk to strangers despite the fact he tried to ask no questions, preferring to allow the dialogue to develop in the direction he wished it to go.

As ever there was a fear for the Marsh gangs, but mostly the people Harry had speech with were openly on their side when it came to circumventing the law. This was Harry, able to pass as one of their own, able to gain their confidence, able to work things round to the matters he wanted to discuss. It was his strength.

He ventured onto Romney Marsh, in winter a dark, uninviting place, a place where a man might die unnoticed amongst the grass and ditches as any wind swept unchecked above. It might have been created by nature just for the smugglers and other brigands. Difficult to cross, easy to lose your way, but a flat terrain for all that.

A bleak battleground for authority against law-breakers.

Hard for soldiers to hide in wait, easy for felons to lie low. Easy for goods to be transported in haste, difficult for pursuers to maintain such speed.

The people who lived here, worked here, the farmers, the smugglers, all knew every inch of the way, just as they understood the weather and all it might bring. The seemingly innocent, often coerced into illegal activity, sometimes by force or threat, lived alongside those who sought an easy income at the expense of others.

Not all the innocent were by any means truly 'innocent'. You could save your life and earn rewards by being less than innocent.

The gangs could enlist a positive army when need be, drawing also from those who lived along the coast. The Marshes were their friends, their sanctuary, their God in a Godless place. They had the measure of the Marshes at all times.

Harry was far from convinced this part of his journey was of any value.

It was like being abandoned on the edge of a very cold witches' cauldron!

Better return to Folkestone. Oliver would want money so a call on Ballerden was important. And he had gathered some information that he hoped would be useful to his friend. He still regarded himself as being on the outside looking in, and longed to be a greater part of what Kindale was about.

It plagued him and played with his mind.

He was deeply engrossed in his own thoughts when two riders trotted past almost unseen. He looked up at the last moment and recognised Grey Jonnie as one of the riders, but had no idea of the other man.

Making no effort to look after the figures (no need to rouse suspicion) he walked on knowing he now had additional information for Oliver. He had just had time enough to see the other man's face and would be able to describe what he had seen. That was good.

Now for Folkestone.

***

Mary Harblow was afraid.

She had known Harry find himself in trouble all too often and believed he had come within a whisker of losing his life on more than one occasion.

So today she was nervousness itself as she waited, waited, waited, hoped and prayed for his safe return.

She began to blame Oliver but it was not his fault. It was just that any association with Oliver Kindale travelled inevitably along a path of risk with trouble, as she called it, the destination. Mary had no desire to be further acquainted with 'trouble' but her head and her heart as one told her 'trouble' was thrusting towards her door.

Just at that moment it was her man who was thrusting through the undergrowth to her front door.

Unsurprisingly she was so relieved she treated him to a welcoming any hero, especially her hero, would appreciate, a welcoming a long lost lover would appreciate. She could be tender but right now her passion boiled over and she was anything but gentle.

Mary wanted everything that was rightfully hers. Harry was exhausted but gave freely. And shortly they were both exhausted and asleep in each others arms.

It was Harry who stirred hearing a horse approaching and was well pleased to see Oliver riding towards the cottage and went out to greet him.

Later, having devoured one of Mary's delightful dinners and sunk an appreciable quantity of ale, the men sat in their chairs either side of the fire as was their wont. Harry's wife, knowing they wanted private discourse and being herself truly tired, cleared away and left them alone seeking her bed for peace, quiet and repose.

Harblow related all the snatches he had acquired on his travels and how he had passed Grey Jonnie as he made his way to the coast. He described the companion.

"Thin. Tall, maybe, and thin. Like a scarecrow. Eyes deep in his head if you understand me. Not good at explaining these things..."

"Y'doing fine, Harry, and I think I know the man. Anything else?"

"To tell the truth, Oliver, looked like he could do with a good meal! Looked half starved..."

"Thank you, Harry, that'll do, I'm sure I know the man, and I expected no less. I wonder where they were riding to? What road were you on?"

"Could be anywhere, Oliver, that way. Would certainly be the road you'd take if Hawkhurst was your destination...." Kindale burst into laughter.

"Harry, my friend, I know full well how you want to tie this up, but in fact it doesn't matter, for I am quite sure a larger group is involved anyway, so Grey Jonnie adding a much feared gang to his entourage makes little difference.

"I have to involve the army, possibly the navy, and will do so through George Gordon. But Chastain is the snake's head, mark my words, and I must snare him at the right time and not before. Then between us we can land a mighty prize, and kill off this dreadful snake.

"We eliminate the head and the body will die, Harry.

"Move too soon and we won't trap all the main players, never mind apprehending all their followers. From now on the danger is very real, and I'll not risk you in too deep, for Mary's sake as much as for yours." Harry somehow managed to look close to tears and was ready to argue.

He had been dreading this outcome. He wanted to be involved even if his life was to be forfeited. Yes, thinking about it, he really meant that. But he also knew Oliver was right. Damn the man!

Standing shoulder to shoulder with Kindale against all that might be railed against them, that was his dream, his frightening, sorrowful dream, and Kindale was dashing that away and all because he was a married man!

Yes, Oliver was right. Mary *did* matter, and Harry didn't want to die although he felt it was his duty if such duty called. Don't be foolish, man, he admonished himself. My duty is to Mary, that is so.

But he looked so downhearted Oliver was moved to cross the room and place a comforting arm around his shoulder.

"My dear friend, I know what you're thinking, and I know the pain you feel, but I am here for the purpose, that is my lot in life and I shall take whatever is thrown at me, but you I will not risk in danger's way. And that is an end to it."

Harry reached back and grabbed his friend's hand.

"I know, I know, I know. But let me play some part, I beg you."

"Harry, you have done well and I still have use for you, believe me. And you'll no doubt taste danger along the way!"

In the silence that followed Oliver was confronted by an image of Charlotte, for what he was explaining to Harry might so easily now apply to him. Not married, no, but having a woman who cared for him. And a sea of anguish pounded the shores of his heart and it was all he could do to turn the tide and free his mind.

He now knew pain.

And he didn't like it. It might yet interfere with his ability to do his job. But nothing now could prevent him thinking about the future, about Charlotte and about how he wanted her.

He didn't want to die, and suddenly realised that he would be faced with death, a risk he had so often accepted at face value, as a debt that might be called in at any stage. Death was one escape from the tasks he undertook that he knew might come any day.

But now he didn't want that inevitability. And he shook with rising despair.

Throughout his life Kindale had accepted an existence without love or compassion in a world where nobody had any particular feelings about anyone else. It had never occurred to him that it was not a way most people lived.

Believing that he cared not whether he should live or die he had embarked on a career that required a concurrence that death would come eventually. It came to all men, and he was content that should his demise be otherwise premature he would still fulfil a useful function being alive in the first place.

He would do what was asked if him, not take unnecessary risks, and ensure that he did not lay down his life in vain.

His coldness suited his position well.

He could think with great and organised clarity, assess each happening as it arose, and make his decisions in a sound and logical way. Never reckless or thoughtless, never allowing external issues to make incursions into the sensible and ordered progress of all he did, Kindale strove for perfection knowing he would not achieve it.

But he would come close, and his strength was his isolation from matters that he regarded as irrelevant, such as emotional ties, and his single-minded determination once he knew he was upon the right road.

And Charlotte stood in his way, the first time another human being had affected him so.

Because of Charlotte he was dreaming of a different life, one where a more natural death might be his fate rather than a savage and brutal end.

The likelihood of being killed never bothered him, and he had always contented himself with the view that as long as he was in the right, had done all that he could in pursuit of his aims, had weighed up the situation and acted accordingly and appropriately, if his enemy should prove his downfall so be it.

In this moment he wanted to abandon that simple philosophy.

Because of Charlotte and his silly dreams he now wanted to live or, more importantly, make sure he didn't die.

And he couldn't be sure that he would survive this time.

He faced the greatest danger and he knew it would be bloody, and he did not want his own blood spilled.

Suddenly he was very angry. He wanted to be angry with Charlotte but he knew that would not do. He wanted to be angry *because* of Charlotte but accepted he should only be angry with himself.

Charlotte had not bewitched him, cast some spell over him. Yet she had. She'd laid her heart before him and asked him to encase it in his own heart. Was that not some form of witchcraft?

No, of course it wasn't. But as he stood next to Harry he was lost in a rough grey mist of turmoil that he had no experience of being able to deal with. How he ached. For a passing minute he even considered taking Charlotte and running away, but that was not the answer, not the way to solve the problem.

His anger grew. How dare he even dream of abandoning his mission when so much depended on him! He didn't have to face this danger alone.

Harry wanted to be with him, Temple too. Then there was George Gordon. Perhaps Major Wendle. Did he have to face this alone?

Yes, he knew he did. He was the only one he could trust, and only one who would think like him, react like him. But that trust in himself was being eroded, and that was the damage that now fuelled his rage.

It couldn't be like this. It was the worst possible situation he had been in and he must relieve the sting of worry by himself. He must calm, he must cast all other thoughts to the skies and concentrate on what he must do. No other interference must be allowed in, not until this was over.

And he yearned for its end, longed for release and the chance to join Charlotte on the long and happy road of life and love.

"I want a stroll, Harry," he said, "just me, my old friend. I will not be long, but I must be alone. Please understand."

Harry nodded but Oliver did not see it, he was already out of the cottage desperately breathing in substantial lungfuls of air as he fought with his emotions and his conscience. He raced deep into the woods and threw himself to the ground, clasping his hands to his face and weeping in torrents.

Overwhelmed with the agonies of his plight he rolled around squealing and screeching, shedding tears copiously, and then crying out for Charlotte and for an end to his suffering.

Once again, he was angry, angry with himself for letting Charlotte pierce his shell, shatter his armour, the very protection that had been his shield throughout life.

He tore at the vegetation and ranted until his frenzy was spent, and then he lay on his back gasping, exhausted, and cursed like a man possessed. But his words were fading in venom and the heat was drawn from his temper, and slowly he regained his composure.

Sitting up, still awash with annoyance, he resolved to complete his work, whatever the outcome, and go to Charlotte free at last. Free of the smothering net that surrounded him, free of the past, free of the harsh lessons he had learned so long ago, free of the demons that had ruled his life.

How they had wrecked him, keeping him in chains, preventing the real Oliver Kindale from rising to conquer his past and building his future.

"Be done with you," he yelled from the forest floor. "Be gone from me. I am a free man, you'll not harm me again."

He laid back and closed his eyes, calmness upon him at last.

His crisis was over, the fever extinguished.

He rose and made his way back and found Harry leaning against the doorway.

"It's alright son," he said with cooling and generous kindness, "I've heard ye from here. But whatever it is, even if you can't tell your old friend Harry Harblow, don't you worry none. It will be alright."

Kindale slapped his shoulder and laughed.

"Thank you, dear friend, thank you. It's nothing I can't tell you about and tell you I shall, if you have the ears and the will to listen."

And so the two men returned to their chairs and their mugs and Oliver explained as best he could.

It was the first time in his life he had shared any personal concerns with anyone, and astonished himself that he should now do so freely. But it felt good, and he knew it was right.

Harry proved a good listener and a good counsellor.

And at last Oliver Kindale was at peace.

Chapter Thirteen

It was cold but he didn't feel the bitterness.

It was as if the icy wind could find no way through his clothing, and his face, exposed to these driving forces of nature, was well used to being battered in this way.

This spot had become his favourite haunt. The snow came quickly and been slow to depart, but it was now lingering only in open places and where it had been gathered up in drifts. The remainder was a slushy mess with paths reduced to muddy byways.

Snow never seemed to like the coast, and this place, *his* place, had been almost untouched lying a few feet from the shingle that gently banked into the sea. It was a remarkable piece of coastline, mainly flat, backed by undulating countryside, and bounded to the south by the cliffs that stretched from St Margaret's to beyond Folkestone.

South from there the Marshes. Sheep rearing country. He knew that it had often been the case that almost as quickly as sheep had been shorn the owlers had started transporting the fleeces to the coast for immediate, and illegal, shipment abroad.

He observed the range of vessels in the Downs before him. Naval vessels, fishing boats, a Revenue cutter. It looked busy and so it would be with a good north-easterly blowing in the sails.

To the north lay the inland port of Sandwich and beyond that the coast swung eastwards around the isle of Thanet and the town of Ramsgate. He could make out the white cliffs on the horizon and recalled his visit there and his meeting with Lt Dugald. And with Ursula Wellfern!

Would he try and contact Dugald? Was it the right thing to do?

Perhaps the navy wasn't the answer. After all he wanted the men landed here before action was taken. And the Preventive services tended to work against each other, rarely presenting a co-ordinated effort against the smugglers!

Indeed, all too often (and George Gordon had confirmed this) they could be a menace to each other! Kindale chuckled quietly to himself.

No, leave the navy out, rely on the soldiers Gordon could muster. Presumably he would have no bother persuading Wendle to play the game his way.

He'd never smoked, but now he almost envied Gordon his pipe. He felt he would like to draw on a pipe right now, and the thought made him realise he was experiencing a kind of contentment, and maybe he was. Perhaps he would take to it once this was over and Charlotte was his life.

A new dawn, with the nightmares over at last, the eternal blackness that littered his memories ready to be drowned and sunk forever. A will to live, that was it.

He no longer accepted the premise that he must die before his time thanks to the nature of his work. He was alive and wanted to live. And he wanted Charlotte.

Even now he couldn't imagine why he had despised her at first, looked upon her as a picture of ugliness, been willing to bed her just for his own pleasure and nothing more.

For the first time in his life he noticed other things, nature at work around him, observing two crows together on a branch. He could almost conceive that they were huddled next to each other for warmth and he realised he was smiling. They were suddenly joined by a starling obviously unafraid of the two much larger birds, as if all such flying creatures must flock as one breed in order to survive the worst agonies of the weather.

He watched a group of men launching their boat further along the beach. The steady slope of the shingle was ideal for the purpose and equally ideal for dragging the vessel ashore. He mused on the fact this coast must've borne witness to many such landings and all too often with goods that should've attracted duty and had been removed from that inconvenience.

Some of the boats traded with ships passing by or lying over in the Downs. And it was all the Preventive services could do to track down a fraction of the smuggling. The authorities found themselves faced not just by the free traders but protective townspeople, and so they were too outnumbered to make a serious impact.

This will change, Oliver concluded. This will end, or be vastly reduced. It truly will.

But perhaps not right away. The purse has been well drained by war and with worse to come, and resources will not yet be organised into effective measures. But it will come. And he began to wonder if he would see the change in his lifetime, and with that consideration he realised he was once again deciding he had a future beyond today.

This was very new to Oliver Kindale, but he discovered he fancied the prospect, and also that such thoughts actually warmed his soul. This was good.

He was thinking very precisely, with great clarity, and without knowing he was doing so nodded his head. He was clear, very clear in thought. He could carry through his mission with nothing to scar his mind, nothing to distract his reasoning and scrutiny. In truth he was thinking deeply and determinedly, with utter focus, for the first time in days and it pleased him.

Thanks to Harry he was now aware Hapling had an excellent knowledge of the French coast from Calais south to far past Boulogne. That was why he was part of this.

Tydeman would be the better sailor, the more experienced smuggler, possibly the more cold-hearted of the two. But Hapling knew the northern French coast intimately.

Gordon could have the pair of them and serve them right.

But they weren't the principal characters in this horrible drama. Kindale involuntarily shuddered at the thought and then felt Charlotte's hands upon his shoulders. He had not heard her coming, for the sounds of her approach had been muffled by the chill wind and the sore rustling of the sea running amok amongst the stones on the front.

He smiled at the waves, the sailors at sea. He thought of the merciless Goodwin Sands just north that had lured and destroyed ships and men with equal pleasure, and endless appetite. Then he turned and drank in the loveliness of his woman's own smile.

Studying her as she slowly retreated to their cottage he saw a very different woman from the one he had first met. Here was his goddess. There was no grand beauty, it was true, and little elegance, but he loved her all the more for it. Her smile routinely melted his heart.

Returning to the sea, he knew now, beyond all other judgements, he could continue in his work unhindered by emotional aberrations. Charlotte was locked in his heart, where she belonged, and no longer needed to wander about as an obstacle to his mental deliberations.

His mind would concentrate solely on matters in hand, and his head swirled with heated satisfaction that it had earned freedom for such concentration. He was thinking better than he had done for some while, so much so that he was able to apply even greater lucidity and intensity to his thoughts. Now he comprehended that he was thinking across an horizon, a barrier of his own making, that distorted his view and misted vital matters, some being of great importance.

Chastain was the leader. Tydeman was the accomplished smuggler, Hapling the man who would navigate a vessel into the French coast to collect the disreputable and disgusting human cargo. Tydeman would therefore be responsible for the landing on Kentish soil, and for garnering all the local support required especially if the army or navy got wind of it.

Grey Jonnie?

Well, ruthless beyond description with a reputation enhanced since his arrival in the county. Was he intent on organising a terrifying gang of massive proportions that would dominate the whole of Kent once the dreadful deed was done?

And one such thought led to another.

In anarchy Grey Jonnie could become the head of the common people, a merciless governor in Kent, with control of the country's vital ports. A man of great authority revered by those hungry for authority and supremacy, however awesome and frightening that might be. That had to be the answer.

They *had* to be stopped.

He could not do it alone. He would have to gift more trust to Gordon who would probably appreciate it anyway.

The sea looked more threatening as Kindale watched the waves and contemplated the nightmare he knew Chastain and Grey Jonnie were planning. He felt anger well up inside him but quickly quelled it; no room for such fury now. He had to employ the coldest of brains and keep personal rage outside.

A small boat was rowed into the shore and he looked over the men who leaped out and hauled their craft up the shingle to what passed as a safe haven, clear of the grasping fingers of the waves.

He didn't think he could go to sea. The sea had to be in your blood, the work had to be learned from the cradle, and he was a stranger in Deal, unlikely to be accepted by these men slaving away relentlessly at their trade.

Who could really blame them for seizing an opportunity to bring more ashore than fish?

If Temple's business as a chandler was going to gather pace, which Temple clearly believed it would, perhaps he could do something there. Temple might welcome him.

Farming too was out of the question.

Charlotte might help him. Or her sister Jack. But then he might become involved with Jack's husband, lying low and providing food by breaking the law. And he didn't want to be on the wrong side of the law. Did he?

Perhaps in Deal there might be no choice!

For certain he would not join any part of the Preventive services. So the possibility of taking good honest work supplemented by occasional good dishonest work could be his course.

He did not have to worry about it now, and he returned his mind to Chastain and Chastain's scheme.

Having considered all the other likely options he was strongly convinced Hapling and Tydeman would sail from Deal, and it would be in Tydeman's remit to ensure the return landing was smooth and untroubled.

They would, in all probability, not steal a boat. No need. It would arouse suspicion and there were navy ships in the Downs. Tydeman would hold sway here by reputation and would agree an arrangement to 'borrow' a ship. That had to be it.

Robert Kettle. Unreliable but well informed.

The man to approach about any arrangement Tydeman might make. And with Temple by his side Kindale might be more acceptable to the man, and be prepared to reveal knowledge if he was well paid.

Kindale would have to weigh up if such knowledge was sound or if he was simply buying nonsense. He would await Temple's return and they would visit Mr Kettle. Temple was well known in Deal and the smuggler might think twice about deceiving him.

Even better to let Temple go alone!

***

It was dark and the wind had eased.

The sea appeared to have relaxed and was seemingly recovering from its exertions, as if preparing itself for the next onslaught.

The sky was ridding itself of the mass of clouds and the moon was in its last quarter thinned to a small arc, barely aglow in the night. The stars were making an impressive show and Kindale absently observed their various degrees of brightness and hue.

Temple had set off on his task only too pleased to have a task to perform, and Oliver and Charlotte stood quietly together in the darkness.

They didn't speak. Words weren't necessary in their relationship. Too many words would've created an invisible wall, a pointless muddle between them. Their affection was unspoken but deeply understood.

It was the sweet charm of their love. Silence. In the evening gloom they could not see each other's faces but did not need to. It wasn't relevant. What they felt for each other was all that mattered. And smothered in this exquisite and engulfing aura Oliver found he could turn his mind to other issues without losing touch with the blaze of fondness that bound them.

Charlotte recognised this and held her tongue if indeed she did have anything to say.

Just being with him, just being able to love him, just knowing he loved her, it was all sufficient and well and good to her. She had her man and would not lose him. She knew she had won. He had come home and would stay.

A couple of nights, no more, and the sky would be moonless and Kindale instantly saw it for what it was: an ideal opportunity for those with malicious intent to reach these shores, and he knew what that meant. Yes, it was happening, it was soon now. A day or two away. That would support the information in Ballerden's letter relating to various dates, places and personages.

Strangely, having decided he had assessed the situation correctly, and could do no more this very night, he allowed his mind to return exclusively to Charlotte and the times ahead.

Oh, how he wanted to live! His eyes searched the skies while his heart throbbed for the woman by his side. He was much comforted by her presence and felt the joyous pleasure of being in love surge up through his body and knew he was smiling and radiating happiness.

He could not believe that he had denied himself such bliss throughout his life. But then he had never known such glorious contentment was possible or attainable. How different his life might have been!

133

What an odd thing is life, he mused. For all that, had he not pursued the route he had taken he would not now be standing next to Charlotte, and, he pondered, perhaps it might not have been a success any other way.

He might have placed himself in danger of more emotional pain that could conceivably have destroyed his heart totally. At least this way his wounds had healed.

Charlotte was a beautiful woman, not outwardly, nature had decreed that she should not be formed in loveliness and bright physical features, but inwardly as a real person. And Oliver Kindale was alive in so many wonderful ways thanks to her inward beauty. Yes, he was alive.

He permitted the thought to roll around his mind at leisure. Alive! Alive!

And once more he wondered about how he might find employment. He reviewed his skills, precious few in number, and concluded his physical strength might be his greatest ally. He could work hard manually, that was for sure, and no doubt that strength could be put to good use by somebody.

Yes, if not in Temple's domain, then perhaps with a shipwright. It would all come right. He would find something and he would do it well, that was his way.

And he would be a good husband to Charlotte.

Together they would face the world and accept what the fates hurled in their direction, because together they could overcome any obstacle and together enjoy any delight that came their way.

He was also feeling at home in Deal.

His visits to Kent had not been many. He knew Thanet intimately and it had played a large part in his earlier life; indeed, Katherine Downford provided for his womanly needs and comforts and he had assumed he was in love with her. Of course he wasn't, any more than she loved him. But she loved his money!

Once, without a penny in his pocket, he had walked along the north Kent coast from Reculver to Whitstable and found the experience exhilarating, his destination less so for a man without means.

The walk had been easy for a man of his fitness, along the top of low cliffs and simple sea shores, with a view of the Essex coast coming increasingly into view across the Thames estuary. Whitstable appealed to him for reasons he could barely comprehend.

Also a smuggling centre the town exuded an air of quaint independence and a determination not to look to the future. It seemed to Kindale to be embedded in a set period and was keen to remain where it stood, unbothered by passing fancies and developing circumstances, its people settled with their lot and unwilling to embrace a new day all the time the old day presented them with all they required.

He was taken by boat to Sheppey.

It felt as if he had been removed from reality and tossed aside in an alien environment. Essex seemed closer. He never lingered on the island completing the job he was paid to do and stole a boat at Harty and rowed himself across the Swale towards Faversham.

These beaches, these creeks, created by nature with smuggling in mind. Impossible for the Preventive services to properly police it was not unusual for those in authority to come to mutually agreeable arrangements with those they should be apprehending.

There was a solitary moment he enjoyed on Sheppey. Not far from the abbey at Minster he chanced upon a vantage point high above the sea and a mile from the coast. He could observe the Medway estuary funnelling into the Thames and see Essex with greater clarity than before.

A busy shipping area.

He had met his contact atop that hill, but was set upon by three men as he later descended. His strength was his fortune. He laid them all out, moaning and groaning, clutching their wounds, their cudgels lying uselessly about the ground.

An hour further on and he had dealt with the man who sent them, a man who would never again send others to do his dirty work, or indeed order any sort of action. They buried him in an unmarked grave but Kindale was not there to see it, let alone to mourn.

He had smiled with satisfaction.

And in Sheerness claimed his reward at the dockyard as arranged. He spent a little on drink, a little on clothes, and substantially more on a young woman who was prepared to satisfy his every desire. Sheppey didn't detain him any longer.

He had once been to Chatham and wished he had not bothered. It was one of the few occasions when failure attended him, and he was obliged to let the navy sort out its own problems. Not that the navy ever paid well, and very poorly indeed for his special talents.

Harry Harblow he had met in Canterbury some years ago and had liked the man from the outset. Kenton said he must work with him and he did so, much to his eventual satisfaction, although there was inevitable mistrust at first.

Mistrust ruled Oliver's life.

Yet tonight he knew he would trust Charlotte with his life. He turned to the silent figure on his right and embraced her and felt the moist treasure of her lips on his. Beguiled, enchanted, besotted, his soul was consumed by her kiss, his heart enthralled by the feel of her tender body.

He had come home, come of age, become a different man. And, yes, Deal would be his home. Deal would do very nicely.

Deciding plainly that Harry and Thomas would not be directly involved (he wouldn't run the risk of their loss) Oliver Kindale had come to an important conclusion.

He would send one or other, as the convenience of the moment presented itself, to George Gordon.

Hapling and Tydeman would be Gordon's reward and he could have them as soon as the party was ashore and heading inland, no doubt with the principal perpetrators, Chastain and Grey Jonnie, in the vanguard.

His planning had to be as correct as anything he had ever attempted, but now his mind was as sharp as it had ever been, and fully focused on the scheme he was setting up, and he felt much more self-assured, just as he had been in days gone past.

Temple returned with news.

"Aye, Oliver, William Tydeman is expected, and will be taking a new boat out. He's chosen a fast one, Oliver, he has at that. Sail, up to twenty men to row, a lot of power there, my friend. It's called the *Maisie Greentail*..." and he saw Kindale's look of incredulity as he reflected on the name. "I have no idea as to the name, my friend, but it's of no matter! She's new and she goes well according to Kettle.

"By the by, I gave him money with more to follow, I told him, if he stays true and stays with the truth, and I showed him my pistol just to remind him of his new obligations! And them obligations mean not talking elsewhere for money.

"If he's threatened he can choose to die by my pistol or someone else's. So that's left it all neat and tidy where master Robert Kettle is concerned."

Kindale smiled.

"And I have better news, my friend. A sort of acquaintance, to term it that way, is an oarsman for this particular run, and I will be taking a drink with him on the morrow. Master Kettle disclosed that while he was examining the rough end of my pistol, if you see where I'm heading."

"Indeed I do. You've done well, Thomas. Some knowledge of the landing arrangements, signalling system, anything you can come by, anything at all. But don't get in deep and make him suspicious. It's easily done, Thomas, easily done."

"I understand you well, my friend. Now I have some more good news.

"It may be that Master Kettle, keen as may be to endorse his understanding and his obligation, and aware of the penalty for failure, wanted to keep the right side of me and for me to feel .... well ... sure of him. So he very kindly gave me a half consumed cask of French brandy, so he says, to toast all that is agreed between us."

Kindale managed to look concerned.

136

"Poison perhaps?"

"Shouldn't think so, unless he meant to do away with himself an' all. We shared a drop or two and he drank from the same cask. So let us do the same, Oliver."

Temple poured their drinks and Kindale, still slightly worried and wearing a furrowed brow to emphasise his position, sniffed like a dog at a tree. Temple laughed heartily and swallowed a great mouthful.

Kindale made up his mind affirmatively in relation to the brandy and took a swig.

His mouth exploded as the spirit then set off in violent search of his throat and stomach. He felt as if he wanted to hold the top of his head to prevent it blowing clean off. His eyes bulged and then watered. Speech was rendered impossible.

But he had to admit he enjoyed it! It was good drink. His only problem now was why the spirit didn't seem to affect Temple the same way. Must simply be used to it, he concluded.

While Temple toasted the times ahead and Oliver's union with Charlotte, Kindale spluttered and struggled to pull himself back together. He drank very gingerly after that and by that medium was able to savour the remainder of his brandy.

Keep a clear head? Too much of that and a dense fog would engulf his brain!

***

Kindale was descending towards Dover when the first hint of daybreak made a weak impact on the morning.

Beth was moving slowly at her master's command. It was still very dark but he could just make out the grim, challenging and daunting shape of the castle on the hill ahead, black with a light here and there, like cats lurking in the thick undergrowth.

He was temporarily sheltered from the wind, slicing icily from behind him, seeking every weakness in man and nature alike, hunting down every less protected part of a human body. The wind had been a welcome feeling at first, for his mind was still addled by the brandy, and it freshened him up and rescued him from a blistering numbness that he could do without.

But now he more appreciated the shelter.

Arriving at the castle he learned that George Gordon had been busy to the south. A soldier mockingly described the expedition as a no more than usual failure.

"Let them go, save the effort," his view on the free traders Gordon was after. "Why bother? It pits men against men, and for what? To save money for the government to squander!" And he laughed without humour.

So Oliver Kindale rode down the steep hill into the town.

Sure enough he ran into Gordon with Whardley in tow and a detachment of six soldiers, all looking dirty, weary and as if they were ready to drink the town dry. Gordon ordered Whardley to return to the castle with the soldiers and make his report to Major Wendle, knowing well that Wendle had already received word.

He saw Kindale, who was keeping out of Whardley's scope of vision in the shadows, and behind his horse, and strolled towards the harbour lighting his pipe as he went.

The two met where a pair of fishermen were repairing their nets and Gordon beckoned to Kindale to move away. It wasn't quiet but the Revenue man knew it was not unusual for ears to pick up voices used indiscreetly. Together they found a more remote place.

"I could earn more if I joined the smugglers, and I don't know why I don't do that," Gordon said, the exasperation and resignation smothering an otherwise sulky and belligerent voice.

"If I spent a year with them I could do this so much better! There are times when you feel almost everyone else is up to something and you're the fool for trying to prevent it. They have a signalling system that I'm blowed if I can fathom.

"No, I can see the results. But how do they organise it, Kindale, tell me that and I'll be a wiser man and one better at his job?

"Last night. I'm a-reckoning it was word of mouth. A string of local people stretched from Folkestone to Dymchurch I'll be bound! Can't see any other way. Some folk are watching me and managing to see me in the dark.

"They signal the boat away from where we're patrolling. I paid well for information, so they knew I'd be abroad and with soldiers too! They watched me coming up from Hythe and as soon as I gets wind they're turning south I head south again. And with that they signals the boat into Folkestone!

"I'm done in, fair done in, Kindale. And you've promised me a success I dare not dream of. Now how are you going to do that, Mr Kindale? Tell me that."

There was a faint glow of light about the horizon as the sun sought chinks in the cloud's armour and tried with all its might to dart thin rays towards the sea and the land. Each quest was dulled and curtained as soon as it succeeded.

Kindale studied Gordon, his face just visible from the yellow and red luminosity of his pipe bowl. There was no look of worry, no look of temper controlled or otherwise, no look of puzzlement.

Gordon was every bit as resigned as the soldier at the castle had been. At that moment Kindale found it easy to believe the Revenue man could change sides without fearing his own conscience.

"Do you know of the *Maisie Greentail*?" he asked.

"Galley. Was to be a Revenue cutter, I'm told, but there wasn't the money left when it was needed. Based at Deal she be used for trading with ships in the Downs and beyond, so I hear tell, probably some free trade into the bargain. Twenty oars, sail. Given a good sea and a good crew could be across to France in hours for that matter!"

But at once Gordon realised the significance of Kindale's question.

"So that's the lie of it, eh? So be it. Do as you have said, Kindale, tell me where and when and what I am to do. Tydeman and Hapling you promise me. Tonight I will settle happily for that.

"Please, Kindale, deliver them to me and make everything worthwhile, give everything I do a true meaning, for I am sore tired and my heart is worn to nothing." His voice pleaded as a child might beg for a treat in the knowledge it would not be forthcoming.

For once the pipe dimmed and the man lowered his head. He was all but defeated, Kindale knew that, and he also knew salvation was within grasp. The hour had come.

Chapter Fourteen

He could've managed quite well without it.

Harry clutched his nervous wife to him and both stared at their unwelcome guest who was doing his best to sound unthreatening and reasonable.

But Grey Jonnie was not an amiable person by nature, and he exuded menace even when trying to be friendly.

"You housed me before. Within a few days I will ask you to house another. He will be brought here to be hidden where you hid me and he will be fetched when the time is right. I am not anticipating him being here more than a day or two.

"Now are you agreed?"

His right hand had moved slowly so that now it was perched atop his pistol tucked in his belt.

Everything about him spelled danger, his whole manner issued forth a warning, his bearing showed he would not be denied.

"You have my word," Harry stammered, more frightened for Mary than for himself, "and our guest will be welcome. We will make him so and declare him to nobody. Whatever your instructions we will execute them and speak to no one.

"You may rely upon it. We have no love of the law or any in authority, if authority he be hiding from."

"It is none of your business who he hides from or why." Grey Jonnie's cold blue eyes were wide and impressive, just as Harry remembered from the previous meeting, and they possessed a level of intimidation that ate into his brain and froze him. Mary, afeared more for her man than anything, tore herself away from Harry and threw herself at Grey Jonnie's feet.

"Spare us, sir, spare us. We are poor and we are no threat. We will do just as you say, I vouch for that upon my heart." Tears rolled down her cheeks. Harry remained stilled, now too scared to move lest Grey Jonnie should choose to confirm the arrangement with brutality.

But the man turned and left, calling through the open door, "He will give his name as Chastain."

And he rode away.

Harry helped Mary to her feet and they clung to each other. It was she who spoke first.

"Should've been an actress, me! That bought him off, husband of mine, so be proud of me."

At first there was a slight chuckle but it soon became a full blooded laugh that enmeshed them both as they swung each other around and then hugged, still laughing together.

When calmness met them they collapsed into their chairs and drank to their adventure, breathless from the humour that had overtaken them, and the relief that had flooded through them.

"Oliver will come soon, and he'll need to know this," Harry admitted. "I may go in search of him but should our paths not cross you can tell him all if he fetches up here.

"You minx! You played that beautifully and I'll swear he knows this Chastain will be safe with us. Aye, I am proud of you. Now come here you little darling."

Mary tried to protest but to no avail. And thus they surrendered to their love as he swept her up into his strong arms and carried her to their heavenly cot.

***

Oliver Kindale was astonished to see his visitor.

"We're anchored in the Downs, Kindale, and I know there's trouble afoot."

Lt. Dugald looked purposeful and rather more worried than when the two had met in Ramsgate.

"Been making enquiries about you, Kindale. I respect your honesty and integrity, and I am also aware that you are as accommodating as I am when it comes to giving the straight and narrow a diversion or two." Kindale nodded.

"That is, if the end justifies the journey to be taken, and only in such circumstances will it do. If we apprehend wrongdoers then it has been worth it. I am at your service, Kindale. I know Gordon and he tells me he holds you in high regard."

Dugald was not particularly tall but his erect posture, with his back straight and stiff, and his slender frame well proportioned, gave the impression of height. He would've been regarded as a military man even out of uniform, for he had the bearing of a man of command. High-cheeked, perfectly clean shaven, with a mop of blonde hair swept back and tied at the rear, his face exuded confidence and control with eyes that appeared ready to search out defects in others, and stood at the front of a brain that could deal with situations in an instant.

Kindale liked the man but was less sure of his position.

On the one hand how had the Lieutenant located him? Gordon quite possibly. Was the naval officer likely to be a restraining hand upon Kindale's shoulder? Had he been sent by higher authority to ensure Kindale knew his every move was being watched?

On the other hand Ursula Wellfern at Ramsgate had organised their first meeting, so she must've had some faith in both men, and presumably believed in Dugald as a useful contact.

He didn't command a ship so would have no say should his captain choose to spoil the plans Chastain and his associates had in hand, and in so doing destroy Kindale's work. The result might be the mere postponement of their operation. Yes, Tydeman and Hapling were wanted men, so too Grey Jonnie, but as yet Chastain and others had done nothing openly wrong.

Their arrest would prove pointless and simply delay what was for them the inevitable.

If you truly believe in what you are doing and you are inconvenienced in the execution of your campaign you re-group, re-plan and start again.

Oliver Kindale thought as hard and as quickly as he could.

He couldn't make a mistake now. Misjudge Dugald and everything could be laid bare. And suppose that the Lieutenant was not all that he seemed and had a foot in another camp, the very camp Kindale was determined not simply to undermine, but to rid of its backbone?

He looked directly into the other man's eyes. They gave nothing away, and if his return stare was anything to go by, Dugald was seeking answers in Kindale's own eyes and also wasting his time doing so. Two men with much in common, and a fact appreciated by both.

Eventually Kindale spoke and keenly observed the reaction. There was none, and none had been expected.

"Tydeman has arranged a boat. Hapling will sail it to France very, very soon, Lieutenant. I think they will leave from Deal, but have no idea where the return landing will be.

"It is vital they have free passage both ways, free of interruption. They will collect men in France and they must be allowed to land those men here. It is essential. After that I have promised Tydeman and Hapling to Gordon on the shore. He will be well advised and on hand with soldiers.

"The leaders will be carrying documents that will condemn them, of that I am certain, which is why they must get ashore and on their way. No chance to drop such documents in the sea and they must be given no chance to destroy or hide them.

"My missing link, Lieutenant, is the landing place. Or rather the stretch of coast from where the actual landing place will be decided. Once I have a better idea of that I can keep Gordon away until the time is right so as not to disturb them.

"Once ashore they will be heading directly for Wingham. I think they'll be looking for an easy and swift journey. I'd wager it'll be this area, perhaps even Deal itself, or St. Margaret's or, of course, further north, maybe Sandwich, possibly even Thanet.

"However, with men rowing I doubt they'll want a long journey, the shorter the better, which is why I'd wager on this coast."

Dugald considered the matter while Kindale fretted lest he had revealed too much. But, he reasoned, Dugald was a man to have by your side and not one to cross or to leave ill-informed. He was too clever by half. The officer spoke.

"If I know what is happening and when and what vessel is involved I can guarantee it safe passage, Kindale.

"I will not say more. You do not reveal your own background, Kindale, so you cannot expect me to make mine clear to you. We must trust each other but in the knowledge we respect each other's work and must rely on us as professionals to complete this mission satisfactorily.

"I am commanded, as is my captain, to assist you. This then is the service I offer you in exchange for your trust. You will know nothing more of the way we work, Kindale, and I shall have no more detailed knowledge of your operations. It is simple. Are we agreed?" Kindale nodded and offered his hand.

It worried him sore but it was a calculated chance and one worth taking.

Shortly after Dugald departed a breathless Harry Harblow arrived with his news.

***

"Well, Harry, there is now paint in almost every part of the picture and we can see more clearly what the portrait resembles.

"I need your eyes and ears in Folkestone and beyond. I need to know which piece of this shoreline will be open to Chastain and his followers on their return. Thomas Temple will be doing the same in Dover, though heaven knows they will not be foolish enough to try and land right under Dover castle.

"They will make all possible haste from the coast, so I cannot imagine East Wear Bay as you describe it will be conducive to rapid despatch. And if they are rowing then for the love of God they would not row further than need be. That makes Sandwich and Thanet unlikely.

"So Folkestone perhaps as far as Dymchurch, St Margaret's Bay, or anywhere along these beaches here either side of Deal, perhaps Deal itself. Tydeman has many friends here. Deal would be on his side.

"I will remain here. Deal is certainly where it starts."

Kindale had explained all that he was prepared to reveal and Harry felt better for it, yet uncomfortable that he might be kept too far from events to come, and knew that was exactly what his friend required. It didn't make it easier to bear.

He was acutely aware the man liked to work alone. Oliver trusted himself and nobody else and Harry was wise enough to realise there were all ready far too many people involved for Kindale's liking. However, he felt quite satisfied that this business was too large for one man and Kindale was more than capable of accurately assessing those he chose to assist.

And in that moment he felt the warm shaft of pride well up within him. He was chosen! And that was good enough for Harry Harblow, and naturally the man was quite right to offer some limited protection as Harry had a wife who needed him, and he appreciated that.

What Harry couldn't understand, and would not ask about, was the woman Charlotte. Kindale had explained her away as his landlady until the night he had confessed all after his fitful turn in the woods near Harry's cottage. Was Oliver truly in love? No, it could not be so!

Charlotte kept herself to herself, rarely spoke, and was nowhere to be seen when not required.

But Harry was not blind and he had noticed the way Charlotte and Oliver looked at each other on the odd occasion their eyes met, and he knew the look of love. It bothered him; love was not in his friend's vocabulary of life, and love might be the diversion Kindale least needed, and the restraint he wouldn't want at a vital moment.

He felt a softness in his own heart. Yes, there was love, Harry was sure. Wait until he told Mary!

The night of his fit Oliver had explained that the woman was more of a comforter than a landlady ought to be, and that he believed his heart might be lost. Harry said nothing at the time but knew there could be more lust than love in this unusual union, yet now he was observing the signs and recognising them for what they were, and in that moment knew Oliver's heart was most probably lost.

But then he became worried in a more troublesome way.

This was not Oliver Kindale riding into battle, not the man Harry knew, but somehow the man was thinking as crisply as ever, resolving matters in his mind with aplomb and being precise and firm about everything he did. Now that *was* the Oliver he knew!

Perhaps Charlotte had sharpened his wits, concentrated his mind, increased his power and scope of thought, and channelled his energies into a truly focused strategy. Yes, that was it!

The mood of the moment captured Harry Harblow and swept his senses into a bewildering state of fantasy, pleasure and excitement. Oliver Kindale in love, by God! And Oliver Kindale ready to take on the whole world if need be, for Kindale was ready and Kindale knew it would all start within hours now.

Harry was thrilled. Suddenly afraid, afraid for Oliver for he knew too strongly that the time was upon them and that death might now stalk them all. But thrilled by a feeling of adventure and the knowledge Oliver's driving force might be held in his heart giving him impetus anew, impetus to succeed but to do so with his usual care and attention to detail.

Yes, this was exciting. And frightening.

"Within the next day or two."

Nicholas Telman was shy of telling Mary Harblow, and Mary herself did not understand its significance, but once he realised that, yes, he *had* to leave a message and return home to Wingham immediately then leaving a message was not so difficult after all.

It had to be done; he trusted Harry and Oliver so why not Harry's wife?

Of course, he had come hoping to be paid.

Mary was quite in the dark but accepted the news, cheerfully offered food and drink, a little of each being agreeable to Master Telman, and then he was on his way north, galloping back to the Canterbury road.

A matter of haste, Mary concluded, and Harry away at Deal.

In time she came to fret. Oliver needed to know that the men would be at Telman's in a day or two, and she started to worry about how she might get this information to him. If only Harry was here, she wished.

Harry was on his way back, bound for Folkestone, elated and afeared, little realising the news his wife had would turn him right round and send him back to Deal. But that is what happened. Harry was the worrying kind, and it concerned him greatly that, at the very time he should be in Folkestone, he was actually heading in the opposite direction

Oliver reassured him for he was grateful for the intelligence, essential knowledge indeed, and sent him back south again without further ado. He also asked him to call on Gordon at the castle and to make him ready. For Harry this was all pleasure undeniably so. It was involvement, participation, and it was laced with danger and every degree of urgency.

He took himself straight to Dover, sought out George Gordon who seemed to share Harry's sense of privilege and excitement at the news, and without any more delay rode across the cliffs to Folkestone.

Folkestone was an anti-climax. Suddenly Harry felt strangely detached and for a few moments he wondered if his friend had deliberately sent him out of harms way, determined to preserve him for the sake of his marriage.

But when he carefully reasoned his way through the maze of knowledge he possessed he decided that his location was imperative as Kindale truthfully had no idea where the men might land, and he was being made use of. That pleased him and comforted him, warmed his soul through.

There had been much for his friend to mull over.

Tydeman secures a boat, Hapling navigates it to a secret point on the French coast, and the pair of them escort whomsoever back to England and a rendezvous with Grey Jonnie and Chastain.

Thence rapidly inland to Wingham where the party will await those who will take them on towards London to complete their dreadful, unthinkable task.

Grey Jonnie reaps his rewards in Kent while Chastain is smuggled back out of the country possibly by way of Harry Harblow's cottage.

They would run rings around authority. Their planning was exemplary and the whole process would be executed in smart time, every step along the way precisely assessed and designed for perfect, untroubled progress.

The French would rejoice.

Chastain was Napoleon's man. In truth there would be no future for Grey Jonnie; he was merely a pawn in a fearsome game, a means to a terrible end, as easily despatched as a man of no consequence when the time came. And he could not see that truth, or if he could he believed he was in too strong a position to be cast aside.

It would be inconceivable to a man like Grey Jonnie that he might be so readily crossed by a mere Frenchman without understanding the forces that his conspiracy was about to unleash. He assumed he was held in high regard, that knowledge of the way he dealt with those that went against him would frighten away any thought of rebellion within his own ranks.

But Chastain, unbeknown to Grey Jonnie, was no 'mere' Frenchman. He held a command of his own and was widely feared in his native land, a land where revolution had been champing at the bit. Chastain had even learned Grey Jonnie's real name, Will Cosney, when the outlaw had steadfastedly refused to reveal it, because he took the trouble to find out who he was dealing with.

This Will Cosney believed he was on the cusp of leading his own style of revolution whereas in fact he was nothing but a puppet, and a puppet that would be destroyed when the moment came, a moment that would so surely follow not long after Chastian's success.

Kindale was clear on all these aspects.

And the day of judgement was nigh. He was determined that Chastain and Grey Jonnie would find him standing before the gates of hell ready to thrust them through to eternal damnation. But he had to be sure they had no chance of escape and just as importantly no opportunity to dispense with the documents that would hang them.

He had to rely on Dugald letting the *Maisie Greentail* pass unhindered. He had to rely on Gordon doing exactly as he was told and moving at the right minute. And both men might easily be driven by the desire to proceed with alacrity and lack of patience, and indeed a lack of trust in Kindale, and strike while they had the occasion to do so.

Relying on them was distasteful for those very reasons.

He needed every ounce of their trust, and in that he knew he was himself relying on their faith in Ballerden as much as anything else. Oddly enough he felt better about Dugald who was clearly under orders from somewhere above and certainly there was a certain level of discipline within the navy.

George Gordon was, in contrast, virtually a loose cannon, a man who was, frankly, free to act on his own cognisance, and that included of necessity acting on intuition from experience gained in his service, his profession.

No, he had to trust these men, and it was Gordon he felt more strongly in favour of.

That was his own experience, his own experience of correctly summing up those he met and knowing who he could use and how, and who he should avoid at all costs. If there was ever any element of doubt he would not chance his arm with a man. Or a woman for that matter!

How he wished he could've done all this without any help whatsoever.

But this business was not for one man to stand against, he accepted that albeit reluctantly.

Dugald, Gordon, Harblow, Temple ... they were now his closest associates and he *had* to make it all come together and he recognised he could not do so without them. He *must* rely on them.

Still the prospect of one weak link stood before him. One man going astray for whatever reason could damn him and bring everything down. And to think that he nearly allowed Charlotte to turn him into that very weak link! There was now no room for mistakes. The smallest error could wreck his plan and open the doors to an unimaginable horror.

This had to work, he told himself over and again. This *must* work.

***

This *must* work.

Fretting and anxious Mlle Descoteaux longed for intelligence of all that was going on around her, and worried continuously lest there should be too little progress or that it should be heading along the wrong path.

She wondered but briefly if she regretted forging this relationship with Chastain, but she swiftly dispelled such concerns; she had wanted so desperately to be here in England where she could keep an eye on him and his unpleasant deeds.

Her blood boiled with rage when she had to exude calmness and subservience in the presence of the monster she detested and wished dead, yet she acknowledged that this was her vocation and in truth there would've been no way she could've been closer to activities. Still she hoped that the day would come that the opportunity would present itself for her to play another crucial part in the downfall of this sickening plot.

This *must* work.

And she must await her time.

Chapter Fifteen

Kindale found he could isolate his feelings about Charlotte and about the years ahead to be spent together, and the thoughts of his mission which were now a totally separate issue in his mind.

They laid quietly in each other's arms, rugs wrapped around them, as the fire, the only source of light, lazily drifted into dying embers, crackling peacefully, gently hissing now and then as if in defiance of its own demise.

Oliver and Charlotte had their own warmth, the warmth of the sanctuary of their hearts, and at this moment he had no thoughts about the hours in front of him and the perils he might face. She was thinking solely of him, her eyes closed lightly and a smile of contentment and satisfaction brightening up her face.

He was looking directly at her face, being no more than an inch from it, although he could barely see its features. Her hot breath spread over his own face every time she tenderly exhaled, and to him it was the nectar of love and he longed to drown in it.

The world could've shrivelled up and died and they would not have been aware of it.

Nothing mattered.

Just being together tight in each other's arms. He thought she might be asleep then she opened one eye, just discernible in the dark, and gave him a toothy, mischievous grin that drove his lips to hers, and passion once again overcame them and made nonsense of their tiredness.

He wanted this hour to be his one special memory, for at the back of his mind was the dread that he might be dead within a day or so.

Earlier Robert Kettle had passed by with the news that the *Maisie Greentail* had just pushed away from the shore, Hapling, Tydeman and Chastain aboard. Kettle retired into Deal a little wealthier than when he left town with his information, and Kindale, momentarily fearing the immediate future, took Charlotte in his arms and made love to her.

Now they slept.

He knew it would take hours to reach the French coast and return. And a few, precious few, of those hours he needed to pass with Charlotte, the goddess he worshipped, the only woman he had truly wanted and wanted so much that he ached and ached.

In a second of terror he had awoken and wanted to gather her up in his arms and run and run and run, run away from destiny, run away from the one piece of work he must complete.

He was soon asleep again, snuggled to her slender frame, unwilling to let go lest paradise should be snatched from him.

Kettle, being an illiterate and largely uneducated person, had used logs to show how many people were on board the *Maisie Greentail*. Seventeen at the oars and Tydeman and Hapling. Chastain would most certainly not row! He would be above such employment.

Kindale knew Hapling would guide the vessel into and out of the French destination, and Tydeman would have organised the return landing, with all its signals and security. No doubt some of the English crew would remain on French soil, their places taken by eager and skilled Frenchmen, men trained and primed for their forthcoming black deeds. After all, the Englishmen would have no knowledge of the plans, and would not have been so keen to partake in this dark venture had they been aware.

And Grey Jonnie, Will Cosney, would be waiting for their return. The documents Kindale so wanted to lay hands upon would be to hand. And the leaders would be escorted to Nicholas Telman's with their men in tow. Straight into Kindale's trap.

It was a moonless night. Little wind. Clouds. An easy sea and one forecast for the hours ahead. It could not have been more perfect for Chastain had he been in league with the devil himself. If there is a God, Kindale thought, he must be a strange God to do business with such a man.

Therefore, perhaps, it is all the devil's work!

Charlotte slept peacefully, assured of her future, the one she had worked so hard for.

She would be good to her man. He would want for nothing. She would be attentive and pleasing, a servant and a whore, and he would please her and her life would be the better for the arrangement. Most satisfactory.

Jess would approve. He would not want her to suffer and never to see and feel the joys and rapture of love.

Peace.

For now, peace.

She understood so little of that which occupied her new man, but she knew it was important and believed it was probably illegal. So what matter? It was a trifle. Half the men of Deal swayed from one side of the law to the other, and earned a good shilling by so doing.

She had herself benefitted.

Wine, brandy, cloth and much more, all had been laid at her feet. Jess was a good man but he knew which way the wind blew and profited from that knowledge. And paid the price for it.

Yes, there had been pain. That is the way of things. But now she had Oliver and her pain was ended.

Oliver Kindale knew that her pain was far from over. He had to return from his mission and start afresh at a life he was so little acquainted with. But he would try because he loved Charlotte and saw in her his chance of redemption, salvation even, and that their future was worth acquiring. Now he knew that more than ever. Now it counted for something.

Peace.

For now, peace.

But also the quiet before the storm. He reckoned the return trip would be about ten hours if all went well and he was self-assured that it would be the same night. They had, according to Kettle, departed soon after sunset so should be back after three a.m., but certainly no sooner.

If there was a stronger wind across the Channel they might be able to use the sail and rest the arms of the oarsmen for at least part of the journey. But no sail anywhere near the Kent coast; too easy to see and besides, precious little wind to fill such sails.

Nevertheless he could take no chances. Although it seemed all too obvious that their plans included putting into the French coast they could also meet another vessel at sea and transfer the men, thus reducing the time away.

He had followed Kettle back to Deal, found Dugald where he expected to locate him, advised him that everything was underway and that there might be options about the journey. The lieutenant agreed that a transfer was unlikely but could not be overlooked. His reasoning was the same as Kindale's: the gang wouldn't take extra risks by involving additional boats.

And what would be the point of taking Hapling, who knew the French coast so intimately, if they were not going all the way to France?

On his return to the cottage he found Thomas Temple in attendance and in an agitated state.

"St Margaret's, Oliver. That's where it'll be. And they're to have lookouts posted from Dover to Deal and beyond lest they must land elsewhere, if you understand me. And my friend, they'll have lookouts inland to.

"I have old friends and favours to thank for this, Oliver, and this Chastain is taking no chances. Tydeman's called in some favours too, and I dare say he's threatened a few as well. There will be people everywhere.

"And any militia at Deal and Walmer castles will learn nothing of this and be no threat. The *Maisie Greentail* will leave the shore as usual and her return will go unnoticed.

"What is this, Oliver, what is this that needs such attention?"

Kindale was so busily weighing up the news that he didn't really hear Temple's question, but he saw the inquiring look the man was giving him when no more words were forthcoming. He wanted to tell him but could not take the risk.

"Thomas, if you value your life and all you hold dear, if you value your way of life and the lives of those you care for, if you value your country, its ways, its virtues, despite its flaws, but above all the freedom you enjoy in a country you understand, then I must succeed.

"It is that important. And I will tell you the answer to your question, and in full, when this is over. You have my word on that."

The two men studied each other until Temple nodded, a dissatisfied man but one who accepted the position between them.

"Thomas, go straight to Gordon. He has no choice but to come from the seaward, and explain why. Tell him what you have told me and remind me of his obligations to our arrangement.

"Tell him to lay off St. Margaret's Bay ready to move once the men are ashore and off the beach. If he can get word to Dugald the navy may be able to offer support, if there is time, but with a weak wind running we can only think in terms of boats being rowed.

"Make sure that if he contacts Dugald the navy officer also knows his obligations to our pact. Chastain must get inland, rendezvous with Grey Jonnie, before I make any move against them. Go now, my friend, and make haste."

He offered his hand which was taken with firmness of spirit, Kindale aware of the fire burning in Temple's eyes, the flames of a man ready to do whatsoever he could, the flames of a man ready to honour his own commitment to the cause.

And Temple was gone.

If Dugald's first visit had been a surprise the next visitor was also a shock, a nasty shock.

***

"You should choose your friends all the better, Mr Kindale.

"But then you will make no more friends, not in this world."

Edmund Whardley was pointing his pistol directly at Kindale's chest, was close enough to kill with a shot, just far enough away to be able to react quickly with the trigger should his opponent lunge at him.

"Gordon's sent me to Winchelsea on some scheme, but I've travelled the other way, see. Knew he wanted me away from all this. But I serve a different authority, Mr Kindale, one that has paid well for me to watch both camps. And in this I am not alone, which may surprise you I dare say.

"I know well what is about tonight and you'll not wreck it. I have been paid good to send you from this world to the next. They know what you're about, Mr Kindale, and they know when I have finished with you that you'll pose no threat to them."

Whardley raised and aimed his pistol in one swift movement. Kindale saw the motion and was about to leap at his foe when a pistol shot rang out. Whardley's eyes bulged with surprise and pain, then closed as death overtook them. His pistol dropped and Whardley followed it, collapsed directly onto his face at Kindale's feet.

He looked up and saw the figure that had appeared unnoticed behind him.

Charlotte, shaking as tears of fear and relief flooded her cheeks, threw down her weapon, and Oliver rushed to hold her. Now he owed her his life.

She shuddered violently in his embrace as he held her close, wrapping her continually within his arms to reassure her, to ease the shock and to lessen the burden. She wept with equal violence and he clung to her, stroking her hair with one hand, kissing the side of her face and kissing it over and over, rubbing her back firmly and all the time aching for her release from this dreadful occasion.

The calmness came and with it a more reasoned shock about her fatal act.

"I had to do it, Oliver, I had to do it..." she wailed.

"Thank God you did, I bless you for that, bless you for my life. If not your bullet then he would have had to die by my hand. I would've had to stop him, Charlotte. Everything is fine, my beloved, everything is fine." And she shook afresh, wept again, and sank deeper into his loving embrace.

"The gun, beloved, why do you have it? But thank God you have."

The tears gradually dried, the shaking then ceased, and they allowed their lips to meet and passion to overtake them. She pulled away quite suddenly.

"Thomas. He made me take it, after the soldiers killed Jess. He checks it for me, keeps it loaded."

But her face was showing more anxiety and she spoke her words hurriedly, her nervousness thrusting its way to the surface.

"Oliver, this is not the only man who would kill you, is it? There'll be others, won't there?" Her voice was broken and alive with concern, and she was shaking again, the fear manifest in all he could make out of her face.

He lowered his arms.

"I cannot be anything but truthful," he said with softness, quietness and caring, "and indeed there may be others. But I will have the advantage of surprise as they will not know Master Whardley has failed. I will be safe, my darling, as I have you to return to, and I will return to you.

"From then we will have each other every day, I promise you so, I promise you," but his words produced a further flow of tears and squeals of terror. He hugged her to him and she kissed him. And both knew this might be the last of their kisses.

Her tears swamped their lips as they fervently made love in each other's arms.

And then she knew it was time for him to go and the agony welled up and smothered her heart and suffocated her mind. She wanted to hold him back, stop him going, but knew he would go no matter what, that she was powerless to prevent this separation.

This man she loved so dearly, wanted so completely, was going off to possible death and even her love, so large, so wide, so deep, could not halt his progress.

"Where can I bury him, Charlotte?" His voice was as cold as it had been at the beginning and it burned into her, increasing her agony ten-fold.

"I'll get me sister, Jack, and her husband. They'll do it. He'll not be found."

"Please, please, please, Oliver, come home. If you must go please come back. I love you, Oliver Kindale, I love you. I don't want to bury you as well." The pain creased her face as the horror of what might be scorched her heart.

"You'll not do that, my sweet. I am alive today because I do things right and make sure they go right and go the way I want them. This will go right, and I'll be back." He found he was scarcely believing the words he was saying, knowing that it might be his last few hours on earth. How could he mislead her so?

The dangers were so great, and greater now than when he arrived in the county not so very long ago.

They were hugging each other, desperately searching for each other's lips, sharing desperate kisses, sharing what joy they could experience at a time of such alarm, a time when both felt the despair and anguish crushing their bodies and squeezing the breath from their lungs.

And then he was gone.

He heard her sobs and muted shrieks as he set off, as he checked his two pistols on the path to where Bess was stabled. He could hear her helpless cries, the call of his name as he rode away, rode away to oblivion maybe, or, God willing, back to her arms. He had no religious beliefs but found a little prayer for his deliverance for Charlotte's sake.

He did not ask for himself.

Now he shut her from his mind. She was enclosed permanently in his heart, safe and secure. But she had no place in his mind and no place in the events that lay ahead. Now he would survive on his wits as he always did. God did not really come into the reckoning.

***

George Gordon had been reminiscing with Major Harold Wendle.

They sat together looking into pitch blackness with just a glow from their pipes to light their faces and then only slightly so. Beyond them the Channel. Beyond them the destiny they knew was now upon them.

153

The chalk cliffs were at their feet and a long, steep drop to the sea, the sea they could hear and which was their only available reminder of where they were.

"You sent Whardley away?"

"Yes, Major, to Winchelsea. He's safely out of it now."

"Tydeman, Hapling and others tonight if we are truly blessed, Gordon. Assuming your man proves reliable."

"I have no doubt about it, Major. So many chances have come my way and so many have gone begging. Poor intelligence sometimes, poor information sometimes and paid for by the King! That is the worst of it.

"And I keep thinking that I need to work where the military will assist me. Instead we seem to get in each other's way. Better off on coasts less well guarded! One day it will be brought together and then, mark my words, Major, we will defeat the free traders."

The two men drew on their pipes and said nothing for several minutes.

"Chatham, Major. Thought the navy would be a good ally. But the Medway. Full of creeks and twists and turns, and marshes and islands, and the navy had other things on its mind. Did they care if men should bring a few welcome items ashore, or ship them out, all free of duty?

"Only when forced to attend to it. Then there was Sheerness, on an island, Major, do you know it?" Wendle grunted that he knew it. "Black place, an island seemingly and in its entirety against law and order! No, that's not fair, but this county is plagued and we tend to put all its people under one roof, a roof of mischief, Major.

"Mostly wool went out of Sheppey. Lot of trade done with the low countries across the sea. No, it would be wrong to tar everyone the same, but there's lots do it."

He chuckled quietly and ruefully. He would not condemn everyone but his experiences in Kent had shown him that too many for his comfort were either actively involved in smuggling or able to be induced by threat or profit, and the whole business was well structured, top to bottom.

Better organised than those trying to prevent the trade! He wondered if Wendle might be offended but it did not upset him, for the army did not always turn out to be the friend of the Excise service.

"I trust, Gordon, that you exclude me and my soldiers from your round denunciation of the country's military services!" Both men laughed.

"Aye, that I do, Major, and I know you're as keen as I am to net our fish tonight.

"The isle of Thanet, Tydeman's usual hunting ground, another coast that burns red hot in my side, Major. I was captured by a gang there not two years ago. Thought my last hour had come, but they relieved me of my weapons, my money, and my clothes, every last stitch, and threw me in a ditch, laughing as they vanished into the night.

154

"The poor woman who found me wandering naked in the early morning light had a shock that might have sent her from this world to the next. Her scream made my teeth rattle." Wendle was laughing again.

"Ah, Gordon, you're a hero, every inch of you, and I suspect she could see that for herself!"

The laughter subsided and they returned to drawing gently on their pipes.

"I haven't been to those parts of Kent, Gordon, but it sounds as if they have little to recommend them.

"There is beauty all around Kent's coasts, Major. It is men who add the ugliness. I did well in my time at Whitstable, caught, if my memory serves me well, sixteen men and one woman actively engaged in bringing ashore boats laden with treasures, all of them free of tax.

"Not one of them in prison or worse. I catches 'em and the law deals with 'em but only in the law's way and leaves me feeling defeated, rightly it does.

"That part of north Kent, right along past Reculver, alive all the time; nice easy shores, easy tides, men can get a boat up in no time."

"And the Riding Officers, Gordon, of little use?"

"Little or less, but much self importance. Makes them a bit more expensive to buy if you follow my meaning." Wendle did, but he said nothing. "And a wrongdoer can easily escape retribution from the law by any number of means these days, Major, not least by parting with money.

"Why do we bother? Until the Preventive services are organised we waste time and money and risk our lives. Been shot twice, Major. In the leg and the shoulder. My leg caught a shot just outside Sandwich and my shoulder was hit in Rye.

"Josiah Barrowford, a companion good and true, honest and diligent and a Revenue man I could rely on, shot down at my side, shot dead, and him with five young mouths to feed. They gave us no chance, and I was lucky to escape with an injury.

"My wife fears for me constantly. Are you married, Major?"

"Not me. Much sought after I am told, so if I live to leave the army I will have a good choice I dare say." There was no sound, then Gordon realised there must be humour in Harold Wendle's words and duly laughed as the Major quickly did.

Wendle spoke, but not to Gordon.

"What is it, Sergeant?" A dark figure, barely discernible, had appeared. Gordon hadn't noticed, but Wendle was wide awake and alert.

"Sir, Mr Temple is here, with a urgent message from a Mr Kindale."

Wendle and Gordon sprang to their feet, goaded by the feel of excitement and terror that flooded through their veins in response to the news. It was always like this beforehand. Fear and exhilaration, unfortunate bedfellows, but successful partners in ensuring the mind is ready and honed for the part it must play.

And Gordon was ready.

***

Kindale was unconcerned.

Gordon had clearly sent Whardley in the opposite direction, and by some distance, so could not possibly be the weak link he had feared.

Edmund Whardley had hinted that there was another traitor in Kindale's close circle and that obviously worried him, but as long as it was not Gordon himself or Dugald that was a matter of some satisfaction.

He trusted Thomas Temple because he trusted Charlotte.

And Harry Harblow was above suspicion.

Naturally Robert Kettle couldn't be trusted but then he wasn't. So was there somebody else, somebody close enough to this whole tragic affair who could undermine his progress?

Ballerden?

Certainly not, or Kindale could not bring himself to think so. But then the solicitor must be close to Kenton, very close, and surely could not be employed by both sides of this argument. There was always, always an uneasy feeling that treachery could lie anywhere along the path, and that it would be no respecter of rank or office.

No matter. Press on.

And so Oliver Kindale went to war, and to the likelihood of his death, or hopefully his salvation and the future he had never previously considered. Either way, he must succeed at once, and Chastain and Will Cosney must be brought to heel and defeated, perhaps slain.

Will Cosney. Grey Jonnie, a man who preferred his title to his real name. A man hiding behind lies and threats and fear. A man who was false in every sense. And the people of Kent would learn that to their cost if they followed him.

But then, as Kindale knew, Kent had a history of rebellion! Wat Tyler, Thomas Wyatt, did Will Cosney wish to add his name?

It would be better if he perished before he was endowed with fame or notoriety. And Chastain dead would eliminate the chance of fires being rekindled in later times. Two men who could easily rot in hell, Kindale decided, and their passing need trouble nobody.

Kindale had learned a great deal about his surroundings, and his education had been improved by Thomas Temple with special regard to moving about the region under cover without rousing suspicion. He had his own stealth, his own ability to hide and travel unseen, and he now understood the terrain.

He could make some pace when needed and do so silently and without drawing attention to himself. That was his strength and always had been, and it was the nature of his calling, the capability to be invisible to meet the requirements of any task. He knew many would be abroad tonight, recruited far and wide.

Deal, Walmer, St. Margaret's and villages beyond, whomsoever they would send and as a result of whatever manner of coercion and obligation was upon them, the people would be prepared of that there was no doubt. Many were simple enough to be led, some would be supportive, others afraid, but none in the knowledge of the real reasons for the work they were doing.

At least if Gordon followed his instructions the soldiers would approach from the seaward and there would be no military presence for anyone to uncover inland. It would add credence to their belief that all was well, and safety was assured for those approaching St Margaret's Bay.

And, Kindale surmised, if Chastain and Cosney believed Whardley had killed their opponent there would be nothing to unduly worry them. After all, Oliver Kindale worked alone. Remove that threat and there was, presumably, nobody to don his shoes and continue with the cause.

If they concerned themselves with Harry Harblow then they would by now be aware Harry was sufficiently far south to be capable of no potential interference. They might even feel that Kindale thought the landing would be there. Even better for their scheme!

The winning cards seemed to be in Kindale's hand, but he had learned over the years that you take nothing for granted and he was ready for any change of plan. There had been no rumour of a decoy run, no suggestion that the intelligence of a St Margaret's landing was false, and he was satisfied in that view.

Besides, there really was only him, and he could not be everywhere, and right now Chastain and Cosney may have assumed he was in hell.

He left Deal by heading swiftly inland and worked his way around towards St Margaret's village, atop the cliffs. There he found a thicket and curled up underneath a large bush for the time being.

***

"They'll all be seasick!"

Major Harold Wendle's opinion of his men going to sea was actually contemptuous rather than defensive.

"But they're soldiers, Gordon, and they'll do as I say. They will still be fighting men when the quarry's in sight. And Captain Gracie here has been a seaman. We'll do the business, have no doubt. And for your part?"

"Three men, but like me, have all sailed. We've all been on the revenue cutters and we know what we're about."

"Right, Gordon, we're under your orders. Your vessel, your command. We support you as soon as we reach the beach. I don't like the idea of nobody to cut them off from the land side, but it can't be helped."

"That's it, Major. We can't jeopardise the operation by having men approach from inland. There'll be more eyes a-looking for us than you could imagine. But it's a narrow way up to the village and a steep climb across the cliffs towards Dover or Deal.

"We need surprise and we need haste. And I'm counting on Tydeman, Hapling and their crew putting to sea straight after the Frenchmen and Chastain meet Grey Jonnie. Back to Deal they'll go, all innocent, like nothing's happened.

"So we must catch them there and then, but I don't see Tydeman and Hapling making a dash ashore or sailing in haste. Chastain and Grey Jonnie must be well on their way before we strike. We must give Kindale the opportunity to deal with them afore we set off after the rest."

Wendle nodded feverishly. He was a fighter, a soldier through and through.

He was ready for action, yearning for a fight, longing to pursue wrongdoers, and apprehend Tydeman and Hapling in particular. There was, after all, the chance of some bounty here, some reward money and Gordon must not benefit from it all!

Indeed, the fever for want of action was present in everyone.

And it was time to go.

Chapter Sixteen

Kindale edged closer to the top of the cliff.

He could hear two men talking very quietly and guessed they were part of Tydeman's lookout and signalling chain.

Their conversation was about other matters and not Kindale's concern. They discussed family, employment, food and the lack of money to pay for it, and the harsh winter that they hoped was nearly over.

Not once did they mention anything about the night's business, but Kindale knew why they were there. Otherwise there was darkness. Blackness. No moon, no stars and plenty of cloud. It would be easy to spot a small lighted signal from a ship or boat many miles out at sea, a sea that was subserviently calm for the devils it served tonight.

He smiled to himself.

They obviously thought they were doing no harm speaking so softly, and that if soldiers approached they would be well warned by other lookouts. And yet he had made his way to within feet of them without their knowledge. Not that Dragoons were ever as stealthy!

There was a whistle from the village.

One of the men said, "Grey Jonnie's here. Spect he'll go straight down to the sea. But still no sign o' the boat. Wonder if there's a change of plan?"

His friend responded:

"Happens, don't it? And Grey Jonnie knows all and knows what them soldiers are about, don't he? We'll soon find out, Sam, that we will."

Kindale heard two horses approaching. A voice cried out.

"Samuel. Samuel Hollerdon?"

"Over here," one of the men replied, and the horses drew close. The rider spoke again.

"Any sign?"

"No, not yet.. not yet"

"Keep your eyes open and do your work well or pay the price with your life. Now, when they appear signal to them to turn north and land south of Walmer. You know how to do that?"

"Yes sire, we know what to do. Tis one of the agreed signals. We're all aware of that."

There was a brief silence.

"Right, come Nick, and we'll ride north. A few more miles between us and the soldiers. And they'll come, I'm sure of that, but we'll be long gone." The other rider spoke.

"No news from Dover then, Will?"

"None, but they can be here too quickly. Let's be on our way, Nick. We can be certain Whardley has done his job well and Kindale lies dead. We only need to outwit Gordon and Wendle now."

As they rode away Kindale knew who the other turncoat was: Nick, Nicholas Telman. The voice confirmed it. Well, it was to be expected, he was always open to the promise of appreciable reward, but there were matters Telman was not acquainted with and therefore unable to reveal.

There was now the added advantage that Kindale was presumed dead!

Then he saw it, a faint light showing twice way out to sea, swiftly lit and extinguished quickly each time, a pinprick of light, clearly a signal.

He heard the flicker of flint and knew the two men were giving their response as directed by Grey Jonnie. He saw the single light of acknowledgement and found himself hoping Gordon was out there and had perhaps also seen the signal from the clifftop, even though he wouldn't understand its message.

All Gordon had to do was follow Tydeman's boat ashore. And it was too dark, dark enough to see less than a hand in front of you, and he knew he was fretting.

But out at sea Gordon and Captain Gracie, both being former men of the sea, had seen both sets of signals finding themselves between the two. They therefore laid off to the north to allow Tydeman to sail directly to the bay unhindered so that they could follow him in.

In so doing they were later to observe the *Maisie Greentail* as she had altered course to the north.

Or rather they heard the boat or at least the voice of command as Tydeman urged his crew to use every last ounce of their strength to reach Walmer. The urging was particularly crude, brutal and raucous, and laced with threats of violence.

In silence Gordon, Wendle, Gracie and the others listened to the *Maisie Greentail's* oars being thrashed through the water. They could not see the boat but knew it was but a short distance away, and they now knew where it was bound. Gordon hoped Kindale was aware, but he was helpless to do anything other than pursue his own and agreed course of action.

Kindale found others abroad and skirted clear of them. They were all part of this grand scheme and were maintaining their stations, no doubt encouraged by Grey Jonnie on his way past. Even now the arrangements could be altered if there was any doubt about Tydeman's safe and unseen landfall.

Walmer, like neighbouring Deal, was far enough from Dover and the soldiers, and sufficiently south to be clear of the navy in the Downs. The military presence at the local castles had been discounted by Chastain and Tydeman as impotent forces of no consequence and even less potential opposition.

Lt Dugald, however, was a sight more cunning and had a small handful of men ashore in Deal, out of uniform with their ears to the ground. If the landing was effected this far north he would be ready.

Wendle had sent word to Dugald on Gordon's agreement, using a trusted horseman to ride to Deal by an inland route. He had not passed close to any lookouts to be spotted.

There being insufficient wind for sail, and sail being more visible at night, two boats from Dugald's ship were being rowed southwards with heavily armed men aboard, ready to move into St. Margaret's Bay once Chastain's men were ashore.

Although Kindale worried and with good reason, for he could not know what was happening, almost every eventually was now in hand with Gordon to the south, Dugald to the north, and Tydeman sailing into a trap all his ingenuity could not overcome, a trap all his foresight and planning had not anticipated.

But there was the darkness.

Nobody could see anything. The *Maisie Greentail* was nearing journey's end, her crew none the wiser about events going on around them. Every now and then a tiny light would flicker to port as she moved along the coast, each light in turn guiding them to the resting place. Tydeman was the complete master; he knew these waters exhaustively, could be sure of every bearing he was taking, and knew exactly how to angle the boat's progress closer and closer to the shore.

Hapling responded with a brief light to every signal so that those ashore were aware of the boat's movements. Coming along behind the *Maisie Greentail* was Gordon, also carefully noting the pre-arranged signalling lights, and mightily pleased with himself. He knew; did Kindale know?

Would it matter?

Let the Frenchmen get inland and then storm the beach and take Tydeman and Hapling. His part of the bargain successfully achieved. Let Kindale take his chance. This was the way he wanted it. Let it be so.

Nevertheless he ached to help Kindale and knew he could not for he had not the means.

No, let it be so.

Kindale was alert and wide awake, shrewd and clever. He would be near Walmer. Gordon could not interfere and determined not to. He would wait for the men to land and head towards Wingham as planned and then deal with his two prizes.

But it continued to trouble him.

Should he let Major Wendle and some men set off after Chastain once Tydeman and Hapling were held? Kindale would surely have had time to act. And he let the arguments rage in his mind, unsure of what to do, certain he should do nothing, equally certain he should intervene.

Kindale deserved help, he reasoned, yet the man had made it clear he wanted none. It was a serious affair but, in truth, he had no idea what was afoot. Wendle might blunder heavy-footed into Kindale's trap and wreck the task Kindale had set himself.

In a matter of minutes now Gordon would have to decide and it was a decision only he could take as Wendle knew nothing of the intricate details of the business. A matter of minutes now.

***

Thomas Temple, believing he was now surplus to any activity Oliver Kindale had arranged, quenched his thirst before starting out on his ride home to Deal.

He felt let down, a man deflated and impotent.

Nearing St Margaret's he found himself challenged by two men and a woman, all waving pistols in his direction. The woman held a lantern so that he might clearly see his predicament and that they might see who was upon them.

"Why, it's Thomas Temple," the woman exclaimed, "and why are you abroad on this dire winter's night when you could be warming a lady's bed." Temple thought quickly, with greater alacrity than he was used to.

"Why, Mistress Gild, m'lady threw me out as I demanded too much of her. And maybe, Mistress Gild, it was so I could come and warm *your* bed!" And he allowed one of his raucous laughs to fill the night and echo around the countryside.

"You're drunk Temple and no good to me in that condition. Get home with ye, wretched man. Let him pass lads."

The woman was the one who had challenged Kindale, no mistaking her, she being taller than her two male companions, in fact towering above them. He rode away pleased to be free but hurriedly dismounted, tethered his horse, and quietly made his way back on foot taking care to make no sound.

He heard what he wanted to hear.

Nancy Gild dismissed the men saying that the *Maisie Greentail* would be all but safely ashore now in Walmer and there was no longer any need for them to be there. She would remain a little longer in case, but she was confident no soldiers would come now or, if they did they would not be in time. No messages had been passed from Dover.

The one thing Tydeman, for all his meticulous planning, had overlooked was the possibility Gordon and Wendle would put to sea, so, unusually for him, he had nobody watching the harbour. The lookouts stretching from the town to Deal were expecting a landward approach by the military and on this dark of dark nights were left with nothing to report.

Temple's heart was throbbing fit to burst under his shirt and cloak, and his head ached with the pressure. He found it most difficult, being in so much haste, to travel without noise back to his horse. Any moment he might stumble or cause a rustling of twigs and the sound would carry on the night air.

He was sweating and swearing profanely in his thoughts. He was gasping for air, his throat dry, and a fury was rising in his breast.

The horse was where he had left it but he had little energy to climb into the saddle so leaned against the beast while he recovered his breath and his senses. Being back on the animal calmed him yet he knew he must ride gently for other lookouts might find him, and a man galloping across the cliffs would be reason enough for a confrontation, and the next lookout could put a bullet in him rather than take a chance.

Oliver had been right.

An air of expectancy hung like a deadly mist. This was important to these people, every one of them. What were they expecting? This was no ordinary landing of contraband. And they weren't all complying through fear.

There was something exhilarating and driving about the atmosphere tonight. There seemed to be promise, optimism, a fearlessness, but there was also menace and there was something quite repugnant about it that Temple couldn't understand.

Only now did he appreciate that what Oliver Kindale was about was vital and was something that needed doing at any cost. It had to be that important.

But where was Kindale? Was he in the wrong place? It worried Temple and disturbed his senses. What could he do about it all anyway?

Would Gordon still be heading for the wrong beach?

The more he worried the worse his aching head became. The more he found to worry about the more complicated it all appeared, and Thomas Temple's mind was not suitably educated, adjusted or able to comprehend the full extent of his worries; certainly it had no chance of delivering a precise answer.

So he did what most simple men would do. He dismissed the crueller parts of his self inflicted nightmare and concentrated solely on anything he could mentally deal with, and thus it was that he decided his great strength lay in surreptitiously following Kindale. And, he had to admit, he had, right from the start, been good at locating the man.

He had done so in his self appointed role as Charlotte's protector.

But on this dark, dark winter's night, with lookouts to be avoided, how on earth could he achieve it?

***

Gordon was indeed heading for the right beach.

Word had reached Dugald, and Kindale was already inland from the shore.

163

Lt Dugald, in one of the boats, was passing Walmer when he too noticed the brief signals from shore and realised there was every chance a another boat, hopefully the *Maisie Greentail,* was being guided in.

His two boats heaved-to on the gentle swell. There was no sound save the sea slapping calmly against the vessels. He wondered where Gordon was, or, for that matter, Oliver Kindale.

The difference between him and Gordon was that he knew where his duty lay and was devoted to its execution. He could make a life and death decision on the instant, based on an immediate summation of all he knew and all he might reasonably guess at.

As his boat floated, and rose and fell with a gentleness that was in its way quite nauseating, he knew where his path stretched and he would only deviate if presented with a change of circumstances, and then only if he considered the move beneficial.

He was consigned to what was, for him, a simple task. Let the men get ashore and proceed inland and then apprehend Tydeman and Hapling, and all else they could lay hands upon. If that arrangement was carried out smoothly then he would decide if further action was needed and the direction it might take.

Also, he allowed for the fact that Gordon might, *might* be to hand and there would therefore be sufficient forces on the ground to deal with their part of the pact. Leading on from this Dugald knew he would have crew to head after Chastain and his followers in case Kindale was not there, or required assistance.

In this he demonstrated a military mind, a mind used to command, whereas Gordon had no such background or training. Dugald would win or lose depending largely on his accuracy in correctly arriving at the right answer, and by that medium won more often than lost.

Gordon would worry about failure and it would curse his ability to make the right decisions, so that failure haunted his career and failure was subconsciously the least he could hope for. Dugald was successful and dreamed of more success, but Gordon had been tainted by defeat over and again so that any achievement was a surprise and a short-lived and much celebrated glory.

Unaware of the other's presence these two men now commanded boats that were resting just off Walmer while the *Maisie Greentail* ran into the slight slope of the shoreline where eager hands pulled her in.

Grey Jonnie greeted Chastain without realising he was greeting his eventual executioner.

He still had no concept of being a convenient puppet in a far greater master plan than he could've ever envisaged. And his purpose was destined to be a short one.

Chastain had even convinced him that the men now arrived in Kent were trusted lieutenants who would carry out the deed and then return to France. Only Chastain was due to make that journey and, in effect, with the keys to the kingdom for Napoleon's pleasure.

The men would stay as the advanced guard. Will Cosney would be dead as would his own band of followers. And that included Nicholas Telman once Chastain was on his way from Wingham.

And of all this Will Cosney 'Grey Jonnie' remained in ignorance, a compliant servant, whose own lust for power and greed Chastain had harnessed to his benefit. A dolt, in Chastain's eyes, who would be no loss once he had played his part.

Cosney had no idea that there were men who were more ruthless than he and that was his weakness. The man of impotent strength who foolishly believes he is the master.

From the shore they set off for Wingham, Telman on horseback leading the way, Chastain and Cosney feeling sufficiently confident to carry a small lamp to guide themselves and the men behind them.

Within minutes they had vanished and were advancing rapidly through the countryside, still dark although the very first signs of daylight were starting to etch themselves on the far horizon behind them. A very faint, hazy ribbon of sky that was barely lighter than the darkness it sought to impose itself on, and very low down, just managing to pull itself up above the sea. But it was there.

Up ahead the almost indiscernible strip on that horizon gave Kindale, with his excellent eyesight, a small but welcome advantage. He was ready, a pistol in each hand, a knife in his waistband, not yet sure what was coming to confront him and, not for the first time in his life, he felt alone.

Not afraid, just alone. Cold and alone. Determined, but only one man for all that.

And not far away a young woman lay weeping.

Only now was the full horror of what she had done and the situation in which she found herself entangling her in the extremes of fear, anger, sublime love and regret that wracked and tormented her mind and soul and tore her apart.

She had killed a man, in cold blood, mercilessly. Shot him in the back.

But he was about to kill Oliver; did that not make it the right deal of the cards?

She had seen her man Jess murdered by soldiers in much the same way, and the killing hadn't stopped there. She had lost so much. Was this her retribution, her right to take another man's life so that she might keep the man who now meant more than anything to her? Her revenge on those who deprived her of everything she had once before?

Charlotte's thoughts ran amok and in all directions and destroyed good reason and sensibility.

She had killed so that Oliver might live, and now he was away facing terrible danger once more. She so desperately wanted to stand with him and know the danger he was amongst, and it hurt with a pain she couldn't understand that she could not.

Jack and her husband had taken Whardley and buried him where he would never be found but she did not want Jack to stay for comfort. Charlotte needed to be alone. If she couldn't be with Oliver in his hour of destiny she wanted to be alone.

She was as alone as Oliver was.

And it was unbearable.

She wanted to scream but no scream would come, so she buried herself in her rugs and wept until there were no more tears to cry.

***

And in Dover another woman was waiting.

Chastain had left hours before and frustratingly Mlle Descoteaux knew not where he was bound. But she had gleaned enough to know the landing was tonight and was at long last able to send a message to Ballerden.

Would it be of any use? Would it be too late?

In Folkestone Nathaniel Ballerden read the letter and contemplated the situation before him. Having mulled over the intelligence in his possession he concluded there was no possible action he could take that might improve the chance of success. He was aware that Kindale was the right person in the right place and if he was not where he should be this very evening then Kenton had seriously underestimated the man.

So in the time honoured way of lawyers he sat down and steadily wrote a lengthy document which in due course he shipped to Kenton. His report was his only possible contribution at this juncture. It was up to Kindale.

Ballerden's report was despatched by a fast horseman, bound for London. At least the authorities would be duly notified and precautions made lest Kindale should fail.

It was indeed entirely in Kindale's hands now.

***

Kindale watched the path of the lantern from his vantage point and moved to a position ahead of it.

Telman was riding slowly along the route across the field and approaching the woodland, and the lantern was keeping pace some short distance behind. Kindale squatted down behind a bush alongside the only obvious way through the trees and waited.

As Telman drew abreast Kindale moved like a tiger and with a great deal more silence. Telman was hauled from the saddle and was dead before his body was dragged into the undergrowth. The knife was returned to Kindale's waistband and he stood erect with a pistol in each hand.

He throbbed with anticipation.

It wasn't exactly fear but there was apprehension. It wasn't exactly excitement but his body was alive and tense, the blood flowing freely through his veins driving him on and on and on.

When Chastain and Cosney were no more than a few paces in front of him he stepped into the path, pistols raised.

"Only hell this way, Chastain," he shouted.

Cosney drew a pistol but Kindale had fired and the man was dead on his feet, his limp body left to fall on the grass. Chastain, having recovered from the initial shock, had grabbed his own pistol and as Cosney slumped forward he took aim.

Kindale did not have time to re-adjust and he heard the crack of the gun and felt the thud of the bullet as it hit his chest. He staggered forward, went down on one knee, and tried to aim but he had no might left to pull the trigger.

His body shuddered as life was sucked from it. The chill was upon his being and it was all he could do to prevent his eyes closing for the last time.

In the dimness a small grin could be seen on the Frenchman's lips. Utterly exhausted Kindale used what little strength he had to try in vain to fire the pistol and wipe the smile from Chastain's face. Where, oh God, was his strength? He found he was praying for enough power to fire his weapon and knew it was truly hopeless. Tears swamped his eyes, tears of pain, tears of vexation, tears of defeat.

His tears were the screams of anguish his mouth would not produce.

Then he heard the crack and metallic roar from behind his head and in that moment saw the blood spread across Chastain's own chest and pour from his mouth. As he himself collapsed he saw the Frenchman fall backwards and knew Chastain was dead.

Lying helplessly face down, unable to move, the agony ripping his body apart, he felt strong hands turning him over.

Temple! Thomas Temple!

And Temple had completed Kindale's task.

"My friend, my friend," a distraught Temple cried, "are you done for? Not if I can help it, my friend." And he removed his coat and wrapped it under Kindale's head.

Oliver Kindale was choking as the blood filled his mouth.

He wanted to tell Temple everything but the words would not come.

He wanted to tell him about the plan to assassinate not only the King but also the Prime Minister, and to leave the door open to invasion. Cosney had believed it was about revolution, but it wasn't.

Kindale could not speak and knew he was doomed.

And just then he wanted to tell Temple how much he loved Charlotte, and again there were no words he could speak. He wanted, and wanted so desperately, to tell him how he finally had a future, a future he craved, a future with Charlotte. Something to yearn for and within his grasp.

He wanted to tell Temple yet he knew his last hour had come. There would be no future, no victorious dance, no loving couch.

His eyes reflected his frustration in the dim early morning light, and then they closed and closed forever.

Temple knelt and gathered his friend in his arms, cradling him, kissing him and crying.

Silent tears, no heaving shoulders, no shaking head, no audible sobs or cries, but the tears glistening on his beard to demonstrate his loss.

***

And so it was that Dugald came upon the scene seconds later.

Epilogue

Kindale died without knowing how successful his mission had been, although he believed the plot would fall apart, as it did, once its main players and leaders lay dead.

Lt Dugald, arriving at the scene, searched the bodies of Chastain and Grey Jonnie and found the incriminating papers that also led to further arrests. Dugald had removed any complications and difficult decisions from the mind of George Gordon.

With both the army and the navy converging on the shore, initially surprising each other, and seizing Tydeman, Hapling and many others, Dugald instantly took some of his crew inland without further thought.

Hearing shots ahead they charged forward and set about apprehending French and English alike as the Lieutenant surged through the battling throng and came upon Kindale and Temple.

The documents he found not only condemned the dead but Tydeman and Hapling too. And for once in his life Gordon tasted total victory. Yet he could not directly celebrate his success for he realised he was mourning the loss of Oliver Kindale, the man who had promised and delivered such gifts, and who now lay dead for his efforts.

With sufficient soldiers and sailors to hand it was easy to round up most of the scattering band. The news and the warning it carried flew across the land like a howling gale. The scheme lay dead and was now beyond resurrection.

Chastain never intended to land at St. Margaret's. As Kindale rightly surmised he needed a very swift journey north to Wingham and the steep climb away from the shore would've meant unnecessary delay. Only Chastain, Tydeman and Cosney knew the truth. The comparatively flatter terrain around Walmer was ideal, and they had deliberately spread the false word knowing it might well reach the wrong ears.

Kindale also died without knowing how the plot was unearthed.

He didn't need to know and he wasn't told. In fact he did once see the person responsible, a French royalist who appeared to visit Chastain in Dover. It was the only occasion she was observed. He never did find out who she was or that she was masquerading as 'Mrs Copwood'.

Veronique Descoteaux could see that revolution in France might spread its evil tentacles beyond the border once it erupted into full scale violence. With the end of the monarchy and the destruction of the aristocracy that walked hand and hand with the new cause, it was possible such revolution could be encouraged overseas.

But that was to be only the beginning as she later discovered.

By abandoning her noble background and joining a revolutionary group she quickly learned that its leaders did indeed plan to elicit support in England, and the assassination of the King was the prime objective in inciting an uprising this side of the Channel.

But the ultimate aim, she learned to her horror, was invasion. Disorder and anarchy in England might lead to its overthrow. The conquest of Europe might readily follow.

Revolution might have been of interest, and there were people who would've been easily swayed such as those gathered in by Will Cosney, but in general the people of England did not want a French invasion and would've heartily resisted it.

Veronique set about finding ways of bringing the plot's utter downfall and immediately realised her best chance of success would be in England once the principal perpetrators were ashore and on their way to London. England was the place to strike.

Nobody in her beloved native France could be trusted amongst the common people. She knew that. However, by chance she later she met an Englishman (perhaps Kenton?) on French soil and came to appreciate that he might be able to help.

Once they were in each other's confidence she could reveal all and he was able to take the information to London.

Thus she set in motion the sequence of events that led to the involvement of Oliver Kindale, and her own part in accompanying Chastain to Dover. The one important thing she gleaned from him was that when he landed with his party he would be carrying vital and damning documents, the very ones Dugald recovered, the ones Oliver appreciated had to be preserved and not destroyed.

Mlle Descoteaux subsequently paid with her life.

Shortly after she learned the joyous news that her goal had been achieved she was found at the house in Dover she'd shared with Chastain with her throat cut. No doubt the group she had infiltrated realised they had a traitor in their midst and concluded it was her. She had been aware that there had been more than one French conspirator in town.

Harry and Mary Harblow shed tears for their own loss. Nathaniel Ballerden rode out specially to tell them about Oliver's demise. Harry never came to terms with the knowledge that Oliver had kept him out of harm's way when he wanted to be at Oliver's side.

Mary knew full well how Harry was suffering, for she was suffering herself as the three of them had formed a close alliance, a warm and precious relationship, now asunder. But they had each other and would survive, and never forget.

Ballerden visited Charlotte and Thomas Temple. His words were brief as he could not reveal the whole story, but they were left in no doubt Oliver was a patriotic hero, yet a man whose heroism could never be disclosed publicly. This was all scant consolation for Charlotte in her wretchedness.

The solicitor bore no words of Kindale's background.

There was money for Temple and the knowledge his role had been vital and was quite heroic in its way.

On his own approach to Walmer he had seen the lantern Cosney carried and had swept stealthily northwards to circle around ahead of it, for he was certain that was where Kindale lay in wait. He arrived too late to save his friend but in time to slay the Frenchman, and in full view of Kindale's dying eyes.

But the greatest shock was for Charlotte. Ballerden explained that a 'friend' of Oliver's had arranged a small pension for her. In fact it was Oliver himself who had done so, a move probably supported by the mysterious Mr Kenton.

No words or money compensated Charlotte for her loss. She was once again a bereaved and broken woman.

Kindale also died without knowing that a few months later Charlotte would bear their son. She named him Oliver. Carrying the child within her may have saved her life for she otherwise felt she had nothing to live for. At least the small amount of money Oliver had arranged helped provide for his young son in his early years.

In time Charlotte accepted Thomas Temple into her life and together they watched Oliver grow into a fine, strong young man, and become an accomplished seaman ... on the right side of the law.

And the three laid flowers on Oliver Kindale's grave throughout each year, in memory of a man amongst men, as Charlotte and Thomas knew him to be.

But for Charlotte there were endless private tears, her agony complete, a woman crushed.

Her collection of memories so very small, her heart overwhelmed with perpetual sadness, a sadness from which there would never be any relief.

Each day was bleak, a lifeless existence following night after night of silent sobbing and sorrowing.

Indeed, a woman crushed.

***

And so England prepared for war. In a few brief years the Martello Towers and the Royal Military Canal would be built in Kent, and once again the county would stand at the forefront ready to repel invasion if need be.

So yes, this might well have been a true story.

Peter Chegwidden in words

Kindale is just one of a widely varied series of books by this author.

And variety is the right word. Something for everybody? If you simply adore a relaxing good read see what else is on offer.

AFTER HUGH

Coming soon is *"After Hugh"*, a book that follows the trials and tribulations of recently widowed Hannah, a very upright, well-mannered and articulate lady, high in moral principles.

Her family tests her instilled beliefs about what is right and wrong, right and proper, and manages to do so to her limits and beyond. And it is as each episode unfolds that Hannah begins to realise how much her beloved husband, Hugh, influenced her life.

Prejudice has ruled her throughout marriage, but at long last she starts to think for herself and gradually becomes a very different, much more tolerant and understanding person.

In doing so she has to abandon long-held and entrenched ideals about life and how people should live it.

Given the impact events largely involving her grand-children have it is little surprising that she has no time for romance.

After all, Hugh was her one and only, and she had never for one moment considered that she might ever love again. But love can creep up unannounced, and with it can come impending disaster in the wrong hands!

Hannah's best friend, Jayne, also lost her husband but in her case to a younger woman. Hannah tries in vain to warn Jayne about the dangers of internet dating, but sadly Jayne learns these lessons to her cost. How astonishing then that when love comes to Hannah she should dive head first into one of its pitfalls.

But eventually she does find true love. Not that she ever sought love, for Hugh was the be-all and end-all of her life. Ultimately love finds *her*, and this time it is truly beautiful.

DEADENED PAIN

A parody of crime novels which satirises almost every aspect of the genre, and does so with humour, drama, romance and poignancy, whilst including all the vital ingredients such as murder, kidnap, theft, a wealth of suspects and life and death encounters.

It follows an unlikely police force as they try and unravel a series of crimes with the body count increasing all the time. Most of the characters appear almost as caricatures as this odd team bubbles along, a team comprised of an extraordinary bag of individuals. And the criminals they're pursuing aren't much better!

There are serious moments, and serious messages (such as those relating to illegal drugs), and plenty of high drama. Moments that will perhaps shock. After all, this is much of the material you might find in a crime novel! There are laugh-out-loud incidents and some that may haunt the reader. Various stereotypes and prejudices are satirised, a reminder that they are far from eliminated in our society. There will be occasions when you nod in agreement, and times when you will smile.

And it all reaches an amazing climax, typical of the genre.

Follow DCS Luke Fuselage and his ill-assorted team as they succeed in making a soggy quagmire out of a level playing field.

SHEPPEY SHORT STORIES

Tall Tales from North Kent

It doesn't matter where you live you'll love this collection of short stories!

Based on Kent's Isle of Sheppey there are eighteen tales with the central theme being relationships.

All kinds of stories to enjoy, from the humorous to the sad, from the satirical to the ghostly, from the saucy to the moving.

There's an introduction to the island (and a map) to set the scene. Just sit back, relax and lap up the fun but be prepared to be touched. It's not all laughter.

TOM INVESTIGATES

A 'Cat's Tail' of mystery and intrigue

With no bad language and nothing to offend this is nonetheless an adult story that might also appeal to younger readers.

Follow the adventures of a tabby cat called Tom as he and his friends try and solve a crime, find a stolen item, overcome a fearsome foe, and indulge in a bit of match-making with two humans.

These are not cartoon cats or any sort of animated cats. The characters are based on the real life cats we see around our neighbourhoods every day, behaving just as we see them behaving.

But here we are allowed into their world, hearing them speak and learning what they are thinking. The story is far-fetched but otherwise there would be no story.

So get in touch with your feline side for a joyous romp of a 'tail'.

Reviews include:

Wonderful Story. If you love cats you will love this story. Imaginative and beautifully told.

(Natali K).

TOM VANISHES

The sequel to Tom Investigates

The inspiration for the Tom books is a real life cat who the author met by chance.

Shortly after *Tom Investigates* was published Tom vanished and was never seen again. Months went by and then as if by magic he turned up on the doorstep of his service providers!

And that remarkable story in its turn became the inspiration for *Tom Vanishes*.

It's quite different to the first story, and tells how Tom is accidently taken to another part of Kent and relates his efforts to get home. Naturally, all the main cats from *Tom Investigates* have a part to play as they try to locate their friend and bring him back.

Nothing is ever straightforward. Problems and concerns abound.

All kinds of adventures follow. There is danger and frustration, but new friendships formed along the way too.

You'll come across Bella, who is looking for a male cat who can be "useful" to her, as well as an interesting assortment of other cats. And there is one outcome to being lost that Tom would never have bargained for!

Does he make it back? Well, read on and find out for yourself.

DEAD CORRUPT

(not yet published)

This is the sequel to *Deadened Pain* and once again follows the inept officers of Birkchester CID as they find themselves hard on the heels of wrong-doers.

As before this is a satirical parody of the crime novel genre but complete with serious messages, this time concerning corruption and modern day slavery. The corruption runs from top to bottom in this tale. Overwhelming passion leads to dastardly crimes and, of course, murder.

Death stalks the air!

The police force has a new PR lady who has her own designs on personal and professional progression, and who proves to be a thorn in the CID team's side. With a new Chief Constable and a new Assistant Chief Constable all in 'new broom' mode life is about to be made sheer hell. And that's without any input from the criminals!

We meet the stereotypical Essex girls, Aurora and Candy; a peculiar assortment of solicitors; two very upstanding, well-respected gentlemen, their two dim-witted enforcers, and their drug-dependent gofer.

There's the farmer from hell who has diversified into all manner of crime, and a solicitor with a most unusual sideline, one that nearly costs an officer his life. The team, in the meantime, are taking incompetence to the next level, as you would expect.

With the first death occurring on the railway British Transport Police, and the aptly named Inspector Beeching, become involved.

DEAD DEPARTED

(not yet published)

Christmas can be murder and it certainly is in Birkchester, administrative centre of Paslow district.

This book completes the Birkchester CID trilogy, three novels lampooning the crime novel genre.

The story begins with three small gangs going to rob the same convenience store at the same time, all unbeknown to each other. But is there a connection after all?

Bodies start to wash up on the beach but are they just red herrings?

And priceless antiquities are stolen from a local museum while all this is going on.

DCI Wilberforce gets toothache and undergoes an extraordinary extraction at the dentist. How could something so simple become a total nightmare ... for everyone else? But fate has a real humdinger lined up for the Force's number one bigot when he is faced with a life and death situation.

And he's not the only senior officer facing death.

However, romance blooms in many directions adding another dimension to the storyline. There are new relationships and older ones gathering pace. One will have a direct bearing on the dramatic climax.

With murder the number one priority the team can do without having to deal with dog rustling into the bargain. But then one of the missing dogs belongs to a close friend of the ACC. Say no more...

DCS Luke Fuselage gets his knickers in a twist, literally, during an illicit night of passion with a fellow officer.

Sometimes the only way is down. And that's where team Fuselage head in this morass of crime featuring more characters than you could shake a stick at. As ever, plenty of suspects. There's a serious message too, this time about the misconceptions over mental health issues.

Printed in Great Britain
by Amazon